Troub
Choctaw County

JOHN R YORK

DocUmeant *Publishing*
244 5th Avenue
Suite G-200
NY, NY 10001
646-233-4366
www.DocUmeantPublishing.com

Published by
DocUmeant Publishing
244 5th Ave, Suite G-200
NY, NY 10001

646-233-4366

Permission should be addressed in writing to the publisher at publisher@DocUmeantPublishing.com
Edited by Philip S Marks

Cover Design by Patti Knoles, www.virtualgraphicartsdepartment.com

Format and Sint-Holo illustration by DocUmeant Designs, www.DocUmeantDesigns.com

Library of Congress Cataloging-in-Publication Data

Names: York, John R, 1948- author. | Marks, Philip S., editor.
Title: Trouble in Choctaw County / John R. York.
Description: NY, NY : DocUmeant Publishing, [2022] | Summary: "A young man named Perseus is cast out of his home of privilege and sets out on a journey seeking adventure and a new life. He heads west with no particular destination in mind until he runs out of money in a backwater town he considers to be in the middle of nowhere. He isn't sure what he should do, but the Fates cast a bit of timely good fortune his way. Two strangers notice him sitting at the counter in an old diner at the edge of town; a young cowgirl and a young Indian from the Choctaw reservation. Before he knows it, he's working at a local cattle ranch. A few weeks later he listens to an old Native American from the Choctaw tribe tell a group of children a traditional story about a mysterious winged creature called Sint Holo. Perseus begins to dream about the mythical beast. During the following months, extraordinary events sweep Perseus and his two companions into a whole new world of discovery, upheaval, and transformation"-- Provided by publisher.
Identifiers: LCCN 2022016688 (print) | LCCN 2022016689 (ebook) | ISBN 9781950075799 (paperback) | ISBN 9781950075805 (epub)
Subjects: LCSH: Choctaw Indians--Fiction. | Young men--United States--Fiction. | LCGFT: Bildungsromans.
Classification: LCC PS3625.O7476 T76 2022 (print) | LCC PS3625.O7476 (ebook) | DDC 813/.6--dc23/eng/20220524
LC record available at https://lccn.loc.gov/2022016688
LC ebook record available at https://lccn.loc.gov/2022016689

This book is dedicated to
my loving wife and best friend, Paula.

If I Were an Indian

If I were an Indian, I'd be so cool,
    I'd be strong and brave, nobody's fool.

I'd hunt all day, and I'd dance all night,
    I'd sing to the spirits, 'till the morning light.

The spirits whisper, "Follow your quest,
    Search high and low for Sint-Holo's nest".

She's trapped in the cave, dark and deep,
    She calls on a brave when he's fast asleep.

I know she's a legend, been gone a long time,
    But I've been dreaming, she's inside my mind.

I know I must find her, for she needs me,
    I'm searching for answers, and so is she.

So, if I were an Indian, that's what I'd do,
    She's ready to return; the stories are true.

Poem by John R. York

Preface

THERE ONCE WAS a young man who lived a privileged life with his parents on the east coast of the United States. He felt aimless and disconnected, not knowing what to do with his life. Little did he know that he was about to undergo a dramatic change in his life.

At the same time, in the Choctaw Nation of southeastern Oklahoma, there was a well-known elderly medicine man and hopayi (a seer) who had recurring visions of a future he found very confusing and unsettling. The visions involved a mythological creature known to all the tribes who had originally inhabited the lands of the southeastern United States. It was a creature from the dark legends. These stories were told and retold by the elders from generation to generation.

It seems unlikely these two events could be related. Yet, in order to fulfill the destiny they were assigned by the laws of the universe, The Fates often spin convoluted webs through the lives of specific individuals who are destined to live through them.

In their journeys, heroes, often improbable and reluctant, will emerge. These heroes must summon great intelligence, strength, and courage to overcome adversity and confront evil. This is such a story, where the unlikely, the improbable, and the reluctant are thrown together with epic consequences.

Acknowledgements

THANKS TO MY proofreader, Paula Payne, and my editor, Philip Marks. Their focus on detail and refinement helped to make this novel a more polished and readable story. Thanks to my publisher, Ginger Marks, of DocUmeant Publishing for her efforts on the interior design and formatting of this book, and especially for her patience and advice in getting me through the process of using a publisher rather than self-publishing. I needed all the help I could get.

Additional thanks to Patti Knoles for her creative work on the cover.

The legend of Sint-Holo appearing in this book is a verbal story told in the oral tradition by Hunter Harris, Native-Legends: a storybook project for MLLL-3043-995 at the University of Oklahoma, spring 2020.

CHAPTER 1

PERSEUS WAS SITTING at the kitchen table examining his breakfast cereal when his mother entered the room. She looked at her disheveled son, sighing as she cast a disapproving look at the box of Lucky Charms on the table.

"Why don't you eat something sensible for breakfast, you know, something with some actual food value and fewer chemicals?" She said this nearly every morning.

Perseus felt obliged to say something, even though she had already lost interest in anything he was doing. She was busy preparing herself a cup of Jasmine Pearl Tea. He thought the stuff tasted awful, and it was ridiculously expensive.

"You know, this cereal is magically delicious, unlike that crap you're about to consume."

"Do you have to be so vulgar, Perseus? My god, one would think you were raised by wolves the way you talk."

He wasn't about to get involved in that little discussion, one he and his parents had frequently. He knew they were not pleased with "how he was turning out," as they would say. They expected him to be more like them, but he knew he was never going to measure up no matter what he did. He was, as they frequently reminded him these days, a disappointment.

His father cautiously entered the kitchen, surveyed the situation, and without a word, headed for the refrigerator to gather up the ingredients for his daily breakfast drink. Perseus didn't know how his father could drink those nasty concoctions. His parents had a lot of nerve criticizing his eating habits.

When the obnoxious whine of the kitchen blender ended, Perseus cleared his throat, causing both parents to turn and look at him expectantly. "You remember that girl you insisted I take to the country club Valentine Ball several weeks ago? Well, she texted me last night. She said I got her pregnant."

There was a collective gasp, coupled with open-mouthed, horrified looks on both of his parents' faces. "Perseus," was all his mother could manage to eke out.

He started to snicker. "April Fools! This is April first. It's April Fools' Day. You should have seen the look on your faces." He was now guffawing.

"There is nothing funny about that, young man," his father said with deadly seriousness.

"Good god, Perseus," his mother added. "What is wrong with you? Have you no sense of decorum or propriety?"

They both shook their heads as they continued to pour their breakfast beverages into insulated YETI travel mugs. Perseus knew that soon they would rush out the door to their respective jobs. They both worked at Howard University in Washington, DC. His mother, Alice, was a law professor. His father, George Percy Fawcett, reputedly the great-great-grandson of the renowned archaeologist, Percy Fawcett, was a professor in the university's history department, specializing in Greek mythology. George married Alice, the daughter of Greek immigrants, in 1990, and that combination of lineage somehow resulted in the justification for giving their only son the name Perseus.

CHAPTER 1

Perseus despised his name. Why would any modern person in their right mind name their son Perseus? His father called him Percy, since that was his father's middle name, although this was not much better. But his mother, being of Greek ethnicity, insisted on calling him by his given name, or as she was fond of saying, his *nomen dedisse*.

"What do you intend to do with yourself today, Perseus?" his mother prodded as she hurried out of the kitchen. The tone of her voice made the question sound more like a challenge, and strongly suggested that whatever he replied would only be a disappointment to her.

Maybe the pregnant joke wasn't such a good idea after all. "I was planning to drive over to Aldie and do some riding."

His father stopped short as he was about to exit the kitchen. "Well, that seems like a fine idea, son. Are you preparing for anything in particular?"

"No. There's nothing coming up anytime soon, but I like it out there at the farm. I thought I'd treat myself to something I really enjoy doing today."

His father gave him a puzzled look, then headed toward the front door. Within a few more moments, both his parents were gone. As the silence engulfed Perseus, he felt a distinct sense of abandonment, if that was the right word for what had just happened. It was April 1ˢᵗ, after all. It was his twenty-first birthday, and neither his mother nor his father had bothered to wish him a happy birthday. Maybe they were playing a joke on him or had something special planned for later.

The northern Virginia weather was still quite cool at this time of year. Perseus, dressed in his classic hunter horse jodhpurs and tall hunt boots, grabbed his leather jacket as he headed out the door. He reflected on his life as he drove his BMW 328i to the equestrian facility outside the little town of Aldie. Now that he was officially of legal age, was he supposed to act mature; to have a plan for the rest of his life; to behave responsibly? He was sure that's what his parents expected of him. Why did he feel so unprepared?

As he drove, deep in thought, time rushed by and he nearly passed the farm. He noticed the entrance at the very last second and quickly whipped the agile Beemer into the driveway leaving black tire marks on the pavement. As he pulled up to the stables, he saw his old friend and longtime trainer emerge from the tack room.

Perseus parked his car and hurried over to the barn entrance. "Hello, Hickory, "You're looking good today."

"Well, I feel pretty good for an old man," Hickory said in his slow, raspy voice. He always sounded like he was about to tell you a story. "I believe today is a special day for you. Am I right?" He had an impish twinkle in his eye. "Happy birthday, Percy. My, my. Twenty-one years old. You're a fully grow'd man, startin' today." He poked his finger into the air for emphasis.

"Thank you, Hickory. You just made my day. I'll tell you what, though, I sure wish I knew what I was supposed to do with the rest of my life. To tell you the truth, I feel kind of lost. My parents don't think much of me these days. I'm sure they expected more from me at this point in my life."

"Don' be too hard on yo'self. A lot of young men don't know where they're aheaded at your age. Some folks don't never get no choice at all. You know, life has a way of just throwin' things out there in our path. When I was your age, my daddy run off and left Momma and us six kids to fend for ourselves. It wasn't what I wanted, that's fo' shore, but it turned out alright, I guess. I mean, here I am with this job and all, right here at this nice farm. I guess they calls that the Fates, you know—destiny."

Perseus was smiling. Hickory always knew what to say to help him sort things out. "I know you're right, Hickory. I'm lucky to have a nice home, this nice car, and my horse, Arion."

"Yes, sir, and you gots nice parents too. They doin' pretty well to provide you with all those things and yo' private schools and all."

Perseus lowered his head. "Yes, you're right. But they're always busy with their jobs and social-standing functions. To tell you the truth, I sometimes feel like I was a mistake. You know what I mean? I'm not sure I was planned, just tolerated." He paused, but Hickory didn't say anything. "I know what you're thinking. I'm just spoiled. I've been given too much, and I don't appreciate what I have."

"No, no. Now I don' think nothin' of the sort. I can see that you wishes you had more of their attention. Ain't nothin' wrong or selfish 'bout dat. You're a special person and a strong person, Percy. You gonna be just fine. You wait and see. Life will be a throwin' somethin' your way sure as horses make road apples."

This made Perseus laugh. "You always know how to make me feel better. I'm going to saddle Arion and practice my jumps. I want to work on negotiating drop fences."

"Alright then. I'll help ya get ol' Arion tacked up. You be careful on dem drop fences now. You hear? Remember to get dem seat bones off the saddle until the peak, then be sure to open on the drop. And watch Arion's bascule and speed. Don't push 'im too hard."

"Will do. Thanks."

Perseus led Arion, his Dutch Warmblood, out of his stall and into the breezeway, and connected the crossties to his halter. Hickory brushed the horse while Perseus collected the tack. He spent the early afternoon riding through the well-manicured grounds of the farm, occasionally practicing specific jumps on the training course. He didn't want to push Arion or himself today. But he was determined to enjoy the crisp weather, the beautiful rural setting, and the special bond he shared with Arion. He had named Arion after the mythical horse Hercules once rode into battle.

Perseus was five-feet, ten-inches tall, with a trim, medium build, and an erect posture. His high cheekbones and strong jawline were complemented by thick, dark-brown hair and hazel eyes. He cut a handsome figure astride his athletic horse. Well educated, he had always been a good student. His pleasant disposition allowed him to make friends easily, and he engaged older adults with poise and self-assurance. It was only in the past year or so that Perseus began to withdraw into himself, wondering where his life was going. He was as perplexed as his parents by his lack of motivation to accomplish anything meaningful.

It was after 7:00 when his parents arrived home from work. His father found Perseus sitting in the study, reading one of the many books on ancient Greek mythology which filled the room's bookshelves.

"What are you doing?" his father asked.

Perseus assumed his father's question was rhetorical, since it was obvious he was reading. "You know, those ancient Greeks came up with some really weird monsters. Do you suppose any of those freaky things ever really existed back then, or did the Greeks just have exceptionally perverse imaginations?"

His father just stood there looking at him, unable to think of a response to such an unusual question.

"How was your day at the university?" Perseus asked to break the silence.

"Well enough, thank you. Ah, how was yours?" He was never sure these days how to deal with his son's increasingly odd behavior.

"Quite nice, Father. I rode Arion out at the farm. We practiced jumping some drop fences and neither of us got hurt. I guess that makes it a good day. It was a pleasant way to spend my twenty-first birthday." Perseus made the last comment as nonchalantly as he could manage. He looked up at his father to catch his reaction.

"Today? Today was your birthday?" his father asked in apparent surprise.

Yep, he had forgotten, just as Perseus thought. *And he was clearly embarrassed that he had forgotten*, which gave Perseus a perverse feeling of delight at putting his father off balance.

His mother, looking through the day's mail nearby, overheard the conversation. She sheepishly came around the corner, a look of sincere contrition on her face.

"Oh, Perseus. I'm so sorry. Why don't we all go out to dinner? We can still celebrate. Maybe we could have some champagne. You're legally old enough to have a glass."

Now Perseus felt like a heel. Plotting his parents' embarrassment didn't make his disappointment over their oversight feel any better. *Why had he done that?* He put the book down and rose from his chair.

"No, it's okay. Really. I'm pretty sore from riding today, and I already ate a sandwich before you got home."

They all just stood there, nobody knowing what to say or how to act. Perseus finally crossed the room and gave his mother a quick hug. She wished him a happy birthday. His father shook his hand and said something banal about being a man. Perseus excused himself and went upstairs to his room.

Perseus had a dream that night, the kind of dream that sticks in your mind. He was in a place that might have been a shopping mall of some sort, but it was labyrinthine in a weird and dreamlike sort of way. When he tried to leave, he couldn't retrace his steps. The mall appeared to have changed and places he had just visited in the dream were no longer where he remembered them to be. He walked down a long hall he didn't recall seeing before and opened a door at the far end. On the other side of the door was a dark shape, something he couldn't quite identify—or even describe. It whispered to him, and he began to follow it when, suddenly, the dream ended.

Two days later Perseus was told, to his great astonishment, that he must move out of his parents' house. They told him that it was for his own good, and that they were convinced he needed this act of tough love to help him get his life together. He was stunned beyond words. They were throwing him out on the street to fend for himself.

At first, he thought it must be some kind joke to get even with him for his April Fools jest, or a bluff to shock him into making some dramatic decisions on his own, but on April 5th, they literally threw him out, telling him to pack whatever he wanted to take with him and leave. He was allowed to keep his BMW, his clothes, and any keepsakes he wanted. They escorted him out the front door, wished him luck, and went back inside the house, shutting the door behind them.

He sat in his car, dazed, wondering what on earth he would do, where he would go. He had some money in his bank account, but not enough to start a new life from scratch. He didn't know how to feel about his parents and their draconian eviction from his home; the only life he knew. His first reaction was disbelief, which quickly morphed into seething anger, then dissolved into a pathetic self-pity.

All he had ever wanted was more of their attention. That need had been an incessant craving, the itch that couldn't be scratched. It was his need for their love; love he could never get enough of. He had always felt that they were very miserly in dolling out their affection toward him. Now this!

Perseus started the Beemer and backed out of the driveway and stopped. He just sat there in his car in the street gazing at the house, his home, *perhaps for the last time*, he thought. Suddenly, to his great surprise, he realized he wasn't really as devastated over this severing from the nest as he thought he should be. He found himself detached from any strong emotion one way or the other. Why was that? Maybe he was in some kind of shock.

It occurred to him that, deep down, he was actually looking forward to whatever adventures now lay ahead of him. It was all just too complicated to get his mind around all of it. He would have to sort it all out later.

His horse, Arion, popped into his head, distracting him from all these maddening emotions. What would become of him? He put the Beemer in gear and headed to the farm, focused on making some kind of arrangement with Hickory. He would know what to do.

He found Hickory inside the stables, grooming horses. "Good morning, Hickory."

"Well, good mornin' to you, Mister Percy. What brings you out here again so soon?"

"My parents."

Hickory looked at him quizzically. Perseus told him the whole story; about how his parents forgot his birthday, how they were disappointed in his apparent lack of motivation, and how they had ultimately thrown him out. When Hickory didn't show any sign of being stunned by this news, it triggered another bout of self-pity.

"I need to make some kind of arrangement for Arion," Perseus said after a pause. "I don't have any way to take him with me. I don't even know where I'm going. I was wondering if maybe you could give him to your nephew, Michael. He's a good horseman, and I'm sure he would take good care of him. I have enough money to cover his stabling costs for a couple of months. Maybe by then you could figure out where he could go." His voice trailed off and he stared into the distance. Hickory said nothing.

He turned away and walked toward Arion's stall. As Perseus drew near, Arion appeared at the stall door, and they put their heads together for several moments. Arion seemed to understand something significant was happening. With a huge sigh, Perseus felt all of the pent up emotions he didn't realize he'd been holding back flood out of him. A large tear rolled down his cheek. Hickory sensed what was happening and quietly continued his chores.

With a sideways glance, Perseus walked silently toward his Beemer. When he returned, he handed Hickory $1,000 in one-hundred-dollar bills. "Here's enough money to keep him here for two months. Can I leave him with you, Hickory? I know it's a lot to ask, but I don't know what else to do. I'm giving him to you. He's my horse, so I can transfer ownership to you."

Hickory waited a few more seconds before answering. "Yes, I'll take care of 'im, and I'll make sure he gets a good home too. Maybe we can figure somethin' out for keepin' 'im here. He's a fine horse, Percy, a mighty fine horse. They might take him in as one of the trainin' horses. Would that be okay with you?"

Perseus thought about that for a moment. "Yes, I think that would be a very good future for him. Thank you, Hickory. Well,

I guess I'll be going, although I'm not sure where. I thought I might just head west, you know, like the pioneers." He smiled.

Hickory smiled back. "You remember what I told you; life has a way of throwin' this kind of thing at us when we least expects it. You gonna be okay. You a good boy, a strong person. You'll do just fine, wherever ya go. Just stay strong and pay attention to them opportunities that life throws out there. They all mixed in with the obstacles."

They said their goodbyes; Perseus, Hickory, and Arion. Then, Perseus strode back to his car. With one final glance at Hickory and Arion, he got in his car and headed west.

it but would soon run out of money. She recommended he go to Oklahoma where there was a lot of opportunity for adventure. "It's Indian Territory," she said, ominously. She drew him a crude map showing the best way to get there through the winding back roads. He thanked her and continued on his journey.

The one-eyed woman's map took Perseus in a southwest direction and eventually out of the Ozarks. He was now traveling through the Ouachita National Forest, a vast forest reserve of nearly two-million acres covering much of western Arkansas and the far eastern edge of Oklahoma. There were several designated wilderness areas of old-growth forests blanketing the rugged terrain. As he drove among the centuries old trees, an unexpected feeling of rejuvenation swept over him. He couldn't explain why, but he felt connected to this place in a strangely compelling way.

On April 21st, as Perseus drew near to the small city of Hugo, Oklahoma, he was painfully aware that he was precariously low on funds. His father had cancelled his credit card, "for your own good," he'd said. As he approached the city limits, he saw the sign, Welcome to Hugo, established 1901: Circus City, USA. *No kidding? Well, that was interesting.*

He drove through the town, past the city limits on the other side, and decided to turn around. This was a small town, but it was larger than most of the tiny towns he'd driven through in the past several days. He decided he should stop here for a while to give himself some time to figure out what he should do next.

He spied a quaint diner at the eastern edge of town and pulled in. The sign read, *Syble's Café*. It looked like a classic greasy spoon, the kind of place that might offer inexpensive but decent food. It was the middle of the afternoon, and there was only one other customer inside. He took a seat at the counter a few stools down from the other customer, and the lone waitress, a nice-looking, older woman, handed him a plastic covered menu.

"Hi there. I'm Syble. I'll be your waitress and cook," she said, offering him a big smile. "Can I get you something to drink while you look over the menu?"

"Uh, do you have any bottled water, like, maybe Perrier?"

She studied him a moment, then chuckled. "Honey, if you want water, what you get here is whatever comes out of the tap."

Perseus had to take a few seconds to recall if he had ever had water from a tap. "Oh. Yeah, I suppose that would be okay. Sure. Does it come with ice?"

Syble laughed. "I'll put some ice in it for you, honey, no extra charge." She walked away still chuckling.

Perseus looked at the menu, which included items for breakfast—served all day, lunch, and supper. He glanced at his Audemars Piguet wrist watch to check the time, wondering if he should order lunch or supper. It became obvious, however, that breakfast was cheaper and, therefore, the more prudent choice. He pulled his wallet out of his back pocket and took inventory of his cash: $43 and change.

Syble came back with a large plastic glass of ice water. "Here you go, honey. Decide what you want yet?"

"Could I get the bacon-egg special with white toast, no butter?"

She looked at him without saying anything.

"Your menu says breakfast "served all day," he said defensively, pointing to the menu. He impulsively looked over at the only other customer, who was watching his interaction with Syble, a smirk on his face. Perseus returned his attention to Syble. "The fact is I'm running a little low on funds. I need to conserve my cash."

Syble looked him over, noticing his seriously wrinkled clothes and generally disheveled appearance. "Sure, we serve breakfast all day, honey. How do you want those eggs? And don't tell me poached." She stated with a thin smile.

"Scrambled, if that's okay."

She shook her head slightly and headed back toward the kitchen, chuckling again. Perseus felt a little embarrassed but wasn't sure why exactly. He suddenly realized that the other customer was still staring at him, so he turned to meet his gaze. They just sat there appraising each other for several seconds.

"You're new in town," the other young man said, eventually. "Just passing through?"

"To tell you the truth, I don't know yet. I guess I might have to stay a while. Are you from here?"

"Yeah. I live north of town a ways. My grandfather has a place up there and I live with him, you know, to kind of help out. He has a small farm."

Perseus noticed there was something a little different about this person: his complexion, facial features, and the way he talked. He wondered if maybe this fellow was an Indian. He'd never met an Indian before. He racked his brain, trying to remember which tribe lived in this area. He could only recall a little bit of his American history about Indians, but he did remember that Oklahoma was once designated as the territory where Indians were forced to go when the Jackson-era government brutally enforced some kind of Indian removal policy.

"My name is Buck," Perseus lied. If this guy was an Indian, he didn't want to tell him his stupid real name.

The other man studied Perseus, as if he was trying to figure something out. Finally, he said, "No it's not."

"What?" Perseus felt the warmth creep up his neck as the thought of being caught in a lie overtook him.

"Your name isn't Buck. I don't think so."

"Why would you say that?"

"You don't look like someone named Buck. You got a fancy car, and a fancy watch, and even though you look like hell, you got fancy clothes. And I can tell from your accent that you're from back east somewhere."

Perseus stared at the other man in amazement. "You're right. My name isn't Buck. The fact is, I don't like my real name and I want to change it. Buck sounds like the kind of name people might have out here, in the west I mean."

"My name is Tommy, Tommy Abbot. I know you're wondering whether or not I'm a Native-American, or you'd probably say, Indian. I'm a member of the Choctaw Nation. All of this land around here is part of the Choctaw Nation, although the white man has stolen much of it since it was given to us," he raised his hands in the air in mock solemnity, "as long as the grass grows and the water runs." He gave a wry laugh. "You're in Choctaw County. Hugo is the county seat. The Choctaw Nation is really big, almost seven-million acres, covering eight counties and part of five more."

Perseus wasn't sure what to say. "Well, my name is actually Perseus, but some people call me Percy." After a pause, he added, "I've never met an Indian, I mean Native-American, before but I'm pleased to meet you, Tommy."

"You running away from something?"

"You seem to be inordinately perceptive," Perseus responded. "What makes you think that I'm running away?"

"Don't take no genius to figure that out. You're saying you're almost broke, yet you have that car and that watch. You don't look like a criminal on the run, so I'm guessing you've left your rich home back east." Placing his index finger aside his nose, as if in thought, he continued, "and maybe your parents cut you off."

Perseus was nodding his head. "That's pretty close. I got kicked out, told I had to figure out what I was going to do with my life. I just turned twenty-one. Guess my parents got fed up with me and thought it was time I went out on my own. Bit of a shock actually."

Tommy chuckled. "I'll bet. But, you know, Perseus isn't a bad name. That's the name of some kind of old Greek hero or something isn't it? That's the guy who cut the head off the lady with all the snakes in her hair, right?"

Perseus was impressed. "Yes, that's right. Perseus from the Greek myths was definitely a hero, a badass really. But in today's world, a guy with that kind of name is a natural target for bullies."

Sybil came out from the kitchen with a plate of bacon and eggs. "Here you go, Perseus. Would you like some coffee with that? On the house." she quickly added. "I can hear everything that's being said out here from the kitchen," responding to Perseus' look of surprise that she knew his name.

Tommy was laughing again, and Sybil joined in. "I guess you can be grateful they didn't name you Sisyphus," Tommy said.

Even Perseus had to laugh at that. "I guess you're right," Perseus added. "Or Uranus, Father of the Titans." Of course, he didn't pronounce Uranus correctly, so now they were all laughing.

"If you need a safe place to hunker down for a spell," Sybil said, "you could stay in your car out back, and help me with dishes in the café in the evening in exchange for three meals a day."

Perseus shoveled a bit of egg into his mouth, then looked up at Sybil. "That's very generous of you, Sybil. May I call you Sybil?"

"Of course, that's my name. So, is it a deal?"

For some reason, Perseus felt compelled to look over at Tommy, who gave him a quick nod of approval. He returned his gaze to Sybil. "Yes, thank you. Thank you very much."

That night, in the cramped discomfort of his car, Perseus had a dream very similar to the one he had the night of his birthday. This time, however, he was in a very large house, wandering through its many rooms. Once again, the place was labyrinthine, making it impossible to find his way back to the entrance. He eventually found himself up in a large attic filled with all kinds of strange objects. As he made his way around a large armoire, he came across the dark shadow-like thing he had encountered in the first dream. It whispered to him. It seemed to be trying to show him the way out just as he awoke.

After two nights of sleeping in his car, Syble told Perseus he could come inside and use the old Army cot she had stashed in the storage room. During the day, between his free meals and before washing dishes at night, he explored the town and discovered a number of unexpected and interesting places. He was surprised to find that Hugo was frequently used as the winter quarters for circus and rodeo companies. The town had a retirement facility for circus elephants and a unique cemetery for deceased circus performers. There was also an annual rodeo around Memorial Day. It became increasingly clear to him that this town was a genuine cowboy and Indian kind of place. One thing was for sure, it was a long way from Falls Church, Virginia—not just in distance but also in culture.

On day five of his new career as a dishwasher, he was sitting at the counter after lunch, nursing a cup of coffee and talking with Tommy, who had dropped by to see how he was doing, when an attractive young woman walked in. She walked up to the counter and called out for Syble, who was in the back preparing for supper. The young woman was wearing a pair of men's Wrangler jeans, a light blue denim shirt, with a red bandana tied around her neck, and a white straw cowboy hat. Her boots were the western work style that men frequently wore. She glanced over at the two young men who were staring at her. She locked eyes with them, staring back in an exaggerated manner. They quickly looked away, embarrassed. She smiled smugly.

Syble emerged from the kitchen wiping her hands on a towel. "Hello, Penelope. You got my order?"

"Yes, ma'am. Just wanted to be sure you were ready to receive it."

"Oh sure. Perseus, honey, be a doll and help bring that beef order in, would you?"

Perseus looked up stupidly at Syble. "What? Oh, yes, sure." He stood up quickly, losing his balance and nearly falling. "Where is it?" he asked Penelope.

She smirked at his awkwardness. "Follow me. It's just outside."

He followed her out to a big, beige Ford Super Duty F-350 with dually rear wheels. She opened the back door of the crew cab, reached in, and handed him a large, heavy box full of frozen meat. He buckled slightly under the weight, but quickly adjusted his balance and headed back into the café, Penelope following close behind. Syble directed him to put it in the freezer, while she signed off on the delivery.

"Who's your new employee?" Penelope asked Syble as she gestured with her thumb toward Perseus.

"Oh, that's Perseus. He's from Virginia, out here on an adventure." Syble offered as she air quoted the word *adventure*. "He ran out of money, so he's kind of stuck here for a while. So, I offered to help him out until he figures out what he's going to do. He's sleeping on a cot in the back room and doing dishes to cover his meals."

Penelope looked Perseus over when he returned, making him feel uncomfortable. She thought he looked like he'd lost his hair brush and was sleeping in his clothes. He seemed sturdy enough though. Her father was looking for someone to help out at the ranch. It was the beginning of the spring calving season, and things were getting busy, but nobody wanted to do the grunt work that needed to be done.

"My dad's looking for some help out at the HB Cattle Company. Everyone just calls it the HB. Pay's $150 a week, plus room and board. It's hard work though. Seven days a week 'till we get the cattle to market sometime in late October."

Perseus looked at her carefully to see if maybe this was a joke, but she seemed dead serious. He looked at Syble who just stared back, and then he looked over to Tommy.

"I'd take the job if I were you," Tommy said. "It's a good outfit."

Perseus looked at Penelope and nodded his head.

"Okay, then. Go gather up your things. You can follow me out to the HB. You start today. I'll wait for you in the truck." She thanked Syble for her order and headed outside.

Turning to Syble, Perseus asked with a questioning glance, "You sure it's okay, Syble?"

"Of course, it's okay. That's what you've been waiting for, isn't it? You need a job so you can make enough money to move on to your next adventure. And who knows, this might be something that changes your whole life, being a cowboy that is."

A cowboy? Is that what he'd just signed up to be? This was a totally unexpected turn of events, but he couldn't think of any reason not to go with it, so he went to the back of the café and gathered up his meager possessions. On his way out the door, he thanked Syble for her help, then hesitantly gave her a hug.

"Go on then," she said. "Before I start blubbering."

He told Tommy he hoped he'd see him around and Tommy assured him that he would.

Glancing back one last time, Perseus followed Penelope out. He quickly got into his Beemer and trailed Penelope's big truck to the HB. *This might turn out to be a real adventure after all.*

CHAPTER 3

PENELOPE INTRODUCED PERSEUS to her father, Bud Wesley, who was clearly not very impressed with the young man's looks. But he desperately needed the help, so he agreed to bring him on. Penelope escorted Perseus around all the facilities surrounding the main barn, describing his initial duties along the way. The list was a grim assortment of thankless jobs, including mucking stalls, hauling manure, feeding, cleaning, and repairing tack. She told him the specific chores changed throughout the season to match the needs of the HB's cattle operations.

Penelope introduced him to the bunkhouse, a separate portion of the main barn. This barn's primary function was to provide stables for the ranch's horses, and included a tack room, storage space for equine hay, feed supplies, and tools.

Perseus quickly regarded the space, noting its austere functionality. There were six bunkbeds, six lockers, a table with six chairs, and a kitchen area equipped with a sink, a coffee maker, and a microwave oven. Two comfortable-looking chairs occupied one end of the room, along with a couple of floor lamps and a book-shelf containing few books but plenty of magazines pertaining to horses, cattle, guns, fishing, and trucks. There were two very basic bathrooms located at the opposite ends of the bunk area. He already felt out of place.

There were currently only two other hands working at the HB. Penelope pointed out which bunks were theirs, although Perseus thought it was pretty obvious just by looking at them. She assigned Perseus the third lower bunk and a locker. In addition to the ranch hands, there was a Mexican couple who lived in a small cabin close to the main house. The wife, Angelica, took care of the housekeeping, including all the cooking. The husband, Chilo, handled all the handyman work, the dogs, the chickens, a few hogs, butchering, and other work when an extra hand was needed.

It was plain to see that the ranch was well organized and in very good shape. In addition to the main barn, there were several out-buildings and storage facilities used for various specific purposes. He was told he must quickly learn where everything was.

Penelope showed him the special barn and yard for the breeding bulls, which Perseus found particularly intimidating.

"The bulls are kept in this barn and the pens behind the barn until it's time to put them in with the cows and heifers of breeding age," Penelope explained. "This monster is a cull bull and that one over there is too young for use in breeding this year, so they'll both stay here." They all looked quite massive, and dangerous, to Perseus and he hoped his duties didn't require him to ever be inside with them.

Penelope showed him the long, covered structures used for protecting bales of hay. There were also bulky, open-ended granaries used to protect huge piles of various types of cattle feed from the elements. Another large shed contained several tractors and machinery of diverse sizes and functions. Perseus was quickly becoming overwhelmed.

At the end of his tour, Perseus was introduced to Chilo, who explained, once again, his initial duties. These chores started immediately. He had to clean all eight horse stalls and bring in fresh straw bedding. He must clean up any manure in the breeze-way and put the nightly ration of hay and feed in front of each stall. Feeding the horses took place at 6:00 AM and 6:00 PM every day. All manure had to be hauled to a special holding area away from the barn.

When the horses were returned to the stables, he was required to remove, clean, and put away their tack, then brush down each animal. There were three more horses in a paddock outside, next to the barn, and their area also had to be cleaned daily. Any horses not used during the day had to be turned out and exercised.

Although this work was considered drudge labor by all the others, these particular horse-related duties were quite familiar to Perseus. During the years of his equine training out at the farm in Aldie, he'd helped Hickory do all these same tasks. He was elated that he would once again enjoy the good fortune to be close to horses.

He was less enthusiastic about feeding and watering the incarcerated bulls and the small cull herd of cattle in a nearby paddock. The bulls scared him and feeding the cull herd required him to learn how to load specific amounts of feed ingredients into a menacing contraption that distributed the stuff into a long feeding trough. None of this was particularly difficult, but it magnified his ignorance of all things related to cattle operations, which ultimately exposed him to teasing by the others.

The other two HB hands, his bunk mates, were rough-cut cowboys who possessed a lifetime of cattle experience. They were also men of few words, but quick to pass judgement. Perseus decided that Slim was the older of the two men; a lean, wiry kind of guy around thirty years old. The man somehow managed to maintain a perpetual stubble on his face, a stubble which seemed to neither grow nor ever get shaved. Günter, the other hired hand, was maybe in his mid-twenties; a large, barrel-chested man with an impressive mustache that drooped well past the corners of his mouth.

It became immediately apparent to Perseus that neither of them was happy with his invasion of their rustic domain. They weren't openly hostile, but, perhaps worse, they acted as if he was not actually in the room most of the time. If he asked them something, they typically ignored him. When he sat in one of the two comfortable-looking chairs one evening, they both told him those chairs were taken.

At night, as he tried to sleep, he could hear the horses in the barn moving about, making all kinds of horse-related noises. He would occasionally hear rodents scamper across the rafters above the ceiling, and there was the nearly constant lowing of the cattle in the distance. There were also mysterious, disconcerting night-noises he could not identify, not to mention Slim and Günter's snoring.

At meals, which were always taken up at the main house in a large dining room, the only person who would talk to him was Angelica, the housekeeper. Unfortunately, her broken English and her strong accent made it very difficult for Perseus to understand what she was trying to say. He often had to just smile and nod, which, more often than not, elicited a derisive snuffling sound from Slim.

Even Penelope seemed to largely ignore him. He had hoped to be able to see her more often and maybe get to know her, but she was always busy doing whatever it was she did on the ranch, so their paths rarely crossed. At meals, she was focused on exchanging information about the operation with her father. On the infrequent occasions when she did favor him with her attention, she was pleasant but remote.

Perseus spotted Chilo fixing a broken stall door in the barn one morning and came over to talk to him.

"Hi, Chilo. Mind if I ask you something?"

"No, Mister Percy, I don't mind."

"How long have you worked here at the HB?"

"I been here all my life," he said. "I came here with my parents when I was maybe only four years old. My papa work here for many years. He was a vaquero, you know, a Mexican cowboy. He die of a heart attack one day. I was maybe then fifteen years old. Mister Bud, he ask me to start working, but I was no vaquero like my papa, so he hired Slim, and I do all the other work. My mama, she was very sad about my papa and wanted to go back to Mexico."

"How did you meet Angelica?" Perseus asked.

"When Miss Hellen get sick with the cancer, Mister Bud ask me to see if my mama know somebody who can help in the house. Mama send this girl, Angelica, from Mexico. She was very young, but she did a good job. Later, we get married."

"How young was she?"

"I think nineteen. I was already thirty, but she liked me, and now we are very happy. Mister Bud, he's very good to us. He is a good man."

"Is that where HB comes from? Hellen and Bud?"

"Si, that's it."

After just one week on the job, Perseus decided he was probably not cut out for ranching. He didn't really fit in. His only happy time was when he was alone with the horses. He thought it would be best if he quit after the first payday and moved on. That night, he tossed and turned in his bunk, wondering if quitting was the right thing to do. Sleep finally overtook him, and he drifted into another dream about being in a place where he could not find the way out, and the same dark figure loomed nearby and whispered to him.

The next day, while everyone else was out working with the new spring-born calves, he singled out one of the horses in the paddock outside the barn. This horse seemed to be particularly skittish and he thought it must be new to the HB's remuda. He had discovered that a remuda is what they called an outfit's herd of horses in these parts. He wanted to work with him to see if he could settle him down a bit. He knew wrangling duties were not part of his job description, but nobody else seemed to be doing anything about getting this horse in shape, and he liked the animal's spirit

Perseus enticed the sturdy buckskin over with some sweet feed. By talking to him softly, and gently stroking his neck, he finally managed to get him calmed enough to put a halter over his head. Then he attached a lead rope to the halter and led him out of the paddock and into the nearby round pen. He expertly unhooked the lead rope and turned him loose. Perseus walked out into the center of the pen and started coaxing the horse to move around the perimeter, twirling the lead rope around with his wrist so that the rope was going in a circle perpendicular to the ground. The horse started out at a trot, then Perseus pushed a little harder until the horse shifted into a canter. After a little while, he pushed even harder, forcing the horse to run at a gallop. When the gelding tried to slow down, Perseus clucked his tongue and pushed him on. Eventually, the horse's focus shifted totally to Perseus.

He let the horse slowdown in stages, maintaining eye contact with him at all times. When the horse was moving at a walk and showing clear signs of wanting to communicate, Perseus stopped swinging the lead rope, turned his back to the horse, and just stood there in the middle of the pen, pretending to ignore him. Within a few minutes, the gelding walked over and stood next the Perseus, who, in turn, stroked his neck.

"You're a good boy," he praised him reassuringly. "I can tell you're very smart too." Perseus reattached the lead rope to the halter, led the horse around the training pen a few more times, and then returned him to the paddock.

He repeated this training technique, one he had learned from Hickory, for the next two days. On day four, Perseus focused on getting a blanket and saddle on the horse, doing it over and over until the activity became routine.

On the fifth day, he brushed the gelding down until he gleamed, affectionately stroking the animal's neck often.

"I'm going to call you Balius. That was the name of one of Achilles' immortal horses," he said quietly.

Balius nickered, bobbing his head as if he approved of the name. Perseus then saddled him up and walked him out to the round pen. He cautiously mounted and sat quietly in the saddle for a long moment, allowing Balius time to get used to the feeling. Perseus was sure this had been a wild horse, probably added to the HB remuda quite recently. He wondered if he might have been captured in one of the annual mustang roundups he'd heard about.

Perseus felt the horse gradually relax under him and nudged him forward. He took his time, using his body to send subtle, yet specific signals to the gelding. Within an hour, he had successfully taken him through all the basic maneuvers. He could tell Balius was going to become an excellent working horse.

Perseus began to wonder what had happened to payday. Penelope told him the pay was $150 a week, but they apparently didn't pay every week. At breakfast one morning, he asked about it. After an uncomfortable pause, Bud told him payday was at the end of each month.

"I was just wondering. Thank you."

"Do you need some cash for something?" Bud asked, a little suspicious that Perseus might be ready to cut and run.

"No, sir. I was just wondering is all."

"I want you to join the rest of us today. We're going to start moving the cow-calf groups to specific pastures," Bud said. "We'll need everyone to help keep them together. Lots of young calves out there, and there's more than a good chance that some of 'em will get separated from their mothers. That creates all kinds of problems. Can you ride a horse?"

Perseus didn't look up. The question didn't seem unusual to him. It was a ranch, after all. "Yes, sir." He kept eating.

Everyone else at the table stopped what they were doing and exchanged glances, a few eyebrows shot up. Nobody really believed him, and Slim let loose a snorting laugh of incredulity, which caught Perseus' attention. He looked up and saw that everyone was staring at him.

"What? I can ride."

After breakfast, everybody assembled in the big barn to saddle their horses. Perseus told everyone he had to go to his locker to fetch his riding boots. While he was gone, Slim went out to the paddock to fetch a horse for Perseus and brought it into the stable's breezeway. It was the new horse that the manager from a neighboring ranch had given to Bud about a month ago.

"Slim, that's not funny," Penelope said, frowning. "He'll get injured if he tries to ride that wild thing."

"Aw, it ain't gonna kill 'im," Slim said. "Kid said he knows how ta ride."

Penelope looked to her father for some help, but he just kept saddling his own horse, saying nothing. She shook her head in annoyed exasperation.

Perseus came out of the bunk room wearing his jodhpurs and high-top hunter riding boots. He found an old John Deere ball cap in one of the empty lockers and put it on to help keep the sun out of his eyes. He looked perfectly ridiculous to the ranchers. Everyone stared at him for a few seconds before exploding into fits of laughter. He halted in his tracks. Slim was holding Balius. Perseus could see where this was going.

He nonchalantly walked over to Slim. "Is that the horse you want me to ride today?"

"Yep. This here horse is the best one for you," Slim said, barely able to contain himself.

"Where'd you get them boots, boy?" Günter asked. "They're awful purdy."

"And them pants," Slim chimed in.

Even Penelope was chuckling. She couldn't help it. *Poor Perseus*, she thought. *He doesn't have a clue.*

Perseus ignored them all and took the lead rope from Slim and walked Balius over to a nearby tie rail. Nobody noticed that he tied a proper bowknot when he tied the lead rope to the rail. Everyone pretended to be engrossed in preparing their own horse while watching Perseus out of the corner of their eye.

After a quick brushing, he put a blanket and saddle on Balius without the expected blowup. This surprised everybody, but they continued to studiously ignore him. Perseus then replaced the halter with a soft snaffle-bit bridle. Everyone headed out of the barn and prepared to mount up. Perseus waited until everyone else was ready before he mounted. He patted Balius' neck, then got up in the saddle and found his seat.

"I'm ready whenever you are," he said to the others, who were all gawking at him as if he had just performed the most amazing magic trick imaginable. Penelope was the first one to recover.

"He said he could ride," she said, smiling. "Come on, let's get moving."

They rode out to the large cow-calf herd that Bud wanted to relocate. They began carefully pushing the animals, moving them slowly, trying not to excite them. Perseus knew nothing about working cattle, but he was good at following directions, and, to everybody's utter astonishment, he was an outstanding horseman. The horse he was riding was also amazing, executing every movement Perseus asked of him.

Penelope kept watching him every chance she could. His style and comportment, his confidence and seat, and the young, athletic horse; they all came together to create a very impressive horse and rider combination that was truly a joy to watch. *Who would have thought?*

At the end of the day, after he had finished all his regular chores, Perseus straggled up to the dining room for some supper. He was still in his hunter riding boots and jodhpurs. Everyone else was already there and halfway through their supper when he walked in. Bud put down his fork and began clapping his hands. Penelope and then Slim and Günter joined him. Perseus looked around the table, and, realizing they must be applauding him, self-consciously dripped his chin.

"You surprised us all today, Perseus. You can, indeed, ride. Yes, sir," Bud said, and everybody else chimed in their agreement.

Perseus didn't know what to say, so he just went over to the sideboard and dished up a heaping plate.

"What I'd like ta know," said Slim in his exaggerated Texas draw, "Is what in the hell kind of boots is those you got on?" Everyone chuckled.

"They're called hunter riding boots. They're commonly used in competitive hunter jumping events, along with these funny-looking pants, called jodhpurs." He paused. "If you think these look silly, you should see the rest of the outfit."

They were all curious now, so he described the required Hunter Equitation competition attire. "Out here, that outfit looks pretty silly, but in the competitions, everybody is required to dress like that. I guess I should go get some clothes that are more appropriate for ranch work. Never occurred to me that I'd ever be doing this kind of riding."

"How the heck did you settle that wild mustang, and when?" Günter asked.

"It's a technique for communicating with a horse that my old equestrian trainer taught me back in Virginia. It's really fairly simple. Just takes patience and the knowledge of how horses communicate. I did it in between my chores." He sat quietly for a moment.

"I want to tell you all that today was a really great day for me. I've trained with horses for many years. At this point in my life, I thought all that training and all the skills I learned were useless. Today, I realized they are the one skill set that is perfect for this kind of work. I don't want to sound all sappy and everything, but today was kind of a turning point for me. Thank you."

Now everybody was quiet. Nobody was sure how to act, then Penelope reached over and put her hand on his shoulder.

"Perseus, you looked wonderful in that saddle today. You impressed us all. We thought watching you get up on that wild horse this morning was going to be a kind of joke, a dangerous joke. But the joke was on us. I think you're a natural horseman, and you're going to make a great cowboy someday, if that's something you want to do."

That night, as he lay in his bunk, he thought about his parents. It had been five weeks since he left home. They had not called him or left any kind of message in all that time. He wondered if they expected him to call them, perhaps to beg them for permission to come back home. He didn't know how to feel. On one hand, he wanted to tell them about the day he just had, how he had impressed all these professional cattlemen. On the other hand, he was pretty sure they wouldn't appreciate the significance of the achievement. They would no doubt consider his current situation as yet another example of his irresponsibility, more waste of time, and yet another disappointment.

He pushed these thoughts out of his mind. He was bringing himself down when he should be basking in the warmth of the HB cowboys' appreciation of what he had done. He also thought Penelope seemed pretty impressed. That was something to feel good about. He focused on the feel of her hand on his shoulder at supper, and gradually drifted off to sleep.

CHAPTER 4

PERSEUS FINISHED HIS morning chores and hurried up
to the house for breakfast. He was always the last to arrive for
breakfast and supper due to the nature of his assigned duties.
He perused the breakfast choices on the sideboard. There were
no boxes of sugar-laden cereals in the lineup, but plenty of other
tempting items. He hadn't thought of Lucky Charms since arriving
at the HB.

All of Angelica's meals had a Mexican influence to them,
which at first made him leery of trying anything. But he eventually
came to realize that just about everything she prepared was good,
and he had discovered chorizo since working here. That's what he
chose this morning. He wrapped a substantial serving of the highly
seasoned sausage in a flour tortilla and washed it down with a large
glass of orange juice.

Bud was already finished with his breakfast when Perseus sat
down. "We're going to put the bulls out with the cows this morning, Percy," he announced. "Soon as you're finished, go on down
to the bull pen area and help me get 'em out and moving to their
assigned herds. Slim and Günter are going to get things organized

out in paddocks. We do natural breeding here, so we're going to put specific bulls out with selected cows and heifers."

"Alright. I'll be there as soon I finish breakfast. Do you want me on the ground or on a horse?"

"You'll need to be on a horse." Bud noticed Perseus' angst. "Don't worry, I'll tell you what you need to do. It's mostly just pushing them along."

"Got it." Perseus was thrilled to have the opportunity to get involved with another real cowboy chore, but he couldn't suppress his anxiety about being around the bulls, especially if they weren't on the other side of a stout, heavy-duty pipe corral.

After breakfast, he quickly saddled Balius and led him over to the bull pen facility where Bud was waiting. The bulls were kept in a series of small paddocks, two bulls to a pen. Bud explained that, although they were going to use two bulls per herd, as a precaution they were going to take one bull at a time to the designated cow paddock to minimize problems related to aggression.

"These boys are reasonably well behaved, but they've been cooped up for quite a while and they'll be excited about getting out into some open pasture with all them ladies," Bud told him with a smile. "The second bull is a backup in case the primary bull doesn't do his job. We run the backup alongside the herd for a couple weeks, so if we have to change 'em out, the herd is already familiar with the backup bull."

Perseus was nervous but stayed focused on the work. These animals were very large, each weighing well over 2000 pounds, and they were downright scary. He realized that Balius probably didn't have enough training and experience around cattle to be doing this sort of work, but it was too late to do anything about that now.

They got the first bull out and moved him down the dirt road to his designated group, about a quarter mile from the barnyard. When they were about a hundred yards from the gate, Slim and Günter rode up to take control. They moved the big bull into a smaller adjoining paddock and closed the outer gate. Bud and Perseus stayed until the bull was successfully herded inside the main paddock, then they headed back to the bull pens to fetch the backup bull.

They brought the second bull to the breeding paddock, but this time the bull was kept inside the smaller, adjacent paddock. He wasn't happy about being kept from getting to the cows and began bellowing his disagreement immediately. The primary bull was already claiming ownership of his herd and returned bellowed warnings of his own. The two bulls, who only minutes earlier seemed quite docile and compatible, were now behaving aggressively toward each other. This is obviously what Bud had been talking about. Perseus shuddered.

This process was repeated for the other three breeding groups and Perseus became more comfortable with each successive move. Finally, he and Bud brought the fourth and final backup bull down the road. This bull, however, was growing more agitated by the competitive exchanges coming from the other bulls as he passed by their paddocks. It became increasingly difficult to keep him moving, and he began swinging his massive head back and forth as he became increasingly belligerent.

As they drew closer to the open gate of the destination paddock, Slim and Günter formed a barrier with their horses near the opening to help ensure the bull didn't try to run off in another direction. The bull grudgingly moved halfway through the entrance but then stopped, apparently checking out the herd a short distance away. Günter dismounted and began closing the gate, while Slim rode his horse right up to the massive animal, leaned over and smacked him on the rump to get him to move all the way inside. The bull took a few steps forward, allowing Günter to get the gate closed, but then he stopped again. The agitated animal turned and lowered his head menacingly at Slim and his horse, who were now inside the pen with the bull.

Slim expertly backed his horse up to the heavy rail fence and attempted to gallop around the bull and deeper into the paddock to get the angry beast to move away from the gate, but the bull suddenly charged. Slim's horse was startled and stopped short, crow-hopping sideways. The abrupt, erratic movement threw Slim out of his saddle and he hit the ground hard. Fortunately, the bull's attention was still focused on the horse as it now cantered further into the paddock. Slim lay still on the ground, dazed by the fall.

The bull quickly lost interest in the horse and turned around to see Slim slowly getting to his feet. It began moving toward him as his horse ran back to the gate. Günter opened the gate to let the horse escape, and, in that brief moment, without giving it any thought, Perseus put his heels into Balius and charged into the paddock. He didn't hear Bud yelling at him to stop, as he flew toward the bull at full speed, whooping and hollering. Balius didn't hesitate for even one second. They flew right in front of the enraged bull, drawing its attention to them. The tactic worked.

The bull stopped dead in its tracks and watched as Perseus and Balius spun around and began rapidly pivoting back and forth, trying to get the bull to turn away from Slim, who was now slowly limping his way back toward the gate. The ploy worked. With the bull's attention averted, Bud jumped off his horse and ran inside the paddock to help Slim get out. When Perseus saw that he was safe, he enticed the bull to the far end of the paddock then raced to the gate, opening and closing it without dismounting.

He jumped off Balius and rushed over to where the others were attending to Slim.

"I don't think I broke anything," Slim was saying. "Just knocked the wind outta me. Reckon I'll have a bruise or two to boot." He looked up at Perseus. "Thank you, Percy. What you did took a lot of guts, man."

"It was a fool thing to do," Bud said. "But that was some darn impressive horsemanship."

"Yeah," Slim said. "If'n you'd got hurt or kilt, I'd a had to start cleanin' the stalls again." They all laughed.

That evening, Perseus was sitting outside the big barn on a stack of bags of horse feed. They had been delivered earlier that day and needed to be put up in the barn. Storing feed sacks was one of his mundane chores, but he thought it could wait until morning. He was tired and there was no threat of rain tonight. It was a beautiful spring evening, the kind of evening a person ought to kick back and enjoy.

There was no moon to light the sky, only the ever-abundant blanket of stars. One of the wonders of this place, Perseus had discovered, was the amazing number of stars he could see. There were very few outdoor lights around the HB, and no city lights to pollute the night sky. He tried to remember if he had ever actually seen the Milky Way before coming to this place. It made him feel small but full of wonder.

The sound of Slim's guitar drifted through the barn. As if on cue, one of the horses nickered. Perseus heard the muffled words of an old cowboy song Slim was fond of playing.

A cowboy's life is hard and dusty.
    He rides alone most every day.
He rides into town with his head hung down,
    Singing yippee ki-yippee ki-yay.

I rode into town in search of whiskey.
    Passing through was my plan.
But there at the bar in that tavern
    Stood the devil of a man.

He said, "Boy, I don't like yer looks,
  Your cowboy hat, or yer horse.
So step outside and test yer courage
  And let the Fates take their course.

The street outside was oh so empty.
  The sun was high at noon.
Stood two men, we faced each other.
  One was sure to meet his doom.

We drew our guns, I drew mine faster.
  Bullets flew, mine met its mark.
He staggered back against my pony
  With a bullet in his heart.

A cowboy's life is hard and dusty.
  He rides alone most every day.
He rides into town with his head hung down,
  Singing yippee ki-yippee ki-yay.

He heard a noise as the song ended, someone approaching the barn, but it was too dark to tell who it was. "Hello, who's there?" he called out.

"Hi, Perseus. It's me, Penelope."

He sat up straight. "Oh, hello," he said, a little jolt of unexpected pleasure perking him up. "I'm just sitting out here enjoying all these stars. I was going to put these sacks away, but I got distracted. I can do it in the morning, if that's alright."

She didn't answer him. She came close enough now so he could make out her shadowed form and see her turn to look up at the sky. "Yes, they're beautiful. I never get tired of looking at them. When there's no moon to wash out the darkness, like tonight, they really pop. Mind if I sit down?"

"Of course not. Pull up a bag," he said cheerily.

"What you did today was pretty brave, or crazy, or both."

"Well, I wasn't trying to be brave, that's for sure. To tell you the truth, I was scared to death. I'm always nervous around those bulls. Don't know if I can ever get used to them." He suddenly felt self-conscious. "I just reacted without thinking. You know, adrenalin, I guess. I was afraid Slim was going to get killed."

"When I brought you out here to the HB, I really didn't think you would last long. You didn't seem like the type who would take to this kind of work, this kind of life. You've surprised me."

"Why did you offer me the job?" he asked, thinking the conversation was taking a strange turn.

"My dad really needed the help, and there you were, looking for something to do. I don't know, I figured it was a temporary fix. But you're not the kind of person I originally thought you were, not at all. Why are you here, Perseus, I mean here in this part of the world?"

He couldn't see her very well in the darkness, even though she was only a few feet away, but he could see her shape and he could smell her. She smelled of hay and horses and earth —and lavender soap. It made him a little dizzy.

"My parents kicked me out of their house two days after my twenty-first birthday. I didn't live up to their expectations; at least I think that's why they turned me out. They're both professors at Howard University in Washington DC, and they wanted me to be more like them, I guess. I just got in my car and started heading west. I don't really know for sure why I'm here. Well, there was that one-eyed woman in the Ozarks who told me I should go to Oklahoma." He thought about that for a few seconds. *Maybe more than just coincidence?*

"Bottom line is, I ran out of money by the time I got to Hugo, but I suppose you're asking me philosophically. I'd have to say I'm on a journey, trying to find myself." He suddenly laughed. "Boy, that sounded corny." He laughed some more. He couldn't see the expression on Penelope's face.

"To tell you the truth, I didn't think I was going to be here very long either," he continued, "and I came close to quitting. But that day I got the chance to work on Balius with the rest of you? Well, that day kind of changed things for me. As unlikely as it seems, and I mean to myself, I think maybe this is the kind of life I was meant for."

Neither of them spoke for several minutes, just sitting there looking up at the stars. Then Penelope said, "I want you to go into town with me on Sunday afternoon, after chores. We need to get you some different clothes."

"Sure, that sounds great."

She got up and headed back to the house. Perseus wasn't sure what had just happened, but he figured it was a good omen. That night, he had another dream like the other ones; lost in a maze, a dark shadow trying to help him escape.

CHAPTER 5

ON SUNDAY, PENELOPE took Perseus shopping as promised. They visited three different stores to locate everything Penelope thought he should have to complete his new wardrobe, including Wrangler blue jeans, a broad leather belt, some western style work boots, leather work gloves, denim shirts, some T-shirts, and a western-style straw hat. She bought him a red bandana to complete the wardrobe. When they were done, Perseus was essentially broke again, but he was happy and feeling optimistic about his future.

On the way back to the HB, they stopped by Syble's to say hello. Of course, he was now wearing some of his newly acquired western wear and looking considerably different than when Syble last saw him.

"Well, as I live and breathe," Syble said as she spotted them coming in the front door. "That can't be Perseus, can it?"

Perseus was smiling so broadly he was afraid his face might crack. Penelope was also smiling, quite pleased with herself and her effort to transform this eastern greenhorn into a reasonable semblance of a cowboy.

"Hi, Syble," Perseus said.

"Hello, yourself. How are things going out there at the HB?"

"Okay, I guess."

"You should see him ride, Syble," Penelope bragged. "Who knew he was an accomplished equestrian? He's doing great."

Perseus was feeling a little embarrassed now, but he was enjoying the attention. "How's business been here at the café, Syble?" he asked, mostly to change the subject.

"Fine. Just fine. I miss my dishwasher though." They all laughed.

Just then Tommy Abbott walked up to Perseus, who hadn't noticed him when they walked in. "Hello, cowboy. Man, have you changed! I never thought I'd see you lookin' like this." He held out his hand, which Perseus shook vigorously.

"Hello, Tommy. What a surprise to run into you. How are things with you and your grandfather?"

"Things are alright, Perseus. Say, I'm glad I ran into you today. I was planning on going out to the HB to talk to you. My grandfather is having his annual bar-b-que next Sunday, and he told me to ask you to join us. It's a big deal, and lots of people will be there. There'll be dancing and storytelling, and food of course."

"Really? Your grandfather specifically invited me? Are you sure?"

"Of course, I'm sure. Grandfather told me he had a vision about you and the future. He's a hopayi. That's a kind of seer, you know, like a person who sees the future. He's also one of the tribe's alekchi, a medicine man. You can come too, Penelope."

Perseus exchanged glances with Penelope, who seemed as surprised as he was. "Well, I don't know," Perseus said. "I'd have to see if I can get the day off, but I'd like to meet your grandfather and see your place." He looked to Penelope again for some clue as to what he should say.

"Don't worry, there'll be other white people there. No war paint or scalp taking, I promise," Tommy said, sarcastically. "In fact, one of the dances will be the Choctaw friend dance. You'll want to get in on that. I'm serious, it would be really great if both of you could come. You won't regret it."

"Okay," Penelope said at last. "Assuming there are no big disasters at the HB this week, we'll be there."

On the way back to the HB, Perseus felt like he was on cloud nine. He was going to attend an Indian, no, a Native-American event with Penelope. Things just seemed to be getting better and better. He told himself not to make too much of Penelope's sudden attention, but everything about this day sure seemed promising. *And what about this vision that Tommy said his grandfather had? What in the world was that all about?* he wondered. He couldn't wait to find out more.

The HB's herd consisted of 300 breeding cows, plus the 10 bulls, a few dozen heifers, and, of course, the new calves. Although this was considered a small cattle operation, it was still a lot of work to keep everything managed properly. In addition to caring for the cattle and horses, the barns, sheds, and pens all had to be maintained, and there were over 1000 acres of pastures with fences and gates to be kept in good repair. All this work resulted in very long days for everyone.

Although there were several dozen acres of unusable marsh and forest along the river and lake bordering the northeast corner of the ranch, most of the HB's 900 acres were good, productive pasture land. There were five oil wells scattered around the HB, but they occupied very little of the pasture land, required no maintenance from the HB's hands, and contributed additional revenue to the bottom line. Given the size of the HB's herd, the usable acreage still fell short of what was needed, so Bud leased another 300 adjacent acres from the Choctaws.

CHAPTER 5

This time of year was always busy for any spring-calf operation, regardless of its size. Late bull calves needed to be castrated and inoculated, and all the calves had to be branded or tagged. The cow-calf pairs required constant monitoring for potential health issues. To manage their pastures, the cowboys moved herds from pasture to pasture every couple of weeks. They also had to keep an eye on the bulls to make sure they were doing their job and not becoming aggressive. Aggressive bulls might injure the cows or calves.

In recognition of his equine knowledge and skills, Bud assigned Perseus full responsibility for the horses in the HB remuda. He still had to do most of the stable cleaning chores, but now he was regularly included in the cattle operations requiring horse-mounted procedures. The days seemed to fly by for him, and he slept like a rock at night. As the week progressed, he grew more excited about the prospect of going to the Choctaw bar-b-que.

On Saturday night, his recurring dream returned. It was more intense than the previous occurrences and pulled him out of a sound sleep. He sat up in his bed, breathing hard. He had the overwhelming feeling these dreams portended something monumental.

Finally, Sunday arrived. Penelope and Perseus headed out to the bar-b-que with a homemade apple pie. When they arrived, they scanned the area for a place to park the truck and were surprised by the size of the crowd. Perseus figured there had to be over 200 people, but it wasn't hard to find Tommy. He had been watching for them and hurried over to meet them as they made their way toward the house.

"Hello." Tommy looked genuinely pleased to see them. "I wasn't sure you'd actually come. I'm glad you did. Grandfather is very anxious to meet you."

This surprised Perseus. He assumed Tommy had made up the vision story. Maybe there was really something to it. Nevertheless, he was anxious to meet the man.

"Come on, I want you to meet my grandfather right away," Tommy said enthusiastically. "What kind of pie is that?" he asked Penelope.

"It's apple. I made it this morning," she answered, obviously quite proud of it.

"That's grandfather's favorite. He's going to want to hide it, mark my words."

They approached a modest ranch-style house where a sizable crowd had gathered around the small, covered porch. Perseus was pretty sure these people were Native-Americans because they were all wearing similar clothing, the kind a white person was unlikely to wear. The people parted as Tommy led Penelope and Perseus toward the front door. There, in an old wooden chair covered with a colorful blanket, sat an old man.

His face was deeply creased by time and the elements. He wore a traditional, red cotton hunting jacket with an applique border and beaded shoulder sashes. Tied loosely around his slight waist was a colorful, beaded belt, and hanging from his neck were three finely woven, glass bead necklaces. Long gray hair flowed from beneath a broad-brimmed, dome crown hat festooned with a magnificent, beaded band. Perseus could not take his eyes off the man.

The crowd grew quiet. "Grandfather, I want you to meet my new friends, Penelope Wesley and Perseus . . ." He stopped, suddenly realizing that he didn't know Perseus' last name. He looked to him for help.

"Fawcett, Perseus Fawcett. It's an honor to meet you, sir." Perseus offered his hand.

"This is my grandfather, Bus Abbot," Tommy continued.

Bus looked Penelope and Perseus over carefully. He took Perseus' hand, holding it firmly. The look on his face was serene, but that look changed when he noticed the pie Penelope was holding.

She noticed the shift in his attention. "I made this apple pie for you, Mister Abbot. I understand that apple is your favorite."

Bud's smile broadened into a toothy grin. "Yes, I am very fond of apple pie, Penelope. And, please, call me Bus. Tommy, why don't you put that pie in the house, for later."

"I told you," Tommy said quietly as he took the pie from Penelope.

"Perseus," Bus said, now looking at him intently. "Did Tommy tell you that I've had a vision and that you were part of it?"

"Yes, sir, he did." Perseus was surprised that Tommy really had told the truth about this. Everyone's attention was now intently upon him, causing him to feel quite self-conscious.

"Did he tell you that I am considered to be a hopayi by my people?"

"Yes, sir, he did, although I don't quite understand what that means. Did you see something in my future?"

"No, I did not see your future, but I saw something quite amazing about the future here in the land of the Choctaw people, and that you are to be a part of that event. I was surprised, since you are not Chahta, one of our people, but I could see that you were chosen because of your strength of character. I think this is a good thing."

"But, how did you know it was me. We've never met until just now."

"This is true, young man, but I could see you as plainly I see you now, and I could see that you were on a journey, a journey that brought you here to our land. When Tommy told me about meeting you, I knew it was you, the young man in the vision. My grandson has inherited some of these abilities to see things that others do not, and he suspected you were someone special."

A hushed murmur passed through the crowd. Perseus turned to see that Penelope was staring at him with her eyes opened wide and eyebrows arched. He shook his head slightly, not sure what to make of this. He returned his gaze to Bus.

"I'm not sure you have the right person, Mister Abbot. I'm actually a pretty ordinary guy. In fact, I'm a big disappointment to my parents. The truth is, I don't really have a plan for my life just yet."

Bus nodded knowingly. "Yes, I know. That is how you came to be on your journey, is it not? You are trying to find yourself, and now you feel you are stuck here in this place, far from your home. But there is a reason for this. You were destined to come here to fulfill a role, to be reborn."

It was so quiet now that the only sounds to be heard were coming from the bar-b-que grills and the horseshoe pits off in the distance. Perseus felt a chill go up his spine as he looked deeply into the old man's eyes. This man was somebody very special, a fact that was apparent in the faces of all the people around him who were listening intently to everything he was saying.

Bus abruptly broke the spell. "But now it is time for eating, then we can dance."

As if somebody flipped a switch, all the people turned and headed toward the tables set up around the bar-b-que grills. Penelope put her hand on Perseus' shoulder causing him to jerk with a start.

"Well, that was pretty heavy," she said quietly.

Tommy moved up beside them. "Let's go down and get some food. Come on, Grandfather, we'll walk down to the tables with you."

Perseus noticed that despite his aged appearance, Bus Abbott seemed to be pretty spry. As they drew closer to the eating area, several young children raced up to meet them. They crowded around Bus, touching his hands and greeting him in what Perseus supposed was their native tongue. Bus looked quite happy with all the attention. The closer they got to the tables, the more people crowded around, trying to coax Bus to go with them.

Tommy herded Penelope and Perseus in another direction, toward the long serving tables. "We better get some food before everybody else starts lining up."

They filled their plates with grilled and smoked meats, corn on the cob, beans, and greens. Tommy pointed out a table, conveniently shaded by a large maple tree, where he wanted to sit.

"I get the impression you had this all figured out ahead of time," Penelope said.

"Oh, yeah," Tommy replied. "You snooze, you lose around here." They all sat down and began to eat. "After this meal, the dances will begin," he continued. "I thought you might like to see the friend dance. It's a traditional dance where male-female pairs dance in place, then they turn and circle around the chanter, then one of the women breaks away from the line and moves around to the other end of the line. By the time the dance is done, everybody has danced with a new partner. "

"You know, in the bad times," he continued, "The white man tried to force all the Native-Americans to forget their customs, their languages, culture, and history. There was a Choctaw man and his wife who started up the traditional dancing again in the 1970s. Now, just about everybody has learned them. There are war dances, animal dances, and social dances. The friendship dance is a social dance. They're all led by a chanter who clacks two sticks together to keep the beat."

Perseus was caught up in the whole experience of being in this place. He wanted to learn as much as he could about the Choctaw. Penelope was a little more reserved in her comfort level. She was born and raised in this county and had absorbed the uneasy, status quo relationship between the two races, white and indigenous. She certainly didn't harbor any overt dislike for the Indian people. She supposed her feelings were essentially ambivalent. She didn't know any of the local Choctaw very well, so this was a completely new experience. She liked Tommy well enough, and his grandfather was amazing.

Tommy introduced Penelope and Perseus to others who eventually joined them at the table. They were all young people, about the same age, and treated the two white people as celebrities. Perseus figured this was probably due to Bus Abbott's vision, word of which had spread through the gathering like wildfire. Penelope didn't see many other whites at the function, despite Tommy's assurances. She began to relax as the afternoon wore on though. Everybody was friendly, and these young people talked and dressed like any other resident of Choctaw County, except for Tommy. Tommy was wearing a traditional jacket like the one his grandfather was wearing, as were many others sitting at tables elsewhere.

One of the young men brought a couple of cold six packs of beer to the table. It was a local brew called T-Town from Nine Band Brewing and the cans were quickly distributed.

"I thought alcohol wasn't allowed on reservations," Perseus said after taking a long swig of the easy-drinking lager.

This comment drew a few chortles around the table. "Injuns can't handle firewater, huh, white man?" someone at the table joked. The person who said this didn't sound like he was particularly offended. It sounded more like a kind of inside joke. Nevertheless, Perseus realized he had ventured naively into murky waters.

"Maybe that's true for some reservations, but not here," Tommy explained. "It's true, though, that alcoholism is a much greater problem among many of America's indigenous people. It has a lot to do with the low socio-economic condition of a disproportionate number of Native-Americans. But we don't want to get into that today. Today is about having fun and meeting new friends."

Others at the table nodded their heads in agreement. One raised his beer and proposed a toast to new friendships. Penelope and Perseus raised their beers as well. They were both impressed with Tommy's obvious intelligence and positive attitude. Perseus considered him a cut above and felt fortunate to have the chance to count him among his friends.

CHAPTER 6

AFTER EVERYONE HAD finished their lunch and beer, they ventured toward an area set up like a small amphitheater, with bales of straw forming a semicircle facing a circular space of hard compacted dirt. Canvas awnings had been erected to provide shade over the straw bales and people were beginning to claim some of these spaces to sit and watch the dances. Dancers, many of them dressed in traditional attire, were congregating opposite the straw bales.

Penelope and Perseus found a place under one of the canvas's covers and made themselves comfortable. Tommy, along with most of the people from their table, sat with them. A man in the middle of the circular area called out something in the Choctaw language while hitting two sticks together.

Tommy explained what was happening. "That man in the center is called the chanter, and those sticks are called strike sticks. He's the guy who establishes the cadence of the dance. The chants may sound like our language, but they're mostly just arbitrary sounds the chanter makes to establish a melody."

"So now, he's calling the dancers out to the dance area. The two people in front will be the dance leaders. By ancient tradition, all our dances go counterclockwise. Perseus wondered if they knew the Earth and all the planets revolve counterclockwise around the Sun and the Earth and the Sun both rotate counterclockwise on their axes. The first dance, and usually the last dance, are always the walk dance. It's meant to represent the long distance most people had to travel to get to these events."

Perseus was mesmerized as he watched the dance. This whole day was so different from anything he had ever experienced, and it thrilled him. He glanced over to see if Penelope was as interested as he was. She was smiling, which he thought was a good sign.

When Tommy told them the next dance was to be the friend dance, he urged them to join in. Perseus didn't want to get out there in front of everybody and make a fool of himself, but then, to his surprise, Penelope got up and turned around, took his hand, and pulled him out to the dance area.

"Do you know what to do?" he asked doubtfully.

"Yes. Well, sort of. We used to do this dance once in a while when I was a kid in elementary school. It was a kind of cultural education thing, I guess. Don't worry, it's pretty basic. It's kind of like the Indian version of square dancing."

"Well, I don't know how to square dance."

"Come on. Don't you want to expand your cultural horizons?" Her laughter had an infectious, child-like quality.

At first, Perseus felt like he had the proverbial two left feet, but Penelope was right, it was a pretty basic dance; side step left, side step right, repeat. Then at some signal from the chanter, one that Perseus never did figure out, everybody turns left and skips, hand in hand with their partner until, at another indecipherable cue, everyone stops and the women move forward one person. The lead woman moves around to the back of the line. So now everyone has a new partner. Every time Perseus got a new partner, he introduced himself and his new partner giggled.

When the dance was over, everybody applauded. Perseus had to admit it was fun, and Penelope seemed to have loosened up considerably. She was telling Tommy how she used to do the friend dance in school. They watched two more dances, a duck dance and a quail dance, according to Tommy.

"We should go back up to Grandfather's house," Tommy suggested. "It's the time when he tells the children a story. I think you should listen."

"Sounds good to me. Are you sure it's alright for adults to barge in on the kids' story time?" asked Penelope.

"It's definitely okay. Grandfather asked me to be sure you were there for this story."

Perseus raised his eyebrows. "Really? I guess we'd better go then."

There were already several children gathered around Bus when Tommy, Penelope, and Perseus arrived. He was sitting in his chair and listening to the children ask about the old time. These were mostly queries about details of stories they had heard from him in the past. They wanted to hear minor clarifications that were important to them. Perseus observed that Bus appeared to take all these questions very seriously and made an effort to answer each one.

Finally, when the new arrivals were seated, Bus held up a hand and the children quieted immediately, watching him intently with obvious anticipation.

"I want to tell you the story of Sint-Holo." He began. There was a collective gasp among the young audience. They were obviously already familiar with the story. For the benefit of Penelope and Perseus Bus added, "The traditional stories of our people are always passed on to the children orally, just as they were told to us by our elders. This is how we connect with our heritage.

"Sint-Holo is a great horned serpent," he continued in his special story-telling voice, "who lives in the deepest caves and in the deepest waters. Although the great serpent is dangerous and sometimes dragged people to their death, especially weak children, he is also a powerful spirit guide who appears to certain people during fasting or in their dreams. When Sint-Holo comes to a person in their dreams, he bestows spiritual gifts upon them. Although he is usually invisible, he may reveal his presence to any youth who has demonstrated a notable degree of wisdom or intelligence beyond his peers.

"One day, a long time ago, there were some boys that were playing on the side of the mountain, not far from here. They were running up and down the side of the ridges when they came upon a dark cave. Curious, the boys entered the cave to see what was inside. Looking at the walls of the cave, they could see pictures painted with pigments made from clay and berries. The pictures showed a horned serpent that covered all the walls of the cave. Slowly, the boys walked deeper into the cave until they came to a pond. The cave was dark, but the water was even darker and very still. Frightened, the boys left and returned home.

"The next day the boys gathered their courage and decided to go back into the cave to play. They went deeper into the cave and started playing in the water. After a little while, they knew it was time to go home. They were heading away from the water when the last boy felt a sharp pain in his foot, and, with a jerk, the boy was dragged away, back into the darkness of the cave. The other boys heard him screaming, and then it was quiet. The other boys ran home to tell their parents and never returned to the cave."

The children listening to the story were all wide-eyed with fright. Bus looked over his audience with a grave expression on his face.

"This is why you should never play in caves. The horned serpent is a creature that preys on weak children. But the Sint-Holo is also a spirit guide that can be seen in dreams and will help you when you are lost. However, when it is time to feast, you don't want to be out when he is hungry.

The children quietly discussed the story among themselves, and Bus suddenly shifted his attention to Perseus. "Sint-Holo has not been seen in this land for generations beyond memory. The legends say he may come again. I have seen in my vision that this may be the time. If you see Sint-Holo in your dreams, you can be certain he is trying to give you guidance."

Then he stood. "Alright, children, it is time for me to go join the old men." Bus stood and headed back down to the picnic; the children hard on his heels.

Perseus sat there stunned, unable to move. Penelope watched him, somewhat perplexed. She was pretty sure something had happened but didn't really understand what.

"What do you think, Perseus?" Tommy asked. "He's a pretty cool guy, isn't he?"

"Yes, he's an amazing person, Tommy. I'm glad you invited us here today. Thank you." Perseus was still staring at nothing, trying to digest what Bus had said. Was he saying that the shadowy thing in his recurring dreams could be this creature, Sint-Holo?

"I think we'd better head back to the HB, Perseus," Penelope suggested.

"Yeah, I guess so." His attention was now drawn to the distant ridge lines of the Ouachita Mountains. He wondered if that's where the Sint-Holo once existed—if he existed at all.

"Perseus?" Penelope was touching his shoulder.

"Oh, sorry. Yes, we need to get going, Tommy. Thank you so much for inviting us. We had a great time. I learned a lot."

Tommy was smiling. "Well, let's get together again some-time soon."

On the way back to the HB, Penelope and Perseus discussed the day's activities. She admitted that she had a nice time and that everyone was very friendly. She also confessed she had some initial reservations. "No pun intended," she said, punching his arm and smiling impishly.

Perseus told her about his recurring dreams. "Do you suppose there's something to the whole spirit-guide thing that Bus was alluding to?"

"Seems a bit farfetched," she said. "I'm pretty sure there's no horned serpent around here. Of course, I'm not a young boy with wisdom or intelligence beyond my peers. The story is quite chauvinistic, by the way. I agree though, what he said about his vision and the reference to your dream is pretty freaky. Is it safe to assume that nobody else knows anything about your dreams?"

"I haven't told anybody about them except you. So, yeah, that story and what he said to me about the dreams is freaking me out too. You know, Tommy has some kind of knack for knowing things about a person too. Maybe it runs in their family. To tell you the truth, the things that Bus said to me today have me rattled. Like I told you, I wasn't sure where I was headed in my life, and my dream has that weird shadowy thing trying to tell me something." He was quiet for a long time.

"Maybe sleeping in the same room with Slim and Günter is giving you nightmares," Penelope said finally.

Perseus looked over and saw she had that impish grin on her face.

"That would sure give me nightmares," she said laughing.

CHAPTER 7

A WEEK LATER, in the first week of June, a man named Bart Oglethorpe visited the HB. He pulled up to the main barn in a midnight black pickup truck hauling an ebony horse trailer. He was the foreman of McAllister Ranch, a large cattle operation located a few miles from the HB. He had signed on with the McAllister Ranch as a troubled teenager, and has spent the last 15 years clawing, brawling, and bullying his way up to his current position. Bart was considered by just about everybody in these parts as the consummate cowboy: rough, rugged, handsome, and as good as one gets with horses and cattle. He was also considered trouble, with a capital T. He always wore a black shirt and a black hat, and he took perverse pride in flaunting his persona as a self-styled black knight.

He was also very ambitious and ruthless, willing to do just about anything to improve his position in life. Bart stayed in close contact with Bud Wesley, frequently offering his services to help Bud out. The help was not due to his largess, however. It was no secret that Bart coveted the HB property. He had been scheming for a long time to find a way to take over Bud's ranch. He also had his eyes on Penelope, who found Bart boastful, pompous, and conniving. She knew he was up to something but couldn't convince her father to see through the man's façade of friendliness.

Perseus watched from inside the barn as this stranger unloaded a magnificent black stallion from the trailer. The man looked as thoroughly cowboy as any man could look, but Perseus perceived something sinister about the guy. He checked himself, thinking that he shouldn't make such rash judgements without even meeting the man. The stallion came out of the trailer already saddled. Bart tightened the cinch and mounted up quickly, then headed out to the pastures where Bud and the others were working with the cattle.

It was late in the day when Bart arrived. After Perseus finished up his chores, he wandered out to the paddock where the others were working. He was impressed by the way this new person handled his horse and worked the cattle. It was clear the big black stallion was special, and he found himself wondering how much of this man's skill with the cattle was actually due to the horse's natural abilities. Once again, he checked himself. Those thoughts weren't very charitable.

It looked as though the crew was about to wrap things up, when the man rode up hard on Penelope and her horse, coming to a skidding stop just short of colliding with her. She and her horse startled and backed away. The man was laughing and saying something to her that Perseus couldn't hear. She looked annoyed, but then Bud rode up and the three of them talked for a while. Perseus couldn't explain why, but he felt a pang of jealousy.

Perseus sauntered back to the main barn to prepare for getting the horses brushed, fed, and settled for the night. Slim and Günter unsaddled their own horses while Perseus replaced their bridles with headstalls and lead ropes and then tied them to a rail to allow them cool down a bit before he brushed them. He took Penelope's and Bud's horses when they rode up.

The visiting man walked into the barn and put his horse into an empty stall, still saddled and lathered up from the hard work.

"I can brush him down for you," Perseus offered when Bart emerged from the stall.

"Don't touch my horse," Bart's tone was shockingly hostile.

Ignoring the rudeness, Bud introduced Bart to Perseus. Perseus extended his hand, but Bart merely turned away, clapping Bud's shoulder as a way of moving him off toward the house. He glanced back at Perseus as they departed, giving him a look that clearly conveyed contempt. *That guy's a real jerk.*

When he was finished with his evening chores Perseus headed up to the house for supper. He was more than a little dismayed to discover that this creep, Bart, had been invited to share supper with them. Perseus decided to hang back, loitering on the summer porch just outside the dining room until he was called in for supper.

When Penelope noticed him, she joined him on the porch. "Anything wrong, Perseus?" she asked.

"Oh, nothing. No big deal," he said, casting furtive glances at the big man just inside. "When your father introduced that guy to me out at the barn, he snubbed me, wouldn't shake my hand. He actually just turned away, then looked back and gave me some kind of dirty look. Seems like a jerk."

Penelope's expression turned sour as she said in a very low voice "I think Bartholomew Oglethorpe is way too full of himself."

Perseus' shoulders lurched back. "His name is Bartholomew Oglethorpe? Ha!"

Penelope shushed him.

"And I thought my name was bad."

"I think he's up to something," she continued. "He's always sucking up to my father, and I'm pretty sure Dad borrowed money from him a couple years back when things got rough around here. Bart's got his fingers in just about everything in these parts. He's got a friend who's an agent for one of the big meat processors, and they're always making deals all around Choctaw County, deals that manage to involve Bart in some way. Did you notice his fancy truck and horse trailer? And that expensive stallion? I don't think he makes enough money at McAllister to afford those things, not to mention all the other stuff he has."

"Hmm. I thought he looked a little too slick. Have you spoken to your father about your concerns?"

"Sure, but he thinks Bart is so generous and helpful. He's even suggested that I consider letting the man take me out, you know . . . on a date." She made a face that made Perseus laugh.

Angelica called everyone to supper. When Bart noticed Penelope and Perseus coming in together, he frowned. He waited until Penelope was seated, then quickly sat down next to her. Perseus sat as far away as possible. When everybody was situated, Bart rose and hurried over to the sideboard to dish up his meal. Everyone else seemed to be oblivious to the little drama taking place.

During supper, Bud and Bart exchanged information about current ranch operations, the same activity and challenges that all beef cattle ranches in the county were confronting. The topics ranged from immunizations, to castrations, to branding, and opinions on the best time to begin weaning. They talked about the general health of the beef market, prices for spring calves, availability of supplemental feed, pasture conditions, and even what the weather would be like in the coming months. Everybody else just listened and occupied themselves with eating.

Bart eventually turned his attention to Penelope, making inane conversation about trivial local gossip, and generally flirting with her in such a deliberate and inept manner that Perseus had to force himself not to laugh out loud. It was obvious to him that Bart's attention was making her uncomfortable, but her father seemed pleased.

Bart eventually asked her how the new mustang was coming along. "The one I gave your father. That one has a lot of attitude, but he can be broken. I could do it for you if you like." He was leaning too far in her direction, getting into her personal space, and causing her to back away.

"He's turned out to be a natural cow horse," she replied. Perseus could see the look of calculated provocation on her face. "Thanks to Perseus, that gelding is coming along much faster than any of us thought possible. Isn't that right, Dad?"

"Yes, indeed," Bud agreed, oblivious to her game. "Perseus here turns out to be a very accomplished horseman, and he possesses some unique training skills."

Slim spoke up, to everyone's surprise. "Yessiree, that boy done saved my ass too. Beg pardon, Miss Penelope. He charged right in on that there horse yer talkin' 'bout when I done got unseated in the middle of the bull paddock with a backup bull that was plum-crazy pissed off."

Perseus was trying to look invisible but could see out of the corner of his eye that Bart was very displeased by this outpouring of praise directed at him. Bart stared at him for a few seconds, then suddenly transformed his demeanor into that of a benevolent and gracious gentleman.

"Well now, isn't that something?" he said, in what Perseus recognized as a blatantly phony display of admiration. "I'm happy to hear your new hand is working out for you, Bud. I know you had your doubts. Where'd you learn to ride? Uh, what's your name again?"

"Perseus. It's Perseus."

"Perseus. Well now, that's quite a name for a man. You are a man, aren't you? Ha, ha. Just kidding, Perseus. So, were did you learn to ride?"

"He was one of them equestrian people, back east," Günter offered helpfully.

Bart cast Günter an annoyed look. "Is that right? Well, that kind of riding ain't at all like Western riding, is it Perseus? I always thought that English riding was for girls." Bart was a large man, and his voice matched his physical size, deep and booming. It was intimidating.

"I was a competitive hunter equitation rider. And, yes, it is quite different from Western style riding. It took me a little time to make the necessary adjustments." Perseus was pretty sure this was not what Bart wanted to hear. He should have just kept his mouth shut. Bart stared at him.

"I think I'll go check things out at the barns and pad-docks," Perseus said as a means of escape. "Thank you, Angelica. Everything was good, as usual. Nice meeting you Bart. Goodnight, everybody." He left as quickly as he could manage.

Down at the barn, he gave the horses a final brush-down and a handful of sweet feed as he tried to calm his nerves. He definitely did not feel comfortable around Bart. There was an intrinsic violent edge to the man. He was cleaning the tack used that day when he saw Bart's horse stick his head out of its stall. Perseus went over to him for a closer look. He was a strikingly beautiful animal. The poor thing was still wearing his saddle and bridle, and he was agitated, probably well past his normal eating time. Perseus was tempted to take the bit out of the horse's mouth but knew that would probably not go over well with Bart.

He was still with the stallion, talking softly to it to calm him, when Bart walked into the barn.

"Hey, get the hell away from my horse," Bart yelled, his booming voice scaring Perseus half to death.

"Oh. I was just trying to settle him a bit. He's such a beautiful and athletic animal. I bet he's exciting to ride."

Bart strode over and grabbed Perseus by the arm and shoved him away from the stall, causing him to fall to the floor.

"Don't you ever touch my horse again you little creep." Bart looked at him with disgust. "You ain't no cowboy, you little piss ant, no more than a horse's turd."

Perseus said nothing. Bart was twice his size and might break him in half if he said or did anything. Bart opened the stall, roughly pulled the horse out, and led it to his trailer. Perseus remained motionless on the barn floor silently waiting for Bart to drive off.

Perseus lay awake half the night, shaken by the experience. He had been stupid to think he could ever measure up to be the kind of person who worked at a place like this; a ranch. He wasn't rough like all the other guys were, and he hardly knew anything about cattle. People here were different, and it was obvious that he was not one of them. Bart was right. He was probably never going to be a real cowboy, no more than a horse's turd. Maybe it was time to move on after all.

He knew he was feeling sorry for himself, but he was lonely. He wished he could bring himself to call his parents, apologize, and ask for permission to come home, to a place where he fit in. He missed Hickory too, the man who always had some words of wisdom to share with him when things weren't going well. That man had a knack for making him feel better about life.

Despite his agitation, he eventually dropped off into a fitful sleep. He dreamed of walking on a game trail that led him along steep mountain ridges, weaving among the trees of a heavily forested area. It felt like he was being pulled along toward some specific place, but he had no idea where he was or where he was going. The trail ultimately took him down through a narrow valley and into a deep ravine.

Suddenly, he found himself standing in front of the opening to a cave. He stood at the cave's entrance, unable to see anything within the impenetrable darkness. He wanted to leave. All his senses told him to run away, but something compelled him to go inside. He felt his way along the cave's wall, making his way deeper and deeper into the growing darkness. Unexpectedly, his foot struck something. Inexplicably, a dim light illuminated the object, it looked otherworldly. His pulse quickened and beads of sweat began to form on his forehead, although he didn't understand why.

He woke up quite shaken, bathed in sweat. He immediately recalled Bus Abbot's story at the bar-b-que and realized this was no doubt what had brought on the dream. It was still early, so he lay there pondering the Indian legend and how closely it resembled his dream as he lay in his bunk trying to decipher the vision. *The vision.* Is that what it was, a vision? Now his mind raced, his plans of quitting the HB just the night before forgotten—at least temporarily.

Over the next two weeks, everybody on the HB was busy from dawn to dusk. Bud asked Perseus to contact Tommy Abbot to see if he would consider signing on the HB crew to help for a few weeks.

"I can't find anybody willing to work," Bud complained at supper one evening, "even though there's plenty of people around these parts sittin' around doin' nothin'. We got to get all those calves branded, castrated, and examined soon, and it would go a lot faster if we could put together three teams."

"I can ask Tommy if he can make time to help us out," Perseus said. "He's a good man."

"He's an Indian, isn't he?" Bud asked, not implying that this would be a problem if he was.

"Yes," Penelope said. "He's Bus Abbot's grandson. Bus is the medicine man for his clan, you know, and a very nice person."

"Yeah. Okay, see if Tommy can help out for two or three weeks. He can ride, I hope?" Bud was anxious about getting help, but the extra person would have to be able to ride.

"Well, he's an Indian, isn't he?" Perseus parroted mischievously.

Bud just harrumphed, in no mood for jokes.

Tommy reported for work the next day. He told Bud he could help out for a few weeks, and he could ride, but he'd have to go back to his grandfather's farm two or three days a week to make sure everything there was alright. Bud thought that was a reasonable arrangement, and he hired him on.

They formed three teams: Bud and Penelope, Slim and Perseus, and Günter and Tommy. The work was hard, and the late-spring days were getting hotter. Calves had to be separated from their mothers and confined in an area where they could be funneled through a chute and into a squeeze where they could be safely processed. The teams worked methodically, trying not to stress the calves any more than necessary to get the job done.

In two weeks time, they had caught up with the spring-calf work and Tommy, Penelope, and Perseus were becoming genuine friends. Perseus had decided, once again, that he wanted to stay on and keep learning about ranching, but his unpleasant experience with Bart was far from forgotten.

CHAPTER 8

NOW THAT OPERATIONS on the HB had settled down into a less hectic, daily routine, Bud had time to go over his books. Conditions in the cattle business had been difficult in recent years, especially for the smaller operations. The market for beef had been lower than expected, and Bud had not been able to hold back any cash in reserve.

His operational expenses were around $155 per cow for an average herd of 300 breeding cows. Even if he could get $600 per weaned calf, his profits would only come to about $100,000, but the following year's costs would be at least $50,000, which did not include living expenses, equipment, fencing, and facilities. He had put off doing some of the maintenance to make ends meet, but it had still been difficult.

Three years ago, Bart had somehow figured out that Bud was in financial trouble and offered to loan him a substantial amount of money to keep things running until the market improved. Bud was getting desperate at the time, so he accepted the loan which was to be paid in full after three years. He used the HB as collateral.

Bud had often wondered how Bart Oglethorpe was able to loan him so much cash money. Bart drove an expensive truck and owned a top-notch horse trailer. His horse, Diablo, was one of the top quarter horse sires in the West, worth many thousands of dollars, probably tens of thousands. Bart did have an excellent job over at the McAllister Ranch, and he seemed to have some kind of business relationship with a guy named Bill Weaver, an agent for a major meat processing company. But things still didn't seem to add up to account for Bart's apparent high standard of living.

Bud, himself, had entered into a couple of contracts with Weaver in years past. He agreed to take on additional cattle purchased by the big meat processor, and they would also pay Bud to feed and care for them. This was a relatively common practice, and the processor contracted with feed lots and ranches throughout eastern Oklahoma. Bud, however, decided it was more work than it was worth. His property was barely large enough to handle his own herd, and the payoff always turned out to be pretty meager.

When Bart offered Bud the loan, making it clear that he wanted the HB as collateral, he told Bud that he greatly admired the property. Bud thought at the time that Bart's interest in his land was closer to coveting than admiration. The 900 plus acres comprising the HB property included an extensive area nestled up to the ragged shoreline of Hugo Lake, as well as a portion of the Kiamichi River. This land was an aggregate of six 160-acre parcels of excellent grazing land allocated to or purchased by Bud's pioneering forbearers. By any measure, it was valuable land.

Looking at a map of Oklahoma, it's clear that those 960 acres of HB land are well within what is still considered to be the Choctaw Nation's reservation. As a result of the 1830 Indian Removal Act, approximately one-third of the eastern portion of what is now Oklahoma was designated by the federal government as the "Indian colonization zone."

The treaty territory, which was divided among the Cherokees, Chickasaws, Choctaws, and Seminoles, was promised to them for "as long as the grass grows and the water runs." This was the treaty language that Tommy sarcastically quoted when he first met Perseus at Syble's café. The Dawes Act of 1887 resulted in a concerted expansion of allotting Native-American land to individual Native-Americans in an attempt to create responsible farmers in the white man's image. The underlying motivation, however, was to break up the reservations. Most of the allotted land quickly transferred to white ownership by sale, by swindle, or by outright theft.

Many of the current white owners of these allocated lands treated this shameful matter of history as an inconvenient truth. It was, after all, their forefathers, not themselves, who acquired this land. "Water under the bridge," as they would say. The current Native-Americans, on the other hand, still struggled to hold on to some degree of control over what was left of their tribal lands. This was one source of the inherent friction lying just below the surface of white and Native-American relations among neighbors in the Choctaw Nation, including Choctaw County. These considerations, however, were not among Bud's immediate concerns.

Bud was worried about the loan issue. He racked his brain trying to come up with a plan that would enable him to pay off the loan and still make ends meet next season. He could cull a large number of his cows, which would increase this year's revenue as well as reduce next year's expenses, but this approach would also amount to a reduction of next year's revenue. He couldn't just keep whittling down his herd or putting off the maintenance of critical equipment and facilities, and he sure as hell didn't want to lay off his hands. There was no way he could run this operation without help.

He decided he should talk to Penelope about it. She needed to be involved in this. She was an adult now, at 21, and someday she would inherit the land and all that went with it—unless he lost it to Bart. There was a time when Bud thought that Penelope and Bart might become a couple, which might have helped to resolve the problem, but it was now apparent that she found Bart insufferable.

On the Friday of the last week in June, Bud finally told Penelope he wanted to meet with her after supper that evening. She had noticed his gloomy mood over the past couple of weeks and wondered what was bothering him. Now, it seemed, she was going to find out. She often went down to the barn after supper on Fridays to help the guys catch up on repairing and cleaning tack. Before supper this evening, however, she told Perseus that she wouldn't be coming down, that her father wanted to talk to her.

"I've noticed that he seems distracted lately," Perseus told her. "Do you suppose there's some kind of crisis?"

"I don't know, Perseus, but he has been unusually quiet. He seems preoccupied with something. To tell you the truth, I'm a little nervous about the meeting."

"I'll keep my fingers crossed." To lighten the mood, Perseus added, "I was wondering if you might want to go camping with Tommy and me for the Fourth of July. We're going to head up to the Ouachita Mountains, around a place called Robbers Cave."

"Camping?" Penelope said, as if he had just asked her to roll around in a manure pile.

"Uh, yeah, camping." It had seemed like such a fun idea, but now he wasn't so sure. "I thought it would be a good way to see a bit of this state other than the HB and Hugo, and I thought you might like to go along. Don't you like camping?"

She laughed; her mind temporarily distracted from her father's meeting. "I don't know. Maybe. I've never been camping, and I don't know if going camping with two men in the wilderness would be considered appropriate for a young, single woman."

CHAPTER 8

His face reddened. "Oh, yeah, no. I mean, we would never dream of doing anything inappropriate. We just thought you might want to be part of the adventure, you know, like one of the guys."

"Oh, so now I'm one of the guys. That's not a very flattering thought, Mister Fawcett." She was smiling coyly now.

Perseus blanched and suddenly began to feel the heat radiate over his cheeks, "I didn't mean you're like a guy or anything. I think you're very feminine, you're actually quite pretty, but you're also, you know, tough, like a cowgirl. It's a good combination. And, well, we're all friends and everything, aren't we?"

She could see that he was getting flustered and very embarrassed. She thought he was sweet, and she knew he was a real gentleman. She also knew that Tommy was a very upstanding young man.

"Let me think about it. It doesn't sound like the most relaxing way to spend a holiday, but it does sound intriguing." She paused for a moment, and her eyes narrowed. "Hey, wait a minute. This isn't some kind of expedition to go looking for that serpent thing in Tommy's grandfather's story, is it?"

"What? No, no. It's just a camping trip. I mean, if there are caves in that area, it might be fun to explore them. And if we happen to run into some kind of monster, well, that would be pretty exciting. Don't you think?"

She laughed, pointing her finger at him. "You are. Both of you. You're going on this excursion so you can go looking for that thing. What's its name?"

Perseus looked like the proverbial cat that ate the canary. "Sint-Holo."

She looked at him for a long moment. He was quite handsome, actually, a very nice, sincere young man. She impulsively leaned over and kissed him on the mouth. They were both surprised by the act. Then they were both embarrassed, looking at the ground and feeling awkward.

Finally, Penelope broke the spell. "Yes, I think I would like to go camping and help search for the Sint-Holo. That is if Dad doesn't have some catastrophic problem to drop on me tonight that is."

He watched her walk away toward the house. *She kissed me. She actually kissed me.* He didn't see that coming.

After Angelica finished up with supper that evening and headed toward her cottage for the night, Bud asked Penelope to join him at the dining table. His mood seemed particularly pensive, and Penelope grew more apprehensive. Her father had always dealt with everything. Even when her mother was alive, her dad was the one who managed every aspect of the HB.

She sat down and folded her hands in front of her, watching him expectantly. He had a folder full of papers in front of him and was paging through them. Although Penelope could tell this was just a nervous distraction; something to occupy his hands while he thought about what he was going to say.

"What is it, Dad?" she said to help him focus. "You're obviously upset about something. Talk to me."

He looked up at her, holding her gaze, then sighed. "The HB is in some serious trouble, Penelope. I haven't discussed this with you before because I thought I could get us through it, but the beef market the last few years has been tough on us. I want to go through the details with you because I think you need to know what's going on. This is your place as much as mine, and you'll be the one to take it over some day. We have some tough decisions to make."

He went through the books for the past five years and showed her how the market slump had whittled away at their profits and dwindled their reserves. He explained the various options he'd used to balance things in an effort to ride out the financial storm.

At last, he told her about the loan from Bart, and the very real possibility of losing the HB to him if they didn't have an extraordinary year. When he was finished, he sat with his face in his hands, his shoulders slumped.

"Oh, Daddy," Penelope said soothingly. "I know you did your best; you always have. I'm glad you shared this with me, although it sounds like it's going to be a tight squeeze. I'm sure we can make it all right again." She reached over and put her hand on his arm.

"We had a good yield of calves this year, more than in the last few years. Prices are up from last year, and they look like they might hold or even go higher. Maybe we could talk to Bart, get an extension on the loan, maybe pay on it over two years instead of the whole amount next spring."

Bud looked up at his daughter with a wry smile. "Do you really think Bart would help us out of this? He's made it clear that he would love to take this land. I've had to kiss his ass for the last three years because of that loan. I know what kind of man he is. It just makes me sick."

She went behind his chair and put her arms around his shoulders. "Now you listen to me, Daddy. This place has been in our family for generations, and we've made it through all kinds of hardships in the past. You've done a great job, and we're not going to lose the HB. We're going to figure something out, and if we have to pay off the loan and struggle through a couple more years, well, that's just what we'll do."

Bud turned around to look at her and she kissed his cheek. "Thank you, darlin'," he said. "You're a true Wesley, and that's a fact. You're right. We will get through this."

That night, as Penelope lay in bed, memories of her life filled her thoughts. She had always felt so content, so loved, and happy. Then her mother died of breast cancer and her world came apart. Following a grieving period she thought might never end, her father, despite his own devastation, helped her through all that, and life continued. She recalled her mother always telling her that life had to be lived to its fullest each and every day, and that had become Penelope's motto as well. They would make it through this rough spot, she was sure of it.

And now, quite unexpectedly, there was a new influence in her life. This young man, Perseus, who came out of nowhere and caught her by surprise. She thought he just might be the one. In some way, a way she couldn't quite figure out yet, this boosted her optimism about the ranch . . . about everything.

CHAPTER 9

PENELOPE COULDN'T HELP but feel guilty leaving her father to go off camping with the boys, but he had assured her it would be fine and insisted she go. He told her the Fourth of July was a good time to get away for a few days. Things at the HB would be on autopilot for the next week or so.

She consulted with Perseus and Tommy about how to prepare for their adventure and was a little apprehensive about how Spartan camping apparently was. They told her this would be a backpacking trip, so they would have to go into town and purchase the necessary equipment, including tents, sleeping bags, and backpacks. They put together a makeshift mess kit, raiding Angelica's kitchen to do so. It was difficult to keep everything light and portable, which would be necessary for hiking around in the mountains.

"You should just take a change of underwear, maybe an extra shirt, and an extra pair of socks," Tommy insisted.

"We'll all be smelly after three days," Penelope protested.

"That's just part of the experience. Believe me, you gotta keep it light. We have to carry everything in and out. You don't want your pack to be too heavy."

Both Penelope and Perseus had some second thoughts about the excursion after the discussion about what they should take to eat.

"This is all, like, freeze-dried stuff. It doesn't sound very appealing," Perseus said. "Couldn't we throw in a few hamburgers or something?"

"And how would we keep them from spoiling?" Tommy asked. "Carry a couple bags of ice up and down the mountain trails?"

Penelope and Perseus exchanged looks of consternation. "How about we take a can of SPAM®?" Penelope suggested. "That doesn't take up much room and, fried up over the campfire, it would be like a feast compared to this other stuff."

Tommy and Perseus both looked at her in horror. "SPAM?" they both groaned.

"Yes. Okay, that's settled. I'll carry it in my pack. You'll see, it'll be great."

They left for the camping trip on Tuesday, July 3rd, planning to return on July 5th.

When they arrived at the Robbers Cave State Park, they were dismayed to discover the place was overrun with holiday campers.

"I guess we should have anticipated this," Tommy said, gloomily. "Maybe we should drive on up the road and see how things are in other locations. I think there's a wilderness trailhead up there somewhere. Probably not many people willing to hike back into those parts."

"Yeah, that sounds like a good idea," Perseus said.

They traveled another 50 miles until they found a trailhead that suited them, called the Choctaw Nation Trail, and pulled their truck into the parking area. There they found some official-looking signs that described the trail as the "Ft. Smith, Ft. Towson Military Road, extending 139 miles of rugged terrain and raging streams."

"That sounds perfect," Perseus exclaimed.

The other two looked at him dubiously. They unloaded their gear and prepared to head out. Since they had started out early that morning, despite the delay in finding a suitable hiking trail, there would still be plenty of daylight. At last, they set out on the trail, heading north, full of enthusiasm and anticipation.

After two hours of hiking, however, their enthusiasm was flagging. "Maybe we could stop and rest a while," Penelope suggested hopefully.

The boys agreed and they spotted a fallen tree close to the trail on which to sit. Groaning, they removed their backpacks and sat down.

"If I have to hike carrying this thing for three days, my shoulders will be bloody," Perseus complained.

The others grumbled their agreement. It was a sweltering hot day, and they were all perspiring liberally. Penelope took out a bottle of water and began drinking.

"Better be conservative with that," Tommy said. "Whatever water we're carrying is all there is."

"What about all the raging streams the sign told us were ahead?" Perseus asked.

"If we find one, we'll have to boil the water," Tommy told them. "Nowadays, who knows what's being put into these waters upstream. You know, there's a lot of oil rigs and drilling going on all around these parts."

Penelope and Perseus looked all around at the seemingly pristine wilderness. "You're kidding," Perseus blinked incredulously.

Just then, as if to underscore what Tommy had just told them, they heard a deep rumble and felt the earth shake.

"What the heck was that?" Perseus asked. "Do they have earthquakes in Oklahoma?"

"Yes," Penelope and Tommy said simultaneously. "It's the *fracking*, at least that's one of the theories," Tommy added. "You know, that's when they inject fluid into shale beds at high pressure in order to free up petroleum resources. Lots of that going on these days in this state."

Perseus just shook his head. "Well, let's get going. I noticed the trail has taken a turn back south. This area looks pretty rugged. Maybe we could go another two or three miles, then we should start looking for a campsite. This map shows some potentially interesting looking places up ahead."

They all groaned as they shrugged their packs back on and continued down the trail. The terrain became more irregular and cluttered with large rocks. The shade of the thick forest provided some relief from the sun, but it was still hot and muggy. As they skirted the ridgeline on a particularly narrow portion of the trail, Perseus noticed something interesting below them, just ahead.

"Hey, look down there," He was pointing to a dark spot he had seen in the ravine. "Do you think that might be a cave?"

"Oh, here we go," said Penelope. "The search for the great Snit Polo."

"It's Sint-Holo," Perseus corrected. "I was just hoping we might find a cave. I think it would be fun to explore. I think that might be one."

Tommy and Penelope chuckled. "Okay, Jack Hanna, lead on," Tommy said.

"You know, my great-great-grandfather was Percy Fawcett, at least that's my father's claim," Perseus informed them. "He was a famous archaeologist who disappeared in the Amazon jungle somewhere in Brazil looking for a lost city."

"Oh, well that's reassuring," quipped Penelope.

Perseus looked for a reasonable way to make their way down into the deep ravine. He picked a spot and led them down toward the dark shadow he'd spotted. Trees were obscuring the area now, but he figured once they reached the bottom, he'd be able to find the place again. The problem was, everything looked different once they were at the bottom.

"Okay, where is this cave, Bwana?" Tommy asked.

"I hope we can get back out of here when it's time to leave," Penelope said nervously. "It's pretty steep."

Perseus was busy scanning the sides of the ravine, but he wasn't finding anything that looked like a cave entrance.

"Could we take another break?" Penelope asked. "I'm hot and tired and getting cranky."

"Uh-oh," Tommy said. "We'd better stop and rest, Perseus."

They dropped their backpacks and found some shade. Perseus told the others he wanted to keep looking and proceeded to move on down the ravine. He was about to give up, thinking what he'd seen from above was probably just some kind of shadow, but when he turned around to go back to where the others were resting, he saw it. It was there alright, partially hidden by an outcropping of rock and some bushes.

As he approached the cave opening, his heart started beating more rapidly. He took a few steps inside, hoping this wasn't just a small cavity washed out by what might have once been one of those raging streams. He noticed that it continued on back and eventually dissolved into darkness, yet he ventured a few more steps toward the abyss. It was an honest-to-God cave. He turned and hurried back to the others.

"I found it," he proclaimed excitedly. "I found the cave. It's a real cave too. You gotta come see it."

His excitement was contagious, and the others scrambled to their feet, their weariness temporarily forgotten. Penelope rushed up to him and put a hand on his shoulder. Tommy did the same thing.

"Maybe we'd better get a flashlight," Penelope said to Perseus.

"We could use our cell phones," he suggested.

"Better not," Tommy advised. "There's no place to recharge them out here, you know. Let's get a flashlight." He turned and ran back to rummage through his pack for the flashlight.

Perseus led them to the cave's entrance, and they all stood and stared at it for a moment.

"Wow," Tommy said. "This thing is really hidden. I'll bet no other human has ever seen it."

At this, they all exchanged looks. "It could be dangerous. Who knows what's in there? You go first," Tommy said to Perseus.

Tommy handed Perseus the flashlight, and he stepped into the cave entrance, the others following close behind. Penelope grabbed his belt as he slowly moved forward, shining the light's beam all around so that they could see the walls and ceiling as well as the floor. Once they were about 15 feet inside, the cave began to narrow. In another 20 feet, the cave walls closed to a narrow crack. Perseus shined the light into the crack.

"It opens back up past this narrow spot," he told them. "I think I can squeeze through."

Penelope pulled on his belt. "I don't know Perseus. It might not be safe. What if you get stuck?"

He stood there thinking about the prospect of being stuck in a cave in the middle of nowhere, and he broke out in a cold sweat at the though.

"I'm not going to try it," Tommy proclaimed.

"Okay, let's go back to our packs and set up our camp down here," Perseus suggested. "I'll have to think about this for a while. If I do try to go through, we'd need another flashlight anyway."

They all agreed this was a good plan, if for no other reason than it at least forestalled the possibility of some kind of disaster.

Their excitement continued as they trekked back to their back-packs, and there was a great deal of speculative chatter about the prospects of what was on the other side of the crack. It required about an hour for them to get their camp set up for the night, which included gathering kindling and larger pieces of wood for their campfire.

There was a small stream running through the bottom of the ravine. Tommy stood at the edge of the water contemplating the significance of this stream. Penelope and Perseus both noticed and walked over to stand next to him. They both began to stare at the water as well.

"Why are we looking at this little stream?" Perseus asked. "Do you think we could drink this water?"

Tommy looked at him. "We could drink it if we boiled it first, like I said before. It looks pretty clear. But I was just wondering what would happen to this stream if there was a rain storm here or somewhere upstream."

They both focused their attention on Tommy.

"What do you mean?" Penelope asked, a niggling of concern already creeping into her thoughts.

Tommy studied the banks of the stream. "If there is a sub-stantial rain in upstream tributaries this creek could quickly rise—a lot. I'm just wondering if our camp is set high enough that we'll be safe."

"How can we tell how high it should be?" Perseus was now also studying the area, although he really had no idea what to look for. "It looks like we're pretty far away."

Tommy pointed out lines of debris on both sides of the stream and explained that they probably marked the maximum flood level. The ravine was deep but also fairly wide at this spot. Their camp was set up on a relatively flat, sandy area that gently sloped down to the stream's edge. It was situated on the inside of a bend in the stream, where material had been deposited over time. The cave, a little farther downstream, was on the outside of another bend, and was no doubt subject to flooding by the stream in the past.

"I think we're okay," Tommy finally decreed. "I don't think there's going to be any rain anyway, but a heavy rain a few miles upstream could hit us here like a freight train without warning."

They all breathed a sigh of relief and returned to their camp-site. Tommy suggested they look around and try to think about various scenarios that might occur during the night so they could be better prepared. Penelope decided they should gather more wood. Perseus returned to the stream and discovered that the water was quite cool. He suggested they put some of their bottled water in a little basin they could build in the stream from nearby rocks to help make their drinking water colder. Tommy scouted the nearby area for a good place to make their latrine.

When they felt they had considered everything, and made the necessary adjustments, they all sat down on seats improvised by rolling three substantial rocks around their fire ring.

"Well, are you ready to explore the inner cave?" Tommy asked Perseus.

Perseus looked off into the distance, ostensibly giving the question some deep consideration. "You know, I think I want to wait until tomorrow morning."

"Why is that?" Tommy persisted.

"I just . . ." He paused, still thinking about the task. "I'm just not quite ready to do it yet. First of all, I'm not sure I can do it. I mean, the thought of squeezing through that tight space and getting stuck has me feeling a little apprehensive. I want to go back there today and just scope it out some more. Second, I can't help thinking about your grandfather's vision and his story about the creature. I'm apparently tied into all that stuff in some weird way. Before we found the cave, the Sint-Holo thing seemed like an interesting but abstract notion. Now, well, it feels much more significant."

He searched their eyes to determine their reaction. They both looked like they might be sympathetic to his concerns. "The dreams . . . those dreams I've had; they seem much more prophetic all of a sudden. It kind of scares me, if you want to know the truth."

Everyone sat silently for a few seconds. Penelope broke the stillness. "Okay, Perseus. We don't have to do this today . . . or at all for that matter. We'll go back to the cave with you and check it out, then, if you think you want to go into the second chamber, you can do it tomorrow. Okay?"

"Yeah," Tommy agreed. "No hurry."

Arriving back at the cave entrance they closely examined the narrow fissure to the second chamber. Tommy noticed that the opening at the bottom of the crack was wider. He scooped out some of the sand that comprised the cave's floor. It was all quite loose, no doubt deposited there from centuries of flooding from the stream. The further he dug, the wider the opening became.

"Look at this, Perseus. I think we could make a substantial opening down here if we scoop enough of this sand away. You could crawl through to the other side without worrying about getting stuck." Perseus agreed this would be the best way to gain access. Even still, he still wanted to wait until the next day, though.

They continued to explore up and down the ravine until it was time to get a fire going and plan their evening meal. Their food supply was limited to freeze-dried packages of either chicken and dumplings or mac and cheese. There were also various packs of jerky, nuts, crackers, and cookies. They decided to do the chicken and dumplings the first night, topped off with a desert of Oreo cookies.

As night gently settled upon the surrounding wilderness above them, the space deep in the ravine darkened more quickly. The overhanging trees and the steep sides of the ravine blocked out nearly all of the sources of illumination. The fire provided them with its flickering yellow light, but quickly faded into inky blackness just a few yards away. The soft sounds of the nearby stream and the occasional snap of the burning wood became tangible objects to help them feel tethered to solid land, dispelling the sensation that they were floating around in some kind of black hole in the universe.

"It's spooky out here," Penelope said in a low voice. "I'm already looking forward to the morning when it will be daylight again."

"Yeah, there's no stars or moon or anything," said Perseus.

"This is the kind of night when spirits walk the earth," Tommy said.

"Okay, just stop that. I don't want to hear about spirits walking the damn earth," Penelope said more loudly with stern insistence.

"Sorry," Tommy said, sounding sincerely apologetic. "You know, I spent my whole life listening to my grandfather telling me his stories about the land, our history, and our culture. Many of them involved spirits of all kinds. It's part of our spiritual beliefs, our understanding of how the earth, the trees, animals and our people came to be. I guess when you're brought up with that stuff it doesn't seem so scary."

"You've never mentioned your parents, Tommy," said Perseus. "Are they still around?"

Tommy was quiet for a while. "My mother died when I was born," he said wistfully. "My father was an alcoholic. He left shortly after that. I've never met him and don't even know if he's alive or not. My grandparents raised me. Grandmother was a very good woman, strong and loving. I miss her a lot. She passed away, maybe four years ago now." He voice quavered.

"Sorry, Tommy," Penelope said. "I'm so sorry." They remained quiet for a while, listening to the fire crackle, then she continued. "My mother died of breast cancer when I was sixteen. I thought I couldn't live without her. I was deeply depressed for a long while, but my dad helped me through that awful time. I know I'm lucky compared to so many others.

"My parents are still both alive and well." Perseus now felt compelled to tell his story. "They never had much time for me though. I always felt like I was a mistake. That's probably just being selfish. I wish I knew how to make them proud of me, but I've just never seemed to measure up in their eyes. I love them both, but we've never been close."

They stayed quiet for a long time. Perseus thought he heard sniffles around the fire. His own eyes were filled with tears. When the fire began to die, they all agreed it was time to turn in. Tomorrow would be a big day.

Perseus was in the midst of another version of his recurring dream when he was awakened by a noise close to the camp. Suddenly, he sat bolt upright in his small tent, listening to a scraping sound. He heard Penelope call his name in a whisper.

"I hear it too," he whispered back. "He struggled to get his boots on in the close confines of the tent, then quietly crawled outside holding his flashlight, but not turning it on. He saw Tommy emerge from his tent, and Penelope poke her head out from hers.

"What is that?" she asked, still whispering.

"It's something large from the sound of it," Perseus said. "Tommy, what could that be? What kind of animals are out here?"

"I don't know, maybe a bear, feral hogs, coyotes. Could be just about anything."

"So, what should we do?" Penelope asked, clearly frightened.

"I don't know," Tommy said.

"What?' Perseus hissed, incredulously. "You're an Indian, excuse me, a Native-American. Aren't you supposed to be one with the land, a tracker, a hunter, a guide?"

"Sorry, Kemosabe. You white men drove us from the land a long time ago and tried to make farmers out of us. My wildlife skills are a little rusty."

"Boys, please. Save the insults for later. There's something large out there and it sounds like it's coming this way."

"Alright, then, on the count of three, everybody turn on your light and shine it in the direction of the sound and start making a lot of noise."

"Ready? One, two, three!" They all turned on their flashlights and started whooping and hollering. In the beams of their lights stood several deer, now wide-eyed with terror. They turned and ran off down the ravine.

They three of them looked at each other and suddenly laughter broke out all around. They pointed, joked, and laughed until their sides began to hurt.

"Oh, thank God. I was scared to death. Just some harmless deer. We're all a bunch of scaredy-cats. You should have seen your face."

When all the quips had run their course, they decided that it was still too early to get up, so they all went back to their tents to try to get some more sleep. Perseus lay on his sleeping bag trying to recall some details of the dream he was having before the deer woke him. There was something different about his dream this time, but he couldn't quite recall why it felt unfamiliar.

CHAPTER 10

PERSEUS'S DREAMS HAD become increasingly more specific, and in the last dream the setting was eerily similar to where they were right now. He finally realized the oddity of his dream as he began to recall the alien-looking object he had stumbled upon in the previous version of the dream. In tonight's dream, the dark shadow-like thing from earlier dreams had reappeared and was in some way linked to that object in the cave. He just couldn't connect the two things. He wondered if the dreams were predicting what was happening here and now or was this camping trip and the discovery of the cave just a self-fulfilling prophecy. He guessed he would find out in a few more hours, assuming he had the courage to enter the second chamber of the cave.

He drifted off into a tenuous slumber but was shaken awake. He groggily looked around the confines of the tent, expecting to find the source of the shaking, but quickly realized there was nobody else inside. It was the ground that was shaking, accompanied by a deep rumbling. Another earthquake? He opened his tent and stuck his feet outside so he could put his boots on. He was pleased to discover the morning air was quite cool.

The others emerged from their tents, both looking disheveled and slightly confused. Everyone looked around the campsite as if to recollect where they were. Their world in the deep ravine was dimly lit by the steel gray light of the early morning, giving everything a slightly monochromatic look.

"Was that another earthquake?" Penelope asked to no one in particular.

"Yes. Sometimes they come in clusters over a few days," Tommy said. "I guess they get more of them up here than we do down in Hugo."

Perseus checked his watch. It was 5:30, about the time he had to get up at the ranch. Well, so much for his hopes of getting to sleep in on this trip. He moved over to the fire ring, which was now just a pile of cold ashes, and began to go through the motions of getting another fire going. He had watched what Tommy had done the day before, and felt a great sense of accomplishment when, about 20 minutes later, a decent campfire was burning.

Penelope put a small aluminum pan of water close to the fire for making coffee. When the water was steaming, she filled three cups and added a tablespoon of instant coffee to each. She announced that there was coffee and the boys each took a cup.

They all sat around the morning fire, sipping. "This is the life," Perseus suddenly announced. "Drinking some really crappy coffee around a campfire in the early morning, a babbling brook close by, and a bunch of crows squawking obnoxiously overhead."

"Thanks a lot," Penelope said, apparently offended by his critical review of her efforts to provide a morning beverage.

"It's a murder," Tommy offered in a sleepy voice.

"What?" Perseus said.

"Murder. A group of crows is called a murder."

Perseus just stared at him. "Oh, so now Tommy Tonto is an expert naturalist. Where were your wildlife skills last night?"

"It was pitch dark, if you recall, Kemosabe," Tommy retorted. "And I did recommend a defense that successfully routed the dangerous killer-deer herd."

"Please, let's not start this again," pleaded Penelope, but both of the boys were grinning widely.

"How did you sleep?" Perseus asked Penelope.

"Sleep? Is that what we were supposed to do on the hard, lumpy ground, with sounds of things crawling around outside the tent all night? Just to be clear, I don't ever want to go camping again. I don't see what's supposed to be fun about this."

"This is an adventure, Penelope," Tommy said. "It's not supposed to be comfortable. It's about the great outdoors, communing with nature, the camaraderie of your companions, eating crappy food, and . . ."

"Oh, shut up," she said, testily, and threw a small piece of firewood toward him.

"Let's have another cup of coffee," Tommy suggested. "I've got something that will improve everyone's outlook." Penelope and Perseus looked at him questioningly. "It's a surprise. Go ahead, heat up another batch of water."

When Penelope served up the second cup of instant coffee, along with a complimentary granola bar, Tommy produced three tiny bottles of coffee liqueur. "Here you go, one for each of you. Add this to your coffee and you'll feel right as rain. They all smiled, and within ten minutes there was, indeed, a new outlook on life among the companions.

After breakfast, they tidied up their sleeping quarters, changed their underwear, and freshened up in the stream. They were ready for whatever adventure day two would provide. Tommy retrieved the portable latrine shovel.

"What's that for?" Perseus asked.

"For digging a hole to the second chamber. Have you decided?"

"Yes. I'm going in. The dream came to me again last night. I'm pretty sure I've been summoned to this place. I don't understand how or why, but I'm pretty sure there's something in that cave that I'm supposed to find."

"Do you have any idea what it is?" Penelope asked.

"Yes, I do, a vague idea anyway. It will be some kind of strange looking object, something quite unusual."

"I think you're right, Perseus," Tommy agreed. "You've been selected. Grandfather has seen it. I feel it too."

They left the camp and made their way back to the cave. When they arrived at the slender entrance to the second chamber, Tommy immediately got down on his knees and began shoveling. It took very little time digging in the loose sand to create a sizable hole exposing a larger opening. Perseus stared at it for a moment, then dropped to the cave floor and began to crawl through.

"Be careful, Perseus," Penelope called after him.

He quickly made it through the opening and stood up on the other side as Tommy and Penelope shined their lights through the narrow opening. As Perseus shined his light over all the nearby surfaces of the cave, he noticed markings on one of the walls.

"There's something drawn on the cave wall in here. It's red, pretty faded, but I'm sure it used to be red. I can't really tell what it is. There doesn't seem to be much of it left."

"Maybe that's the drawing of Sint-Holo, the one in the story," Tommy suggested.

"Yeah, it could be I suppose. I'm going to go in a little farther." He moved slowly and deliberately, checking everything each step of the way. After several yards, he saw that the cave curved toward the right and the ceiling was lower. He continued around the curve and had to start bending over to keep from scraping his head on the roof of the cave.

"Perseus," Penelope called out. "We can't see you anymore. Where are you?"

"I'm still here. The cave took a right turn. I'm okay. I've spotted something just ahead. Hold on."

His flashlight beam revealed an ovate object on the floor of the cave. Scattered around it were piles of debris which seemed to be stone fragments fallen from the cave walls and ceiling. Shining his light all around the area revealed a concave depression in the cave's ceiling just above the object. When he crouched down to examine the thing closely, his heart began to pound. He was pretty sure this was the thing he had seen in his dream. But what in the heck was it?

He heard something behind him that made him jump. He turned around quickly and saw two flashlight beams moving around on the wall ahead. Unexpectedly, Tommy and Penelope appeared from around the bend in the cave.

"There you are," Penelope said, relief evident in her voice. "We were afraid something happened to you."

Their lights were trained on Perseus kneeling there with an odd expression on his face.

"I found it, the thing in my dreams," he said. He turned around and trained his flashlight beam on the object.

"Oh my God," Penelope said in a whispered voice. "What is it?"

"I don't know, but it looks like it's some kind of chrysalis-like covering. I think there's something inside." He gently placed his hand on the object, which elicited a very slight glow. He heard Penelope gasp.

"I think it was encased in the rock, just there." Perseus pointed his light at the depression, then down at the debris on the cave's floor. "You see this rock debris around the thing? Maybe those earthquakes shook it loose. It might have been sealed up in there for ages."

Tommy came and knelt beside him. "Whoa, this is totally amazing. What are you going to do with it?"

Perseus looked at him. "What am I going to do? I have no idea. I have no idea at all."

"This is your show, brother. You were called or summoned or chosen or something, I don't know what for sure, but I am sure this decision is yours." Tommy shifted his gaze from the object to Perseus. "What do you feel in your heart?"

Perseus felt Penelope move closer and lay her hand on his shoulder. "It's incredible, whatever it is."

He realized tears were rolling freely down his cheeks. It had all seemed so unreal until this moment. He felt an emotional upwelling so strong that he began to shake. Penelope knelt beside him, trying to soothe him with her nearness. He took a deep breath.

"Okay. I'm okay now. Thank you for being here with me. I'm sure that I have to take this with me. I don't know why or where or what will happen next, but I'm sure I can't just leave it here. I'll need your help."

He gave his flashlight to Penelope, then leaned over and gently picked up the chrysalis-like object. He was surprised by its light weight. It was much lighter that he expected, maybe only 15 pounds or so. He estimated it to be nearly 30 inches long and roughly 12 inches in diameter in the middle, tapering down to around 4 inches or so at both ends.

They carefully made their way back toward the narrow passage. Penelope was the first to go through, then Tommy. Perseus passed the chrysalis through the opening, handing it off to Tommy, then made his own way through. They walked the short distance back to the camp and set the object on the ground next to the fire ring. As they studied the strange object, each of them took pictures of it with their cell phone and exchanged theories about what it might be.

"I don't think we should show these pictures to anyone just yet. In fact, I don't think we should tell anybody about this. Let's give it some time. I have a strong feeling that there is something inside this thing and it would be best to keep it a secret for now."

"What about Grandfather?" Tommy asked.

Perseus slowly nodded his head. "Yes. If it wasn't for him, I doubt that I would have ever figured out that I was supposed to go find this thing. He should know about it, and I'd like to hear what he has to say. If this is some sort of mythological creature from the past, maybe it should belong to your people, if it belongs to anyone at all. Who knows? If it is the kind of creature your grandfather described, it might become a disaster."

"Like Jurassic Park," Penelope added, ominously.

They both looked at her, eyes wide. "Holy crap!" Tommy exclaimed.

They sat on their rock seats and examined the thing for a long time, unable to take their eyes from it. They all touched it several times and agreed there was something going on inside the casing.

"How could anything live so long entombed in solid rock inside a cave?" Penelope asked Perseus.

"Well, I know that there are some organisms, when exposed to extreme conditions, go into a state called cryptobiosis, which is the reversible cessation of metabolism. That may be a stretch, but I guess it's possible."

"How in the world do you know about something like that?" Tommy asked.

"One of my last attempts to get a college degree was taking a couple of biology courses. I just remember learning about crypto-biosis. It was so radical I guess it just stuck in my memory. I'm not saying that's what's happening here. It just popped into my head.

Heck, for all I know, what's under that covering could be some kind of radioactive space debris from a million years ago."

That comment caused them all to view the chrysalis with renewed trepidation.

"Okay, so what are you going to do with it?" Tommy asked.

"I'm going to take it back with me . . ." He stared at the thing for a few seconds. "I don't know where I'm going to take it." He looked at Tommy, then Penelope. "Do either of you know where there's a remotely located safe place we could keep this thing for a while? Maybe your grandfather would have some idea of what to do."

"Maybe, but I am pretty sure something like this would get my people all worked up. It would have to be planned carefully."

"I know where there's an old, abandoned cabin on the HB," said Penelope. "It's out by the lake and nobody ever goes out there anymore. It was built by one of the first settlers in my family, so it's not in very good shape, but it might be okay for keeping this thing secret and safe for a little while."

Perseus and Tommy were nodding their heads. "That sounds like a pretty good idea, at least for a few days. We need time to think about this, and to consult with your grandfather too," Perseus looked to Tommy for some agreement. He gave a thumb's up.

"Let's plan on leaving first thing tomorrow morning," Perseus suggested. "We may have to leave some of our stuff here so we can fit this in my backpack."

It was mid-afternoon when they first heard the distant rumble of thunder. Nobody gave it much thought, and they busied themselves with sorting out their belongings, trying to decide what could be left behind or somehow added to already full backpacks.

Perseus re-examined the chrysalis, trying to determine how sturdy it was and how it should be prepared for packing out. It felt like tough, rubbery skin, slightly flexible, but it still held its original shape when he tried to compress it. He detected what felt like a slight movement inside, but it was so subtle he figured it was likely just his imagination, which he admitted was running wild. The chrysalis felt neither warm nor cold; rather it seemed to take on the ambient temperature.

He decided it would be alright to just stuff it into his backpack after wrapping it in his sleeping bag. It would stick out a little, but he could conceal it by draping the extra T-shirt he had brought over the exposed part. There would even be room for a few other things if he tied them to the outside of his pack.

Another clap of thunder, this one considerably closer, startled them. They all exchanged concerned looks. Tommy instinctively re-examined the flood line on the opposite bank, then made a visual 360 around the camp.

"Are you thinking maybe we're not far enough away from the stream?" Perseus asked.

"I don't know for sure. It all depends on how much rain comes with the storm and where the storm actually dumps the moisture. To tell you the truth, if there was a flooding amount of rain, we probably wouldn't want to be in the ravine at all."

They all stood around alternately looking at the stream and the darkening sky. Suddenly, there was a blinding lightning strike directly above them, instantly followed by a deafening clap of thunder. Penelope screamed, and they all instinctively ducked.

'Hoy crap!" Perseus shouted. "Maybe we ought to get out of here pronto."

Tommy just nodded his head, and they all scurried into their tents to start packing. Only a minute later a deluge began pummeling the campsite, accompanied by strong, gusting wind.

The little one-man tents collapsed, and the occupants struggled to escape the now soggy, clinging material.

"You gotta be kidding me!" shouted Perseus.

"Let's salvage what we can and get out of here," shouted Tommy. The thunderous tumult of the deluge that surrounded them was so deafening that they had to shout to be heard over it.

Without a moment's hesitation, they recovered their backpacks and began to stow their gear, but the intensity of the storm made doing anything nearly impossible. Perseus concentrated on getting the chrysalis into his pack, abandoning any effort to cover it with his thoroughly soaked sleeping bag. At a signal from Tommy, they left whatever remained in the campsite and followed him toward the spot where they had originally descended into the ravine.

Tommy kept glancing at the stream, which was rapidly rising and gaining in velocity. When they arrived at the rugged little gully they had used as a pathway to the bottom of the ravine, they stared transfixed as they gazed up at the pathway that was now a cascading watershed fed by the torrential rainstorm.

With a sigh, and a look of determination on Tommy's face, he began to lead them up the ravine a few paces to the side of the now impassible gully. Every step they took up the slopes of the ravine was a constant struggle as the path had become waterlogged and slippery, making it difficult to gain their footing.

Suddenly, Penelope, who was behind Tommy, lost her footing and began to slide down the slope toward the ever-swelling stream. Perseus, just behind her, managed to catch her as she began to slip past him. Struggling, and feeling the first icy grip of panic taking control, they used every ounce of their strengths to get to a large tree about halfway up the side of the ravine, where they anchored themselves, hoping to ride out the storm.

They huddled close together, shivering, both from being soaked and from fear. Stunned into silence as they sat trembling together, their exhaustion and the noise from the storm overwhelmed them. They felt the wind intensify, but it was a different kind of wind, like breathing: incredibly strong, then less so, in and out, alternating every few seconds. The sudden change in intensity caused their ears pop. They huddled together as the niggling fear of being blown back down the ravine and into the now raging stream captured their imagination.

The tree that they were clinging to began to shift under them. Before they could wrap their minds around what was happening, the massive roots of the tree emerged from the rocky soil and were thrust into the air, the fury of the storm toppling the tree. But the fates had other plans for them. Rather than being flung down into the ravine, the trio had been thrown backwards, rolling behind the roots, and into the gaping pit left behind.

The pit quickly filled with water coming down in sheets off the slope above them. Before they knew it, they were up to their waists in a muddy sludge. Struggling desperately, they managed to escape the hole and reach another, smaller tree which they hoped would keep them from sliding down toward certain death.

As they struggled against the forces of nature, they began to feel like the storm was going to last forever. There were several more terrifying lightning strikes nearby, each one accompanied by a deafening crash of thunder. All three of the companions were seriously wondering if they would survive this powerful act of nature. Perseus was thinking that he would never forgive himself if anybody was killed or hurt seriously. This stupid adventure was his idea. He was crouching between Penelope and Tommy, and he put his arms around both of them, as if trying to shield them from any harm.

Just as it had come, the storm abated with surprising suddenness. It took several minutes for everyone to realize the worst was over. They began crying and laughing in relief all at once as they began to grasp the reality that they had survived.

With renewed vigor, they continued their struggle to escape the water drenched ravine. The going was extremely difficult due to the mud, loose rocks, and downed trees. When they finally reached the top and found that the trail was still intact, they spontaneously cheered and hugged each other.

"You should see yourself," Tommy said pointing to Penelope and smiling broadly.

"Yeah? Well, you look like a mud ball, mister." She looked Perseus over and started laughing and pointing.

"What?" He was covered, head to toe, with dark mud and leaves, and he was hugging the mud-covered chrysalis.

"You need a shower," she said, still laughing. "We all do."

An awkward silence ensued as they each became aware of the real danger they had endured. Long moments of silence passed between them as they contemplated how to feel after escaping their near-death experience.

Penelope began to sob. Both Tommy and Perseus went to her to try to comfort her, but their emotions were just as shattered. *What does one say after such an experience?*

After the initial shock of their ordeal abated, they began the long hike back, but after a few miles, Penelope insisted they stop. Their exhaustion and hunger finally caught up to them. A fallen log that had been placed alongside the trail to serve as a resting place for hikers, provided just the spot. She rummaged through her sodden, muddy pack and withdrew a package of English muffins that she had sealed in a plastic bag and the can of SPAM she had insisted on bringing. The boys watched eagerly as she opened the can and sliced the meat with a small knife. She placed two slices between each muffin and passed them out. Perseus stuffed his muffin in his mouth almost in one ravenous bite while Penelope and Tommy followed suit.

"See?" she said, eventually. "I told you this would be one of the best meals you would ever eat."

CHAPTER 11

BY THE TIME they arrived back at the truck, the day had become bright and sunny with only a few puffy clouds drifting lazily across a brilliant blue sky. There were two hikers who had just arrived and were still preparing themselves for a hike. As the three companions emerged from the trees and into the parking lot, the hikers gasped.

"Are you guys alright?" they asked with genuine concern. "What happened?"

"We're alright," Tommy answered. "We had to battle one of those raging streams the sign refers to."

The two hikers stood and stared at them as they walked by. "Is it safe on this trail?" they asked.

"Oh yeah," said Perseus. "Just stay out of the ravines. You'll be okay."

They watched the hikers tentatively enter the trail, occasionally looking back, no longer sure if they had made a good choice.

Tommy found a bucket in the truck bed which they took turns filling at the potable water faucet near the trailhead. They took turns dousing themselves to try to rinse off their mud-caked clothes and bodies. However, the effort was only moderately successful. They knew that their water-logged boots were probably ruined, but even if they were salvageable, they couldn't stand sloshing around in them anymore, so they took them off for the ride home. Although everything was thoroughly soaked, the extra T-shirts they each had packed were at least less muddy than the ones they were wearing, so they changed into them.

Tommy grabbed the canvas tarp that was stored behind the back seat of the crew cab. They used it to cover the front seat in a pointless effort to spare it from the mess. Perseus volunteered to sit in the back seat with the chrysalis, electing to remove his jeans for the ride home, "as long as nobody looks."

When they drew close to the HB, Penelope directed Tommy to turn onto a dirt side road, where they quickly encountered a field gate. She got out and opened the gate, motioned him through, then closed it. She led them to a secluded area in a stand of old trees. There was an overgrown path at the edge of the trees which led to a rundown cabin.

"I think we should keep the egg-thing in here until we decide what we're going to do with it," she said. "It's not that far from the main house, so we could come out every day to check on it."

Perseus got back into his soggy jeans and went inside the cabin to check it out. It was plenty dusty, with cobwebs in every nook and cranny, but he thought it looked suitable. The two windows even had glass still in the panes. He gingerly laid the chrysalis in one corner.

"Do you think it survived the storm?" Penelope asked.

"Well, if it survived a few thousand years buried in rock inside that cave, I think it should be able to survive a little water and mud. I'm not sure there's actually anything alive in there, Perseus continued pointing to the chrysalis. "I think it will be alright here. Thank you, Penelope."

The three of them silently stood in the middle of the ramshackle cabin gazing at the artifact.

"All I can say is," said Tommy, "that was one heck of an adventure, Perseus. I felt like we were in some kind of Indiana Jones movie or something."

"It was exciting for sure," Penelope agreed. "I'm glad it's over though. Way too much excitement for my blood."

"Thank you, guys, for helping me on this quest," said Perseus. "I couldn't have done it without you. I guess only time will tell if it was worth the trouble, not to mention the near-death experience." They all chuckled. "Tommy, do you think we could get your grandfather out here on Sunday to take a look at this thing?"

"I'll tell him about it. Frankly, I don't think you'd be able to keep him away. Remember, it was his vision that started this whole thing."

Tommy dropped them off at the HB and headed back to his grandfather's. Penelope and Perseus were grateful that there was nobody around when they arrived. They hurried off to get cleaned up before anyone got back knowing that they would never live down the ribbing they would get if they were caught looking like they did.

July was a relatively slow on the ranch, a time when the main task each day was to monitor the herds to make sure there were no problems, or to deal with them if there were. Every of couple weeks they rotated the herds to fresh pastures. Every evening, after all his chores were done, Perseus rode Balius out to the abandoned shack to check on the chrysalis. None of them spoke of the thing other than to Bus Abbott.

When Bus finally visited the shack on Sunday to inspect their find, he was stood staring at the chrysalis for several minutes before he spoke.

"I didn't think such a thing really existed," he said to the others' surprise. "The object of the quest in my vision was vague. I knew it was supposed to be something significant, perhaps something out of our legends, but this is most extraordinary. I am even more surprised that you were able to actually find it." He looked long and hard at Perseus, as if he was trying to figure something out. "It was you, though," he said after a long pause. "I thought that part of the vision had to be a mistake, but it was you. The Great Spirit sometimes works in ways that are difficult to understand." He stood there, looking off into the distance, nodding his head.

"You mean, because I'm white, rather than one of the people?" Perseus asked.

Bus slowly nodded his head. "Sometimes it's not about what you are, but who you are."

"Believe me, I don't know why it was me either," Perseus said. "I have a feeling there's more in my future than just finding this thing."

"Yes, it will be so," Bus replied. And he was reassured that it was, indeed, this young man who had been chosen. Bus knew there was more to the vision, but there was some part of it he still couldn't decipher. So, he kept silent.

Ten days after placing the chrysalis in the shack, Perseus rode out to check on it. When he entered the shack, he saw immediately that the leathery case was moving. It appeared as if there was something inside straining to get out. He moved closer to it, setting the lantern down on the rough board floor. Something was definitely happening. It was a good thing he had arrived when he did, but now he realized that he wasn't really prepared.

As he stared at the object, wondering if there was something he should do, he noticed a small tear inching across the membrane. When he saw a single claw-like talon emerge, he gasped. Whoa, was this really happening? His heart raced. As the rent in the casing grew longer, more of whatever was inside became visible, but it was impossible to comprehend what he was seeing. Even after it was almost completely exposed, Perseus still had no idea what it was. It was still contorted into an oblong ball from being in the chrysalis, and it was slimy with some kind of viscous fluid.

He moved the lantern closer to the creature and began helping it remove some of the matter which had encased it for ages. When it was completely free and lying on the floor, trying to get itself unwound from its fetal position, Perseus realized that this creature was like nothing else on earth. It suddenly looked Perseus directly in the eyes and made a sharp squeal, causing him to flinch.

Perseus stared at it, completely mesmerized. It looked ungainly as it tried to move about, but it was moving resolutely toward him. Although Perseus was frightened, he did not move away, but rather held out his hand and gently touched it. He stroked its still slimy skin, noticing that what appeared to be scales, felt more like finger nails. The creature began unfolding its front appendages revealing bat-like wings. It stretched its neck, all the while, never taking its eyes off Perseus.

Using the bandana from around his neck, Perseus began wiping the slimy fluid from the creature's body. Within 15 minutes, it was staggering about, fully revealed. Perseus was having a hard time trying to describe the creature. If he had to compare it to something, he would have to say it looked somewhat like a large, reptilian bat, except it had a longer neck, a moderately long tail, and short, stocky hind legs.

Its head was something Perseus thought probably only a mother could love. If you combined a vampire bat's face with the long snout of a fox or a possum, and covered it in odd-looking, dull golden scales, you could arrive at a reasonable description. Its nose, if that's what it was, was a bizarre arrangement of fleshy and bony protrusions which gave the impression of spikes or horns. But Perseus thought they appeared to be something more suited for some purpose other than defense or aggression.

The little guy had managed to crawl up onto his lap and was making a sound that resembled purring. The strangest thing about the hatchling was that it never took its eyes off of Perseus. He could swear it was studying him.

Suddenly it stood up on its stubby hind legs, spread its wings to their full span, stretched its neck and issued a high-pitched cry. Then, it folded itself back up and nestled into Perseus' lap, but it was still looking at him. He figured it must be hungry. Of course, he had no idea what such a creature would eat. He just hoped its diet didn't include humans. He had a granola bar in his pocket, which he unwrapped and broke into small pieces, offering them to the little guy. It ate greedily. He put the creature down and went outside to fetch a canteen of water. Balius was snorting his unfamiliarity with the scent of the new creature now covering Perseus.

Back inside the shack, Perseus patiently gave the creature water he poured into the bottle cap. He would have to bring some dishes or pans of some sort to use for food and water. Once the little guy seemed to be ready to settle down, Perseus made a nest on the floor out of his light jacket. He picked the creature up and carefully placed it on the jacket. It looked up at him. Its compelling amber eyes looked almost golden. They reminded him of human eyes in some way. They looked intelligent.

He talked to it soothingly and told it he would be back tomorrow. He hated to leave, but he couldn't stay here all night. He waited until it seemed to be sleeping, then headed back to the bunkhouse. Balius continued snorting his distaste for the alien scent all the way back to the barn. On the ride to the bunkhouse, the magnitude of what had just happened hit Perseus.

"Good heavens," he said to himself. "Now what in the world am I going to do?

The next morning, after breakfast, he surreptitiously caught Penelope alone just outside the dining room. "Something extraordinary happened last night. There was something in that chrysalis after all, and it hatched while I was checking in on it. You won't believe it."

"What is it?" she asked wide-eyed.

"That's just it, I don't know. I can tell you this though, there is nothing like it on the face of the earth. It looks like some kind of dragon or, heck, I don't know what. Do you think you can ride out with me tonight and look at it?"

"Are you kidding? Try to keep me away." She looked around to see if anybody was nearby, then leaned over and kissed him. "This is so exciting." Then she ran off toward the barn to prepare for the day's work.

Perseus stood there for a few moments, savoring the kiss she had just bestowed on him. Then he strolled down to the barn to continue his morning chores. During his late morning break, he went into the bunkhouse and used his cell phone to do a little research on what his little creature might be. It kind of reminded him of a dragon, so he looked at several sites about such creatures. He found one site that described several different kinds of dragons, all according to myth and folklore. He decided the thing his creature most closely resembled was a wyvern.

The artist rendering of such a creature looked very similar, so he supposed that's what it could be: a wyvern. Funny name, he thought. All the descriptions seemed to indicate that a dragon or wyvern or any other creature of this ilk was a reptile, but he was pretty sure his wyvern was a mammal. It sure didn't look or act like a reptile, other than its scales. Maybe they weren't actually scales. He did more research.

There were a few mammals that had scale-like hair; a creature called a pangolin had scales, and other animals like the armadillo, hedgehog, and porcupine all had scale-like skin. So, it was possible that it could be a mammal. The thing that perplexed him the most, however, was how any living thing could survive all those millennia in a state of metabolic suspension.

Whatever this thing was, it would be the most astounding discovery since, well, maybe ever. This had all kinds of implications, including some very troubling possibilities. Every scientist would want to examine it, put it in a lab and study it. Others would want to exploit it in one way or another, like putting it on display. What if it had dragon-like powers described in the legends, like breathing fire? Would the military want to own it and control it? Maybe it would be considered a public hazard. He wondered how large it would grow. Thoughts of *Godzilla*, *Lord of the Rings*, and *Game of Thrones* raced through his mind. He suddenly felt sorry for the little guy. It probably wasn't going to fit very well in the modern world.

That evening, Penelope told her father she was going to take a ride around the ranch with Perseus. This didn't seem to have the impact on him that she was anticipating. He took the announcement in stride, only telling her to be careful if they were in any of the paddocks with bulls. She noticed he was smiling when he said this and wondered if the comment was meant to be a double entendre.

She met up with Perseus at the barn. He had her horse saddled and ready to ride. Slim and Günter were in the bunkhouse watching television and didn't seem to notice that he had left. As fast as they could without drawing attention to themselves, they rode to the cabin. Perseus had brought some things with him, including a couple of small pie pans for food and water, a towel to replace his jacket, and a variety of food he liberated from Angelica's supper table.

When Perseus opened the cabin's rickety door, a waft of extremely foul odor hit them, making them wrinkle their noses. He pushed the lantern in ahead of their entry and saw the little creature sitting near his jacket, looking up at them expectantly. It stretched out on its hind legs, spread its wings, and raised its head, emitted that same high-pitched cry as it had done the night before, then folded itself back up.

"Oh my God," Penelope said slowly. "What is that?"

They moved closer, closing the door behind them. Perseus knelt down close to the creature and set the lantern on the floor. It immediately crawled its way into his lap and began that purring sound it made. He stoked the creature's neck.

"That is so adorable," Penelope said in a sing-song voice. She knelt down beside him.

"Yeah, well there's nothing adorable about this smell. I guess I need to figure out what to do about his waste. First, I guess I'll have to find it."

"What's his name?"

"Name? He doesn't have a name. He was just born last night. I don't even know if it's a boy or girl. I guess it has to be Sint-Holo."

"That's such a complicated name, though."

"Well, it's a Native-American name, I guess. We should probably consult Bus or somebody. I don't think we should call him Jimmy or anything like that. Tommy would have a fit. Too white."

Penelope giggled. "Can I touch him?"

"I guess. Just be careful. He probably has to get to know you. This thing has a mouthful of teeth you won't believe."

Penelope started talking baby talk to the creature, who had now shifted its attention from Perseus to her. She held her hand out palm up. It looked at her hand for a moment, then into her eyes. "It has extraordinary eyes, Perseus."

"I know. She looks like she's trying to figure you out or something. I think she's intelligent."

"You just said, 'she'," Penelope said, shifting her gaze to Perseus.

"What? I did? I'm not sure why I said that, but all of a sudden, I got the impression she was a female. Strange. Here, try to give it a little of this cheese I brought."

"Cheese? Should you give a one-day-old cheese? By the way, do you have any idea what she is?"

"I'm guessing she might be a wyvern. It's a particular type of dragon."

"A wyvern, Wow. Here little one, want some cheese?"

The creature looked at the offering, leaned over to smell it, and then took the cheese with its mouth. Penelope slowly reached over to pet it. "Would it be okay if I touched you?" she asked. It made the purring sound.

"I think that means it's alright."

When Penelope stroked the creature's neck, it responded by closing its eyes. "She likes me. I was there, you know, when Perseus found you in the cave." It opened its eyes suddenly and looked back and forth between Perseus and Penelope, making a chattering sound. It sounded as if it was excited.

"She acts like she understands," Perseus said.

CHAPTER 12

SHE WAS STILL confused; still very disoriented. She had been asleep so very long. Now, here she was with humans. How did she even know these creatures were human? It was difficult to process all the images that were appearing inside her head.

It had been a fortunate coincidence that her protective casing had been doused with water and mud soon after the mountain had released her. The most desperate need of her kind upon being liberated from the rock was moisture. After countless ages of entombment, her body was desiccated in the extreme. Once exposed to the air, it was a matter of life and death to find a means of hydration quickly.

She was aware that this male human who was present when she broke free and took her first breath of air, was responsible for taking her to where she could be exposed to the life-giving water. Now she knew there was another human with him when this happened, a female, and she saw her for the first time tonight. She had a lot more to piece together before she could venture forth. She knew she was fortunate to have these humans willing to protect her.

She was what humans called a wyvern. Her kind had dominated the world at one time, superior in intelligence and in numbers to the primitive humans who shared the land with them. Humans had one brain, while wyverns had two brains; one specifically focused on cognitive processes and a second for storing memories.

When offspring were born, their second brain was already completely populated with the knowledge of the mother. This was the process that she was going through now, integrating the memories and knowledge of her mother into her cognitive brain. It would take time for all the synaptic connections to form. It was a time for resting in a safe place, allowing her mind and her body to grow. And she would grow quickly.

Humans and the wyvern had mostly lived side by side in peace and harmony in the old times. On rare occasions, the wyvern even tried to communicate with a human through their thoughts, but this was considered to be a futile, even dangerous activity, due to the humans' proclivity toward fearful and superstitious reaction to things they did not readily understand. They were not well suited for thought-based communications.

There were many more wyvern than humans in those times, and the wyvern were much larger and stronger. The humans did have some advantages, however. They had appendages which included hands with opposable thumbs. They could accomplish things that wyvern could not, such as building and farming. They had spoken languages, while the wyvern communicated through thought images. This allowed humans to indulge in cooperative efforts more easily than her kind.

The humans were also violent. This trait rarely became a problem for the wyvern because of their larger numbers and size. Humans were predisposed to conquer, to dominate, and to control everything around them. They often killed senselessly and brutally.

A wyvern only killed out of necessity, for defense or food, and they rarely fought amongst themselves.

When the changes began, and much of the land became inhospitable to living creatures of every kind, humans killed off many of the animals they depended on to survive. They turned their attention to her kind and the two intelligent species waged war on each other for the first time. It was a dark time.

The wyvern decided to go into seclusion rather than continue the ugly war with the humans. Suitable males were chosen to breed with the females and the cycle of rebirth was begun. Thousands of eggs were deposited in caves and crags all over the land in the hope that one day the world would change again and provide more favorable conditions for her kind. They knew it was a gamble, but they ultimately decided it was their best hope for the survival of their species.

Each embryo contained all the knowledge of its parent, stored in its second brain waiting to be tapped if the time ever came when it would see the light of day in a new world. That time had apparently arrived, but whether or not they could survive in the world they would find themselves in, several thousands of years later, would depend on how the modern humans would react to a species considered to exist only in legend.

CHAPTER 13

THE MEAT PROCESSER agent, Bill Weaver, called Bart to tell him he was on his way to Hugo and needed to meet with him immediately, it was urgent. They arrange to meet at Syble's Café. At 3:15 Bart was sitting in his big black truck in Syble's parking lot when Weaver pulled in next to him. He got out of his truck and the two men went inside the café.

"What can I get you boys?" Syble asked.

"Just give me a coffee, black," Bart snapped. He was not happy to have been called away from his work.

"I'll have an iced tea, sweet," Weaver said more politely.

There was nobody else in the place at that time of day, so Syble went back into the kitchen after serving them their drinks.

When she was out of sight, Bart spoke in a low, annoyed voice. "What's this about? Why're you pulling me out from my operation in the middle of the day, in the middle of the week?"

Weaver looked at Bart, showing no sign of being intimidated. "We've got some trouble, that's why. Your bookkeeper, Miss Peasen, is starting to ask questions that don't have good answers. She apparently had a meeting recently with the accountant at the Choctaw Agriculture Office to compare notes on last year's processor contracts. The accountant called me this morning, wanting to go over my records with me."

Bart pounded the counter with his fist. "Damn." He sat there a few moments, looking out one of the many windows surrounding the café's interior. "Alright. I'll take care of it. Meanwhile, are you sure you covered up our end of the paper trail?"

"As good as can be expected, but if anybody takes a close look, there will be numbers that don't add up."

"I understand. Maybe we should ease up on the Choctaw Nation's cattle ranches this year. We can make up the difference with a few places west of here. I have some contacts out there."

Weaver nodded.

"By the way, things are lining up for me to take over the HB. There's no way Bud's gonna be able to pay off that loan, I'll make sure of it. Once I have control of that spread, we'll have more opportunity to raise the stakes."

Weaver smiled. "Sounds good. Just let me know when the coast is clear with the bookkeeper issue. Just text me something innocuous, like, 'problem solved'."

"Don't worry, it will be solved."

Two days later the McAllister bookkeeper and the Choctaw accountant disappeared without a trace. Their vehicles were parked in their driveways at home and there was no sign of any foul play in or around their homes or work. They just seemed to have vanished.

Bart visited the HB during the last week in July. He was getting impatient about his planned takeover, and he asked Bud to go over his operation projections for the year. Considering the loan obligation, Bud felt like he has no choice.

After reviewing the HB's accounts, Bart realized that Bud might just be able to pay off the loan after all. "Well," Bart said, feigning delight, "you've done a great job of managing things here, Bud. It may be a bit of a tight squeeze, but I think you're gonna come out of this alright. Too bad. I'd of liked to have this place." He said this as if he was joking, but he wasn't fooling Bud at all.

"If nothing goes wrong between now and market time, we'll probably make out just about right," Bud said, trying not to sound too optimistic. There were always plenty of things that could go wrong in this business.

Bart left the HB in a foul mood. He might have to take measures to make things more difficult for Bud. He thought Bud was a loser. The HB had been in the family for several generations, and it had never gotten any bigger or more prosperous, despite the fact that it was on some of the best pastureland in the county. If he had this place, he could squeeze out a lot more productivity. Then there was that hot little daughter of his. He'd like to get his hands on her someday. If he played his cards right, maybe she would come with the property.

Tommy called Perseus that same day. "Hi Percy. I was wondering if you and Penelope could meet me at Syble's later. You guys real busy out there?"

"Things aren't too crazy. What's up?"

"Syble wants to talk to us . . . says she has something important to tell us. She sounded pretty upset."

"Oh, well, I guess we could get over there. Let me find Penelope and see if she can get away. I'll call you back in a little while."

He found Penelope bucking hay off a delivery truck at one of the hay covers. "Hey, that's my job," he told her. "Why are you doing that?"

"I like the exercise," she said, sweat dripping down her face. It was a hot day. She removed her bandana and wiped her brow just under her hat. "Don't you think I can do this?"

"Are you kidding? I know you can handle it, as long as you're not doing it because you think I'm shirking my duties."

She smiled. "Then come on up and help me."

He grabbed a couple of hay hooks hanging on one of the nearby poles and climbed up on the back of the truck. "You get the bales down here on the edge of the truck and I'll stack 'em."

They worked in silence for a while. "Tommy called a little bit ago. Said that Syble wants us to come down to the café today. She's got some news or something, I guess. He said she sounded upset."

"Really? I wonder what that's all about."

"Don't know. Guess she wants to tell us in person. Do you think we could get down there later?"

"Sure. There's not that much going on around here until next week when we start weaning the calves. Slim and Günter can handle things here for now. We'd better go soon, before she gets involved in the dinner rush. She'll be too busy to talk to us then."

"Okay, let's get this truck unloaded."

They met Tommy at the café just before 4:00. There were already a couple of early diners in the place, but Syble had an extra waitress on for the evening business. Syble came out from the kitchen with a look of worry in her eyes. It was obvious that she was stressed. Quietly, she led them over to a table in the far corner of the diner.

"Sit here," she motioned to the table and chairs and sat down herself, looking around as if to make sure nobody was close enough to overhear their conversation.

"What's going on, Syble?" Penelope asked.

Syble was wringing her hands. "I overheard a conversation between Bart Oglethorpe and that man from the meat processor, I think his name is Bill, or something like that. You know, I can hear just about everything anybody says out here when I'm back in the kitchen, during the slack time that is."

"Bart and that other guy met here around 3:00 in the afternoon a few days ago. They were talking about having some kind of trouble with Jeannie, you know, the bookkeeper at the McAllister, and the accountant from the reservation Ag Department. Something about them meeting and asking questions that didn't have good answers. That's the way this guy, Bill, put it. Bart got real mad and pounded the counter, then he said he would take care of it."

"Well, you've probably heard that Jeannie and that fellow from the reservation Ag office have disappeared."

"I did hear something about that, now that you mention it," Penelope said.

"It's been the talk of the town down here. Sheriff figures there's been foul play, but they can't find any evidence. But here's the other thing, the main reason I asked you to come here. Bart tells this guy that he's going to be taking over the HB pretty soon, says he'll make sure it happens, and then they'll have more opportunity, whatever that means. Is your father planning to sell the HB?"

Perseus could see that this news upset Penelope. "No, he's not." She sat there, obviously mulling this news over in her mind. "Thanks for telling us about this Syble. You're the greatest, and this is important information. Thank you."

It was starting to get busy with the early crowd, so Syble excused herself, leaving the three companions to themselves.

"What's going on, Penelope?" Perseus asked. He could tell she was fuming.

She sighed heavily. "You have to promise that you won't tell anybody what I'm about to tell you."

Both Perseus and Tommy nodded. "You have our promise," Perseus said.

"Dad borrowed a lot of money from Bart a few years ago when things weren't going well. He used the HB as collateral, and the loan is coming due early next year. That's what the meeting was about, that Friday evening when Dad said he wanted to talk to me. If we can't pay the full amount, Bart plans to foreclose and take over the ranch. It might be close, but we think we can take care of it."

"What a creep," Perseus said. "I really dislike that guy. His name should be Black Bart."

"I wonder what he meant when he told that guy he would make sure it happens." Tommy mused.

"Whatever he has in mind, it can't be good," Penelope said. "I think I want to get a beer. You guys want to go over to that little hole-in-the-wall joint down the road? I think it's called the Red Barn. They have some pool tables, so maybe we could shoot a game of pool."

"Sure, let's go," Perseus agreed.

It was about 4:45 when they parked their trucks in the Red Barn parking lot. There was a taco food truck parked out front, so they each got a taco to complement the beer. The place was already busy with serious pool players, so the prospects of getting a table without getting involved in some kind of impromptu tournament seemed pretty slim. They found a small table in one corner of the bar and claimed the seats. Before Perseus sat down, he turned and walked up to the bar and ordered three beers.

"How's the little wyvern doing?" Tommy asked.

"She's doing pretty well, I think." Perseus took a long drink of his beer, washing down the last of his taco. "It's amazing how fast she's growing, and she's really smart."

"And so cute," Penelope added.

"Grandfather is still trying to come up with a plan for what to do about her," Tommy said. "He thinks when word gets out that there's a dragon-like creature that has reemerged from the past, the world will go crazy. He's afraid for her."

"So am I," Perseus said.

"Oh no." Tommy and Perseus looked up to see what had caught Penelope's attention.

Bart had just burst in the front door with three of his cowboy thugs, causing everybody to look up to see what was going on. A few people recognized and greeted him just inside the door. He was swaggering around, checking out the crowd. It was immediately obvious that he and his buddies had been drinking before they arrived. He suddenly saw Penelope sitting in the corner with Perseus and Tommy.

"Well, well. What do we have here?" he bellowed. Everything in the room stopped as the other patrons quickly realized there was probably going to be trouble. Bart staggered over to their table.

"Penelope Wesley. What in the hell are you doing out with this little creep and an Injun?" He slurred. What's the world come to?"

Penelope held up her hand. "Please, Bart, could you just leave us alone?"

He sneered and gave a derisive laugh, then turned to look at Tommy. Hey, Injuns ain't supposed to be in here. It's illegal for an Injun to drink firewater on the reservation. Don't you know that, boy?"

"Technically, this is not the reservation. You white men stole this particular piece of our land from us a long time ago."

"I think we're gonna have to run you out, boy." But then Bart turned his attention to Perseus. "And this here is the new hand at the HB, if you can believe that." His gang snickered stupidly. "His name is Pussius. Now ain't that a purdy name for a little sissy boy?"

Perseus kept his mouth shut. He was trying to work out an escape plan. Penelope attempted to intercede. "Bart, please, just go have a beer and leaves us alone."

Bart ignored her. He pointed to Tommy and Perseus. "You two, get out of this bar. You don't belong here, and you're not welcome here." Bart's friends started crowding around the table.

The three companions definitely did not want any trouble, so they all got up to leave, but Bart grabbed Penelope's arm and told her to stay a while. "Let go. You're hurting me," she cried.

Perseus couldn't take it anymore. "Let her go, you big jerk." He pushed on Bart's shoulder to little effect.

Bart let go of Penelope and grabbed Perseus by the neck. Perseus was terrified that Bart would knock his teeth out. Tommy tried to intercede, and in the few seconds that Bart was distracted by Tommy, Perseus kicked him in the groin with all his might.

Bart instantly dropped to the floor, holding himself and screaming in agony. His three cowboy buddies then proceeded to brutally beat Tommy and Perseus. Mercifully, others in the bar finally jumped in to break things up, pulling the drunken thugs off the now bloodied and battered boys. Penelope helped get them outside to her truck for a quick escape. When they arrived at the HB, she immediately took them to her father up at the main house. Bud and Penelope doctored them as best they could, and in the end decided the two victims didn't need to go to a hospital. But they had been beaten up pretty badly.

Perseus told everybody that he thought it was time for him to move on. "I think it's pretty clear that Bart is a dangerous man, and he seems to take some perverse pleasure in insulting and hurting me. The first time I ever met him, when he came down to the barn to get his horse after having supper up here, he called me a name and threw me to the ground."

Bud was very angry about the attack, but he knew there was not much he could do about Bart. "I'll call the Sheriff and tell him we want to file an assault charge against those men."

"That will just piss him off even more. I'm sure he'll want revenge for me kicking him. I'm as good as dead already." He looked around the room. "I'm scared, okay? That guy scares the crap out of me, and I don't want to die, and I'm pretty sure he'll want to kill me now."

"Listen, Perseus. I want you to stay," Bud said. "I know this was a bad experience, but there is so much more that is good around here. Think of all the things you've learned and accomplished since coming here. We need you. I need you."

"I need you," Penelope added.

Everyone looked at her. For some reason this pronouncement surprised Tommy and her father. Perseus had hoped he might hear her say this someday, but certainly not under these circumstances. He didn't know what to do. After more thought, he realized he didn't really have enough money to go anywhere . . . and there was the wyvern, of course.

"I think I just need to go to bed. I can think about it some more tomorrow."

"I'll drive Tommy back to his truck at the Red Barn," Bud offered.

As Bud and Tommy drove off, Penelope walked with Perseus to the barn. "Do you want me to go feed and water the wyvern, Perseus? I don't think you should go out there tonight in your condition."

He had forgotten about feeding her. "I should go do it. I'm not in that bad of shape. I think I'm mostly just feeling sorry for myself. Maybe we could go out there together."

"Yes, I'll go with you, but let's take the truck."

When they opened the door to the shack, the odor wasn't nearly as intense as it had been during the first few days. They had tried using cat litter in a large tub situated in one corner of the room, hoping the creature would get the hint. It worked. Not only did this solution reduce the smell, but it also made clean-up a whole lot easier.

"Hi, little girl," Penelope cooed. She set the lantern on a small table they had previously added to the shack's interior. They had also borrowed an old bench from the barn and installed it in the room as the only other piece of furniture.

Perseus sat heavily on the bench, not greeting the wyvern. She immediately sensed something was wrong and made her way over to Perseus. She hopped up on the bench next to him and looked at his face, clearly examining his wounds and making odd sounds.

"I'll be alright," he said to the wyvern. "I got beat up by this big oaf named Bart."

"Yeah. A big oaf. That's a word for somebody who is a bully and a jerk."

The wyvern was looking intently at Perseus. "He grabbed Penelope and was going to throw Tommy and me out of a place where we were all having a beer and talking," Perseus continued.

"A beer. It's a drink made from fermented grain and some other stuff. I don't actually know how to make beer, but it's alcoholic."

"That means it makes you feel kind of light-headed."

"Who are you talking to?" Penelope asked, her face squished up in confusion.

Perseus looked up at her. "What? Oh, I was just explaining . . ." His voice trailed off and he slowly looked back over to the wyvern. "Hey. She can talk."

"I didn't hear her say anything," Penelope said, now even more confused. She immediately grew concerned that Perseus may have suffered a concussion.

This was the moment Perseus realized that the creature was intelligent. "She was sending me thoughts, or something like that. They weren't exactly words, more like thought pictures. It's hard to explain, but I could understand her, and I think she understood me too. She was asking me questions."

"Perseus, are you sure? Maybe you hit your head."

"No, I'm sure." He looked at the wyvern. "Penelope says she can't hear your thoughts."

Penelope suddenly gasped. "Yes, I did. She asked me if I took care of you after you were injured."

"She says she can only communicate with one individual at a time. Perseus, this is amazing."

Suddenly, the shack door opened and Tommy walked in. The little wyvern moved around to hide behind Perseus, hissing a warning to the intruder. Then she recognized that it was Tommy and came back out next to Perseus, screeching her greeting with outstretched wings.

Tommy chuckled. "Hi. I thought you guys would be out here, so I came back. Seemed like we should be together after what happened at the Red Barn."

"Hi, Tommy," Penelope said. "I'm glad you came. We've just discovered something remarkable. This little girl can communicate."

"What?" Tommy looked around the room, a little confused. He got a very odd look on his face. "Yes, I was attacked by the bad people too? I'll be alright." He finally focused in on the wyvern. "Holy crow, she's talking to me. Well, not talking exactly, but I can understand her."

"It's pretty amazing, isn't it?" Perseus said.

"Wow, and look how big she's getting," Tommy observed. "I bet she's twice as big as she was and it's only been a couple of weeks since she came out of that egg thing. How big will you get?" He directed this question to her.

"She doesn't know how to describe the maximum size, but it would be much larger than a human," Tommy told the others.

"It's going to get pretty hard to keep her out of sight if she gets that big," said Perseus.

"What are you going to do with her?" Tommy asked.

"I don't know. If I was chosen in some way, as your grandfather seems to think, I can't understand why. I'd have to say it was a poor choice. I mean, who am I? What can I do? If her fate is in my hands, then I'd have to say she's in trouble. But maybe it's not really in my hands. If she's an intelligent being, won't she have to determine her future for herself?"

The wyvern had been watching him intently as he said this. She moved even closer to him, climbing up onto his lap, now looking almost directly eye-to-eye. "*You are already fulfilling your purpose, Perseus. You are allowing me to live and grow. For this, I am grateful.*"

This was not exactly what she said, because she was projecting thought pictures, but this is how Perseus perceived her thoughts. When he shared what she had told him with the others, it seemed to settle the question for the time being.

"Do you have a name?" Perseus said out loud.

The wyvern seemed to be looking for an answer in her database brain. "*We do not have the equivalent of names as you are thinking of it. Would it be good for you if I were to have a name?*"

Perseus repeated the question. "Tell her, yes, that would be very good," Penelope said.

"Should we call her Sint-Holo?" he asked Tommy.

"It's kind of strange that the legendary serpent in our folklore is called Sint-Holo, because there is no such thing in the Choctaw language. What I mean is, the words don't have any other meaning. My grandfather and I have discussed this. If you are wondering if this has a special meaning to our people, I don't think so. You could call her Penelope, the Sint-Holo, or anything else, and it would be fine for some and offensive to others. It's like that with everything, is it not?"

Perseus thought for several moments. "Maybe we could name her Filia. That's the Greek word for friendship."

"Why a Greek word?" Tommy asked.

"Well, it kind of sidesteps the whole native, non-native language quagmire, and she's like a mythical being, which has its roots in Greek mythology. And the word friendship seems like an optimistic wish for how our two species will interact. Is there a Choctaw word for friendship?"

"Ittikana. Ittikana means friendly or friendship. I think the idea is good. It's a good name."

"Which version, the Greek or the Choctaw?"

"Well, I guess I'd have to say the Choctaw, Ittikana," Tommy said hopefully.

"I think that's a pretty name," Penelope agreed.

"Alright then." Perseus looked directly at the wyvern. "We would like to name you Ittikana, which means friendship in the language of the local Native-Americans. Tommy is a member of the Choctaw Nation, and that is also where we found you."

She made a sound that combined her screech and purr. *"This is a good name. I believe I understand the implication."*

Perseus repeated the translated thought to the others, and everybody seemed happy with the decision. They all agreed to help take care of her and to keep her existence a secret, only telling others if they all agreed.

Later, as he lay in his bunk, Perseus struggled with all the ethical issues associated with Ittikana's status. It appeared that she was intelligent and able to communicate, and think, and had many other abilities normally only associated with humans. What category of being would she be considered and what rights would she have, if any? He worried about what would happen to her once the world found out she existed.

CHAPTER 14

TWO DAYS AFTER the Red Barn incident, Bud got a call from the County Sheriff. According to several locals, Bart Oglethorpe was swearing to get revenge on a man named Perseus for injuries sustained in a brawl at the Red Barn a couple days ago.

"Do you have an employee out there named Perseus?" the sheriff asked.

"Yes, I do, Sheriff. His full name is Perseus Fawcett," Bud replied. "I'm surprised to hear you describe the incident as a brawl. The fact is that my daughter, Penelope, and her friends, Perseus, and Tommy Abbot, were attacked by Bart and several of his associates. They beat the crap out of the two boys. They're still recovering."

"That doesn't surprise me. Bart is trouble, that's for sure, but I'm just passing on what others are telling me. I think it would be a good idea to keep that fellow out of town 'till this thing blows over."

"I appreciate you giving me the heads-up, Sheriff. We were considering pressing assault charges on that bunch, but Perseus was afraid that would make matters worse. He's probably right. We'll keep him here and make sure there's someone with him all the time. I don't think Bart would come out here to the HB looking for that kind of trouble."

"Alright then. Give me a call if it looks like there's gonna be a problem."

At supper that evening, Bud told everyone of the sheriff's call. They all decided to start carrying weapons with them when out working, and to always work with a partner, never alone, especially Perseus. Everybody seemed to agree with these precautions as if it was no big deal.

"So, you're all going to start carrying guns to work?" Perseus asked, obviously startled by this decision. "Really? I mean, are you saying there's a chance that we might be forced into a gun battle with these guys?" He was looking from face to face around the supper table.

"Now, now, Perseus," Bud said in as calm a voice as he could muster. "This is just a precaution. Bart can be obsessive about some things, but I don't think he's going to come out here with his gang and start a shooting war. The word will get around that we're armed, and that should deter him from doing anything stupid. We're not going to make you carry a gun if you don't want to."

Perseus just stared at Bud in disbelief. Finally, he snapped out of his shock. "I don't want to be a problem, Mister Wesley. Maybe it would be best if I just leave. I mean, never in my wildest dreams did I ever think I would need people carrying guns to guard me from some town bully."

"Are you anti-gun?" Slim asked, surprised by Perseus' reaction.

"No. No, I'm not against guns, not at all. I just don't want to be the cause of a gunfight, and I'd really rather not be in one." He realized he was breathing hard. He knew he needed to calm down. He looked at Penelope to see how she was taking all this. He thought she had a sympathetic look on her face, or was it disappointment?

He excused himself and left the table. "I'm going to the barn to finish my chores."

When Perseus had turned his back to leave, Bud motioned for Slim to follow him and pointed to the holstered revolvers lying in a row on a small table next to the door.

The next three weeks were tense, but this was the time of year when the calves were weaned from their mothers, so the days were busy. The process was drawn out because the cows had their calves at different times between February and early April. Their target for getting weaned calves to market was September and October. This was also when the bulls needed to be pulled back in from the cow herds and put back in the bull pens.

Perseus was still upset by the situation he felt he had created. He decided not to carry a gun, but everyone else wore a pistol on their hip, and Bud carried a rifle in a scabbard hung from his saddle. It reminded Perseus of old western movies about cattle drives and gunslingers. When they were out in the far pastures, they sometimes caught glimpses of a lone rider along the distant tree lines. Everybody assumed it was either Bart or one of his thugs looking for an opportunity to catch Perseus alone.

He continued to be frightened, but he was also embarrassed. His self-esteem was ebbing day by day and he flirted with the temptation to run away. He still didn't have the funds to get far though. Besides, he knew he couldn't just leave Ittikana behind. How would he transport her? She was growing so rapidly it was alarming.

He considered calling his father to get his input and advice. He knew this would almost certainly end up being an exercise in futility because his father was always too preoccupied and consumed with his own concerns. He would probably lecture Perseus about being more responsible, more focused, and accuse him of allowing his imagination to run off into delusions of fantasy.

But what if he took a picture of Ittikana and sent it to his father? Wouldn't that convince him she was real? He tried to imagine his father's reaction, but he found that he couldn't come up with anything other than disbelief or indifference, although that was probably unfair. It occurred to him that the life he was living out here in Oklahoma, as a hired cowboy on a cattle ranch, being pursued by a bad guy named Bart, and everybody he worked with toting six-shooters, was so far removed from his parents' limits of reality that they would never believe this was his actual situation. The extraordinary fact that he had found and rescued a legendry wyvern from a cave that he had dreamed about, or that a Native-American Choctaw medicine man had told him about a vision that their son would find this creature, was simply beyond their capacity to accept.

Perseus felt like these thoughts should be making him feel blue or depressed, instead, they made him laugh. For some reason it reminded him of the April Fools' joke he had pulled on his parents the day of his birthday; very inappropriate, but funny. Of course, they hadn't thought it was funny. He supposed someday his parents would have to come to grips with the life that was now apparently his own reality.

One evening, after supper, Perseus was out at the barn doing his usual end of day chores, when Penelope strolled into the barn.

"Hi, Perseus. Mind if I hang out with you for a while?"

"That would be great. We've all been so busy lately; I haven't seen much of you. I kind of thought maybe you weren't so happy with me these days."

"No, not at all. I've just been trying to give you a little space. I know you've been upset, and everything is so complicated right now."

"I'm glad you came down here to talk to me, Penelope. I'm frustrated, to be sure, and it's not just about Bart. I'm still afraid he's going to do something awful, but I've kind of gotten used to living in the shadow of death, something only a man with balls of steel could endure." He looked up at her with an impish grin.

She giggled and slapped him on the arm. "This situation is intolerable," she said. "I keep hoping it will all just settle down. This is a critical time of year for the operation, a sort of make-or-break time. We don't need this kind of distraction. But I want to know what's on *your* mind. Are you still thinking of moving on?" She was looking down at the ground when she asked him the question.

She had been following him as he walked along the side of the barn with a water hose. He stopped and looked at her. "I'm not going to move on, at least not willingly. I've had plenty of time to think about all this, and I don't just mean the whole Black Bart thing. I'm still struggling with myself, trying to figure out who I am, but I am beginning to understand that a guy has to put a stake in the ground at some point."

"I've been worried about what my parents might think about me doing this kind of work and living this kind of life. Well, I finally realize that I don't need to live my life for them. I like this place and the things we do here. I like myself a lot more than I used to, though I know I've got more to learn and more maturing to get through. And . . . I like you too, Penelope. You and your father are important to me, and I want to continue to be a part of all this."

She was peering into his eyes, looking like she liked what she was hearing, when there was a heavy *thunk* as splinters of wood from the barn exploded inches from where they stood. The sound of a gunshot followed almost instantly. They instinctively dove to the ground and Perseus quickly positioned himself between the direction of the shot and Penelope. They began crawling toward the barn door and moved inside. They waited for a couple of minutes but there were no more shots.

Bud and the others ran down from the house, their guns in hand. "What happened?" Bud yelled.

Perseus poked his head around the barn door and saw who it was. "Somebody just took a shot at us. It came from that direction," he said pointing.

Bud ran up to Penelope. "Are you alright?"

"Yes, Dad, we're fine."

Bud holstered his gun and grabbed his daughter and held her tight. After a moment, he held her at arms' length, as if wanting to see for himself that she was unharmed. "That sonofabitch has gone too far." He was seething.

"I don't think he would actually try to kill us, would he?" she said to her father. "It was probably just a way to let us know he's still out there or to scare us."

"I don't care what he's trying to do. This has gone too far. I'm going to call the sheriff. Slim, you and Günter take the truck and see if there's anybody lurking around within gun range of the place. Be careful. Shoot first and ask questions later if you find anybody."

"Yes sir," Slim said with a grin. "I would like nothin' better than to put a hunk o' lead in that varmint."

The next morning, they discovered several gates had been opened and the cows and calves had rejoined, requiring them to start sorting and separating them all over again. Bud was furious. He told the others to start getting things back in order, he was going to the McAllister Ranch and confront Bart with all this treachery. Everyone tried to talk him out of going.

"Daddy, please. That guy is dangerous. You don't know what he might do if you get in his face."

"Enough is enough," he replied. "I'll call the sheriff on my way and tell him what's going on and that I'm heading over to the McAllister. Don't worry, I'm not going to gun him down or get in a fist fight with him. People like him have to be pushed back or they just keep bullying until they break you down."

Perseus was thinking that Bud was the bravest man he'd ever known. And he was right about bullies. They have to be confronted or they'll never stop, never leave you alone. They thrive on others' fears.

Bud called the sheriff, who said he'd meet him at the McAllister Ranch. He arrived before the sheriff but couldn't find Bart anywhere. Everybody claimed they didn't know where Bart was. The sheriff still hadn't arrived when Bud got tired of waiting and decided to go back to the HB to help sort out the cow, calf problem. He was still fuming.

He was driving down the gravel road that connected the McAllister Ranch to the highway, going faster than he should have. He saw a lone rider up ahead, nearly obscured by a thick cloud of dust. Something was obviously creating all the dust, but Bud didn't give it much thought. Then he realized that the rider was a large man on a black horse, waving a lariat over his head. Before he could completely process what was happening, a herd of cattle materialized from out of the dust and were stampeding out onto the road from around a small hilly rise.

Bud was going way too fast. He slammed on his brakes, but it was clear that he was going to plow into those cattle if he didn't do something fast. He swerved the wheel to the right, not seeing the large maple tree until it was too late. His truck careened into the tree head-on.

Penelope kept looking at her watch. She thought her father should have been back by now. They were all out in the pastures sorting out the calves from the cows when she saw the sheriff drive up to the house. She expected to see her father drive up behind him, but he didn't. She watched the sheriff get out of his SUV and head up to the house, and she turned her horse in that direction. Perseus saw what was happening and chased after her on Balius.

She rode hard and jumped from the saddle before the horse came to a full stop in front of the house and ran up to the porch where the sheriff was talking to Angelica. Perseus was close on her heels.

When the sheriff heard her coming, he turned to meet her. She looked at him expectantly. "Where's my father?" she asked breathlessly.

"Penelope, your father had an accident out at the McAllister Ranch. He ran into a tree on that gravel road going to the highway."

"Is he okay? Where is he?"

The sheriff wore the answer in his expression. "I'm sorry, Penelope, he didn't survive the accident. He hit the tree going pretty fast."

She looked at him in disbelief, shaking her head. "What do you mean?" she said, tears already welling up in her eyes.

"He died at the scene, sweetheart. I'm so sorry."

Stunned, Penelope froze. Perseus could see she was about to collapse and ran up the steps just in time to catch her. He held her in his arms, on the floor of the porch, rocking her back and forth as she cried out in great sobs of grief.

"Nooooo! Nooooo! Oh my God!" she screamed over and over. "Noooo!

Slim and Günter rode up and knew instantly that something awful had happened. They slowly climbed the stairs, looking down at Perseus holding Penelope. The scene before them was breaking their hearts.

"What happened, Sheriff?" Slim asked.

The sheriff told them that Bud was out at the McAllister place looking for Bart, and he was supposed to meet him there. Bud got there first, and when he couldn't find Bart, he took off in a rush. Nobody knew where he was going. Bart was out driving some cattle and the herd was crossing the road just as Bud came tearing up the road right at that exact spot. He swerved to miss the cows and hit the tree.

Slim and Günter exchanged suspicious looks. "Well, ain't that a tragic coincidence," Slim said cynically. "Just happened that Bart, the foreman of the ranch, was out by *hisself* movin' a herd of cattle right in front a Bud."

"Now, I know what you're thinking, and I admit it's suspicious, but there's not a shred of evidence that this was premeditated. I don't need a couple of pissed-off cowboys going around gunning for Bart. We got enough trouble in Choctaw County as it is."

Slim and Günter just shook their heads and went over to where Penelope had collapsed. They knelt beside her, knowing there was nothing they could say or do. Angelica also came over to sit next to them, stroking Penelope's hair and speaking soothingly to her in Spanish.

"I'm sorry, folks. Really sorry. Bud was a good man, one of the best. His body will be at the funeral parlor on Jackson. They'll be wanting to know what arrangements . . ." He could see this was probably not the time to discuss such things. Without another word he turned, walked back to his SUV, and left.

The next several days were a blur. Of course, Penelope was inconsolable in her grief. Perseus tried to help her with funeral arrangements and all of the necessary legal details that accompany the death of a head of household and owner of a business. She did not want to think about most of these things, so he muddled through it as best he could.

It turned out that there were no other direct family members to notify. Bud had a brother who had passed away four years earlier, and Penelope's mother had two sisters living in other parts of the U.S., but they were not close. There were, no doubt, second, third, and fourth cousins scattered around somewhere, but no easily available information about how to identify or contact any of them.

Everybody in the local community was shocked at the news and there was a great outpouring of sympathy in the form of cards, emails, phone calls, and visitors bearing food or flowers. Penelope, however, was too numb to appreciate their genuine sympathy. Perseus just kept trying to reassure her that he would take care of it, whatever "it" happened to be. But since he had no connections to her family, such as it was, or the community, or the business details of the HB operation, this proved very difficult.

He arranged for Tommy to conscript a couple of his friends from the reservation to help Slim and Günter keep things on the HB running smoothly. This was a critical time in the annual cycle of the beef business, and it was close to the time when they would have to sell their cattle, which included making arrangements with a buyer and the transportation of the cattle to a feed lot. Perseus was grateful that Slim essentially took charge of operations, updating Perseus everyday so he could try to pass on the information to Penelope.

The funeral was the most difficult day. Perseus thought that Penelope seemed to be in some kind of trance, barely able to respond to the sympathies extended by those attending the service. For her, it was as if her world had ended. Her father had been so young. It was just inconceivable that he was gone forever. Her feeling of loss was so profound it was crushing her. She was only at the service because Perseus had told her she should be there, and she was counting on him to guide her through it all.

Tommy and his grandfather attended the service. When Penelope realized that Bus was standing in front of her, she momentarily emerged from her despair. He held her hand in his and was looking into her eyes. When he saw her focus on him, he told her how sorry he was and then began chanting something very softly in the Choctaw language. She had no idea what he was saying or what it meant, but she felt a strange easing of her pain. He then patted her hand gently and gave her a faint smile before moving on. She would later tell Perseus this was the only moment she could remember from the entire day.

The day after the funeral service, Bart Oglethorpe visited the HB on the pretense of extending his sympathies to Penelope. Angelica answered the door and was unsure what to do. She asked Bart to wait on the porch and then hurried to the living room where Penelope was going through the motions of looking at some business papers. Angelica nervously announced that Mister Bart was at the door, and anger immediately flashed over Penelope's face.

She jerked open the door. "What are you doing here?"

"I wanted to extend my sympathies for your father's death. I also wanted to tell you that I could help you run the HB, now that your father is gone."

She could detect no sign of genuine sympathy in his face. "You've got a lot of nerve coming here. You've been nothing but trouble for us. You're not welcome here. Get off my property."

He stood silent for a moment, a malignant frown forming on his face. "You better think it over, Penelope, otherwise you should start looking for another place to live." He turned and stormed off to his truck.

She turned and went back inside, so furious by his audacity she wanted to smash something. She didn't notice that Bart drove down to the barn rather than heading out toward the highway. He was looking for Perseus. If he got the chance, he would take care of the little bastard once and for all.

Bart entered the barn, surprising Perseus, who was working with Slim and Günter shoeing horses. They all stopped what they were doing and stood together to face Bart. Bart strode up to them and got close to Perseus. Although his heart was hammering away, Perseus didn't flinch, but kept his eyes locked on the big man.

Bart quickly eyed Slim and Günter. He noticed they had their hands resting on the revolvers hanging from their hips. He saw, too, that Perseus was holding a hook knife for trimming hooves.

"You would be wise to clear out of these parts, boy. You don't belong here." He wanted to smash Perseus' face in, but the state's gun laws made it perfectly legal for these idiots to shoot him, and it was plain to see they were hoping for the chance. Having said his peace, he turned and left.

Perseus stood there until he heard the truck pull away, then he let out a breath he didn't realize he was holding. "Thank you, guys. Thank God you were here! I'm pretty sure he would have done me in otherwise."

"Well, he's lucky he didn't try anything," Günter growled. "I wouldn't lose any sleep over puttin' a bullet in that man's head."

Perseus shuddered at the thought.

CHAPTER 15

A FEW DAYS after the funeral, Günter came riding in hard from one of the far pastures. He found Slim and told him that there were several dead cows and more in distress out in the paddock near the lake.

"Looks like bloat," he told Slim excitedly. "I left Tommy out there to try to find others that might be having the problem and to look for anything unusual."

Slim quickly found Perseus to tell him of the grim discovery. Perseus told Slim to go back out with Günter and he would follow as soon as he could. He didn't want Tommy alone out there, but he needed to tell Penelope.

He ran up to the house and asked Angelica if she knew where Penelope was. "She jus' go with Chilo. Maybe with gallina."

Perseus had by now picked up several words of Spanish. He knew she meant they could be with the hens in the chicken coop. That's where he found them. Chilo was telling Penelope that something had made a big hole in the enclosure, which seemed quite odd.

"Penelope," Perseus gasped after running from the house. "We have a problem out in the far pasture. Günter says we've got some dead cows and others that are in distress. He said it looks like it might be bloat."

Penelope was still in her dark state of mind, but this seemed to snap her out of it. She looked at the hole in the chicken coop. Now this bad news about the cows. "Bloat," she said, and Perseus could see her face darken. "That is caused by eating something that almost certainly does not exist naturally in those pastures this time of year."

She looked up at Perseus. He could see her mounting anger was bringing her out of her depression. "Bart," she spit the word out. "Let's go."

They got into her truck and headed for the pastures to join the others. There, spread over the 40-acre pasture, lay several cows and a few calves. It was clear some of them were already dead, while others were having difficulty breathing and their left sides were noticeably distended.

Slim met them at the truck. "It's bloat alright. We found lots a flakes of alfalfa and white clover layin' around in this pasture and the one next to it. You know them cows is gonna go fer that stuff if'n they can get it. It was put here sure as horse turds. Only one person I ken think of who'd do such a thing."

"Bastard," Penelope hissed. "First things first. We have to get this fixed right now. Perseus and I will comb the pastures and pick up any flakes of hay we find and put them in the back of the truck. You know what to do, Slim. You and Gunter go get the big truck and load up some portable corral and the squeeze."

"Yes, ma'am." Slim quickly went to get Günter.

Tommy was standing by. "Tommy, give me a hand getting this hay picked up. You walk along one side of the truck and I'll take the other side."

Penelope told them they should start in one corner and methodically scour the pasture from one end to the other. There were cattle still glutting on the forbidden hay, and they tried to chase them off, but it was tempting stuff. Penelope called their vet from her cell phone and told him what had happened. He promised he would come out as soon as he could get there. It would be a race against time.

When Slim and Günter returned, they raced to set up the portable corral, using several pipe corral sections to form a chute leading to the squeeze. The veterinarian showed up just as they were getting the first cows and one calf into the enclosure. One by one, they put an animal in the squeeze so they could insert a tube through the mouth and into the rumen to relieve the gas with an anti-foaming agent. There were two serious cases where a surgical instrument, called a trocar, had to be used to cut an opening in the animal's side and a bloat needle inserted into the incision to relieve the gas.

At the end of the day, they had managed to save all but one of the cows that were still alive when they started treating them. A total of twelve cows and calves were lost. Their jubilation at their relative success was overshadowed by their anger. This had clearly been an attempt to kill off enough animals to decrease the HB's fall revenues, which would make it more difficult to pay off the loan. By now, everybody on the HB knew about the loan, and all they stood to lose if the HB went to Bart.

That day's incidents, Bud's apparent murder, the shooting attempt at the barn, and the personal threat directed at Perseus, left little doubt who was behind all of this treachery.

"I'm not going to take this any longer," Perseus announced. "I'm going to do whatever it takes to bring Bart down, and I'm going to do everything I can to make sure you don't lose this ranch, Penelope."

For the first time that day, Penelope realized that Perseus was now wearing a holstered gun on his belt. "Perseus, I appreciate all you've done, but I don't want you to do anything that could get you killed. You know Bart is a vicious person. You can't just go gunning for him!"

Perseus gave a single, mirthless laugh. "I have no intention of going gunning for him. Are you kidding? But I've had it. We're going to close ranks and make sure he doesn't get the chance to do any more harm to us, or the stock, or anything else on this place. I realize that until now I've been a bystander and an unlucky target for Bart. The most important thing is to save the ranch, and if we can figure out how to put Bart in a box, we'll get'er done, as Slim would say." They all chuckled and then voiced their support.

Perseus was glad to see that Penelope had come out of the dark place she had been in since her father's death. He knew it was too soon for her to just carry on, but today's disaster seemed to help her become more focused on the immediate problems of survival. And this was essential if she was to have any chance of keeping the ranch out of Bart's hands.

After supper that evening, Perseus asked Penelope if she felt up to going out to see Ittikana. She didn't hesitate with her answer, yes. It had been almost two weeks since her last visit and Penelope was shocked at how much the wyvern had grown.

"Oh, my gosh!" she exclaimed. "How can she grow so fast? How big do you think she'll get?"

"She doesn't seem to really know how to judge her full size. She was sending me thought pictures of comparisons that didn't make any sense to me. I'm guessing she can get pretty large though. I was planning on taking her outside tonight. That's why I was hoping you'd come with me. We can't keep her in this little shack much longer, and we can't really keep an eye on her out here either."

"Does she know you're taking her outside?"

"I told her last night. She's excited and a little frightened."

Ittikana was nuzzling Penelope when she suddenly stopped and rose up to look Penelope in the eye. She was now tall enough to stand on her hind legs and be eye to eye with Penelope. This startled her at first, but she quickly realized that Ittikana was examining her thoughts.

"*You are sad,*" she told Penelope. "*What has happened?*"

Penelope turned to look at Perseus, surprised by the creature's abilities. Perseus saw the look of despair cloud her face again. She turned back to face Ittikana.

"*Yes, I am very sad, Ittikana. My father was killed a short time ago, just since the last time I saw you.*" Now a tear trailed down her cheek.

To Penelope's utter surprise, Ittikana leaned over and licked the tear. The look in the creature's eyes changed dramatically, her eye color actually darkening. "*I share your sadness,*" she said simply and lay her head, a head Perseus thought only a mother could love, on Penelope's shoulder. The gesture so moved Penelope that she reached out and hugged Ittikana.

Perseus watched quietly, hoping this wouldn't throw Penelope back into an incapacitating depression again. When the two females parted, Penelope seemed to recover her composure.

"*Do you want to go outside?*" Perseus directed his thought to Ittikana.

"*Yes,*" she replied.

Perseus opened the shack door and stepped outside several feet. "*Come on out, Ittikana.*"

She seemed hesitant, moving just to the threshold so that her head stuck out the door. She carefully scrutinized the adjacent area and sampled the night air with her complex-looking nose.

"*It's alright. Come on out,*" Penelope coaxed.

Ittikana moved a few feet past the open door and looked up toward the stars. "*This is much more magnificent than the memories of it all. The stars are beautiful.*"

She moved farther into the open in her ungainly fashion, her front appendages being primarily for flying. When she was several yards away from the shack, she abruptly stood on her hind legs and spread her wings to their fullest extent above her body. She lowered her head, and in one swift, powerful jump she was airborne. The sound of her wings beating the air drowned out the other night sounds, and she shrieked out her joy as she rose higher and higher above the two humans watching her, open-mouthed. She dove and climbed and dove again, flying in a large circular pattern around the cabin.

Perseus began to think she might just keep flying and head off into the distance, too distracted with her obvious happiness at being free to return to her human handlers. But she eventually did settle back to the ground, making a somewhat rough landing. Her body design was more suited for hanging than standing, but Perseus guessed she would become more adept with practice. She was an impressive sight when in the air though. He estimated her wingspan at around twelve feet, possibly more, and she was only six weeks old. It was going to become increasingly difficult to conceal her.

Her excitement was so pronounced it was not possible to sort through all the emotions she was projecting. Perseus could not understand what she was trying to communicate.

"Slow down, Ittikana. I can't understand what you are saying," Perseus pleaded.

She shrieked her jubilation, then lowered her head, nearly touching her chin to the ground, and hissed in a most frightful way.

"Whoa!" Penelope exclaimed in shock. "Calm down, girl."

Ittikana's delight was contagious, making both Penelope and Perseus laugh. Her ungainly manner notwithstanding, she seemed, literally, to dance around the humans. Finally, she settled down and sat back on her hind legs in her usual resting position.

"*Thank you,*" she told them. "*I saw some interesting large animals while I was up there in the sky. They look like they would be a good food source.*" It seemed to Perseus that her eyes were sparkling with anticipation.

"No, Ittikana. Those are called cows and they are the source of our livelihood around here. They are not for eating, at least, not by you, unless Penelope gives you permission to take a specific one." Perseus explained what Ittikana had said, much to Penelope's dismay.

"I'll have a talk with her," he assured Penelope. "I think we should bring her in closer to the main buildings. Having her out here is pretty inconvenient, and she's getting too big for this little cabin anyway."

"Not to mention she apparently needs to be taught what she can and can't do. If we bring her in, everybody on the ranch will certainly see her. How do you think that will go over?"

"I don't know, but we have to confront that situation eventually, don't we? Tommy's grandfather never did tell us what he thought we should do with her. She' going to need to be protected, Penelope."

"Yes, I know you're right. Frankly, I don't know what else we can do. Let's take her up there right now, under cover of darkness. We need to discuss this with her and warn her about all the livestock she'll be close to. We can't have her eating our cattle and horses."

So, they explained to Ittikana what they intended to do and told her she would have to follow rules, which she understood and agreed to. They also tried to describe the possible reactions other humans might have when they saw her, and they told her there were other humans she would be meeting right away. She under-stood. Her inherited memories about humans were vivid and quite worrisome, but she decided not to reveal those memories to her humans just yet.

They eventually convinced Ittikana to get into the back of the pickup truck. There was nothing in her inherited memory to prepare her for something like this. Perseus had to agree to ride in the back with her to get her to comply. She quickly became very interested in the experience and asked Perseus many questions about how this apparatus worked. She was very happy about being outdoors and took in all the nighttime scenery as they headed back toward the barn.

They tried to sneak past the big barn, but Slim, ever vigilant these days, heard them approaching, came out to see who it was. At first, he thought they had a calf in the back of the truck, but when he came around to take a closer look, he screamed.

"What in tha name of all that's holy is that thing?" He actually drew his pistol.

"Don't shoot, Slim," Perseus said, moving between him and his passenger. "This is Ittikana. We found her when we went camping back on the Fourth. She's called a wyvern, a kind of dragon."

Slim stared at the creature, trying to get his brain to come to terms with what his eyes were seeing, but his mind would not compute. "Uh-huh. Well, what's it doin' here?"

"We're going to keep it here, at least for a while," Penelope informed him. "It needs to be protected, Slim. As you can imag-ine, this is a very rare creature."

"Well, it's also a very ugly critter," Slim said, reluctantly holstering his gun.

Ittikana hissed.

"Careful, Slim," Perseus warned. "She can understand what you say. What you think, actually."

"Uh-huh. Are you a tellin' me that there thing ken talk?"

"Yes, well sort of. She can receive your thoughts and can send her thoughts to you." Perseus turned to look at Ittikana for a moment. He was asking her to say hello to Slim.

"Aah!" Slim shouted and backed away. "That just ain't right. My God almighty, that ain't right. I'll have ta think about this some."

Günter came out to see what all the commotion was about and had a similar reaction. All said, Perseus thought the initial introductions seemed to go well enough. Nobody got hurt. He asked Slim and Günter if they had any suggestions for where they might keep her. Günter told them that she looked kind of like a giant bat and maybe she could roost in the nearest hay shelter.

"Maybe she'd wanna hang up there in them trusses. Ain't no hay underneath at the far end, so she won't be a messin' up the hay. Know what I mean?" Slim was trying to be helpful, which Penelope and Perseus thought was a good sign.

"That's actually a pretty good suggestion," Perseus admitted. He shared the idea with Ittikana, but the concept of a truss was a little vague to her, so she told him she wanted to see it.

They all went to the far end of the hay shelter to show Ittikana the trusses and explain the concept of roosting. She studied the structure for some time. The hay shelters had no sides, only a tall roof covering, so she realized now that she would not be cooped up in an enclosure.

"Yes, I like this place," she eventually told Perseus. She stood up in the back of the pickup and spread her wings. Startled by her now formidable stature, Slim and Günter hollered and quickly stepped back several yards. She flew up to the wooden truss structure and easily grabbed the bottom chord with her hind claws, then she worked her way into a corner using her thumb claws to grab the truss webs so she could snuggle up between the bottom chord and the corresponding top chord. When she was done, the humans could barely tell she was up there.

"Are you alright?" Perseus asked her.

"*Yes, this is very nice. Much better than the old building.*"

"Good. We're all going to go to sleep now. I'll see you in the morning. Remember, no eating the animals around here."

"*No. I will not eat the animals.*"

Perseus relayed the conversation to the others.

"Well, don't that beat all?" Günter said, pulling at one end of his long mustache.

Slim and Günter went back to the bunk house. Perseus lingered outside with Penelope. He could see she was tired, but he was hoping he could have just another few minutes with her before she returned to the main house. She was leaning back against the truck, looking up at the stars.

"It's been a pretty interesting day," he said nonchalantly.

She shifted her attention to him. "Yes, to say the least."

"Perseus, I want to tell you something. If it hadn't been for you, I don't know how I could have survived these last two weeks. I know it's been like I've been in a trance. I'm still struggling with everything. It's just so hard to believe that Daddy's gone. But you have been so patient and so, . . . well, you've just been there for me to lean on. Thank you, from the bottom of my heart."

She turned to him and put her arms around his neck. Their eyes locked. He wanted to kiss her, but he thought he should let her decide. He didn't want her to feel like he was taking advantage of her at this very delicate time. She leaned closer and their lips met. It was a long, sweet kiss, full of sadness, but also tenderness and promise.

"I want to say I love you," she whispered. "But I can't say that right now. I need time to do some healing. Do you understand?"

"Of course, I understand, Penelope. I'll be here when you're ready."

CHAPTER 16

PERSEUS WAS KEENLY aware that the HB Cattle Company was moving into a hyper-critical period. He knew they needed to successfully negotiate a sales contract for their cattle and get them to a feedlot and then prepare the cows and bulls for the winter months. He felt confident he could help deal with all the cattle-related issues. Slim and Günter, who were old hands at this sort of thing, and Penelope, who was as good as any cowboy, were working diligently on this final stretch of the beef cattle cycle. Perseus even felt fairly comfortable with his own abilities now, but he was aware that the others were looking to him for leadership, as unimaginable as that would have been several months ago.

His main concern, however, was the wyvern, but it was difficult to concentrate on her while he was preoccupied with the ranch. For the time being, Ittikana seemed quite content where she was, but he knew the time was coming when she would want to move on to the next stage of her development, whatever that was. And even more disconcerting was the knowledge that it was just a matter of time before her existence would become public knowledge. Those were the concerns that weighed heavily on his mind.

He finally decided he was going to call his parents. He wanted to tell them where he was and what he was doing. He hoped that they were concerned and would want to hear from him. He was also hoping he might get some advice from his father regarding the wyvern, maybe even from his mother. She was a lawyer after all, so maybe she would have some legal advice regarding the creature's rights.

He procrastinated for several days, telling himself he should wait until he was fairly certain they would both be home. They were, after all, in a different time zone, so he had to take the hour difference into account. Finally, he brought himself to dial the number. He was nervous and realized he was pacing as the phone on the other end rang.

"Hello." It was his mother.

"Hello, Mother." There was no immediate response. "It's Perseus."

After more silence, "Perseus." Maybe she had already forgotten about him. "Where are you?"

No "hello," no "how are you." His stomach was tied in knots and his heart began to beat a rhythm all its own. "I'm in Oklahoma. I thought you might like to know what's happening in my life. Is Dad home?"

"Oklahoma? What in the world are you doing out there? Are you in school?"

He heard his father asking who was on the phone. His mother cupped her hand over the phone, but he could hear her response. "It's Perseus. He's in Oklahoma." There was another pause and then he heard his father pick up another phone.

"Hello, Perseus? What are you doing in Oklahoma?" his father said, sounding as incredulous as his mother about his location.

"This is where I ran out of money and had to find a job," he said honestly. "I'm working on a cattle ranch called the HB Cattle Company outside of Hugo, Oklahoma." There was more silence.

Even though it was only a few seconds, it felt like an eternity before he was able to continue. This call didn't seem to be going well and he was beginning to regret even making the call.

"How are you guys? Is everything alright back there?" Perhaps if he made the first attempt to bring the conversation around to something more congenial, his parents would follow.

"We have been wondering where you've been," his mother said in a scolding tone of voice. "You just disappeared."

"You kicked me out of the house, Mother. Where did you think I would go? Maybe camp out in the garage?"

"Don't get sarcastic with your mother, Perseus," his father said. "You could have called. It's been months since you left."

"Mother, Dad, the phone works both ways. You never called me, not even a text. You kicked me out of the house. I guess I thought you might actually be concerned about what would become of me, might want to know if I was alright."

"We asked you to leave to try to jolt you into doing something with your life. Of course, we care about you and your future," his father said a bit harshly.

"What are you doing in Oklahoma?" his mother interjected. "You're not in prison, are you?"

Perseus pulled the phone away from his ear and looked at it, unable to believe the question that had come out of its speaker. He put it back to his ear. "What? Prison? You've got to be kidding. All this time away, no communication between us, and all you can come up with as a possibility for my situation is prison?" It was as if she had punched him in the gut.

"Well, what are you doing, son," his father asked.

"I told you, I'm working on a cattle ranch."

"Doing what?" his mother demanded, "Punching cows?"

Perseus had no idea what punching cows meant, but the sarcastic tone of her voice made him realize that she was not going to think much of anything he could possibly be doing on a cattle ranch in Oklahoma.

"It's just general ranch work, Mother," he replied, trying desperately to control his temper. "Listen, I just wanted to call you to let you know I'm okay. I'm working and meeting new people and learning new skills. I do a lot of work with horses. I know it's been a long time since I left." He decided to leave out the reminder that they kicked him out. "I think about you both all the time, and I wish things had been better between us."

Now, there was another long lull in the conversation. Perseus knew his parents weren't very good with this sort of thing. He decided to change the subject.

"Dad, I wanted to talk to you about something, maybe get some advice. You too, Mother. What I have to tell you is quite fantastic, but I assure you it is all true."

He told them the short version of how he came to find the wyvern. He described how he brought her back to the ranch and watched her tear free of the chrysalis and, with the help of his new friends, was now watching over her. He told them how she came to be called Ittikana. Then he continued to explain his concerns about her future in a human-dominated world. He told them she was intelligent and growing fast. It wouldn't be long before it would be impossible to keep her existence a secret.

When he finished, he waited, hopefully, for their reaction and input.

"Perseus, are you using drugs or some kind of hallucinogenic?" his father asked.

"No, Dad. I'm not on drugs. This is not a joke or a hallucination. It's very real."

"Why can't you just grow up, Perseus?" his father asked angrily. "You've got to stop living in some kind of childish, ridiculous fantasy world. Will you never grow up?"

"I thought you might be interested in this creature because of your work with ancient myths, Dad. This is something that came out of the mythological past. It's an amazing discovery."

His father hung up.

"Hello?"

"Perseus, you are such a disappointment," his mother said, sounding genuinely sad. "If this was supposed to be another one of your inappropriate jokes, it was not funny. Try to stay out of prison." Then his mother hung up too.

"Hello? It's not a joke!" Perseus heard the connection go dead. He was so worked up over the way the call went, he thought he might vomit. His parents were just casting him off, plain and simple. They really didn't have the capacity to care about his wellbeing. They were done with him.

Perseus felt depressed at the way the call had gone. The phone call was a mistake, and yet, he supposed it was good to finally understand where things stood between him and his parents. They keep telling me that I'm a disappointment, he thought. Well, they're pretty disappointing too. He lay around in his bunk for the rest of the day rehashing the call over and over again.

He finally dragged himself off his bunk and headed out to complete his evening chores, ending with Ittikana's feeding. She, of course, detected his emotional distress and asked him why he was feeling sadness. He told her he didn't want to talk about it, but she felt a strong sense of empathy and decided she would try to explain how she could relate to his feelings.

"I do know what it feels like to be cast out, desperate about the future, and afraid. My memory is full of sadness and struggle to survive. As the human population increased in the old lands across the big sea, they systematically attacked us, intent on driving us out. They did this to many other creatures as well, including other humanoid sub-species.

"My kind decided to search for other lands where there were no humans. They came here to this land and found very few humans. Much of the land was covered with ice but there was an abundance of food. Later, the land began to warm, and the human populations increased. They began to hunt our kind and kill only to destroy, not for food. In an attempt to ensure our survival, our mothers deposited the next generation underground, sealing us in the rocks."

Perseus told her that he found her in a cave. He believed her sealed packaging was released by an earthquake.

"How do you know these details about your past?" Perseus asked. *"The time you just described must have been many thousands of years ago."*

"These memories were transferred to my second brain by my mother. This is the way our kind keeps track of our history."

"You said your mothers deposited the next generation in the rocks. How many others like you do you think there could be?"

"I do not know, probably thousands."

"Oh, wow. I wonder if more of you have come back to life recently."

"Do you know of any others of my kind?"

"No." He wondered to himself if perhaps the recent increase in earthquake activity had been the cause of releasing Ittikana's chrysalis from the cave ceiling. If so, there could be others of her kind out there in the mountains . . . maybe *a lot* more. "That would be a really interesting surprise for both our species," he said out loud.

"What do you mean, Perseus?"

He decided to change the subject. *"The world is very different from the world in your memory. First of all, there are now hundreds of millions of humans in this country, and many of them are just as violent and intolerant as they were back when your mothers decided to hide your generation. Humans also have much more powerful weapons for killing things in this age. I guess I should also tell you that humans can now fly."*

This news clearly startled Ittikana. "*How can this be? Can you fly?*"

"Sure, anybody can. We don't fly like you do though. We use machines to fly, a machine like the truck that brought you over here."

He spent almost an hour trying to describe what the human dominated world was like. When he was finished, Ittikana felt a deep sense of despair. Their survival strategy was apparently not going to work. This new future-world did not sound like the kind of place her kind could survive in.

Perseus asked her how large she would grow, but once again she was not sure how to describe her potential size, only that it would be much larger than she was now.

"*I expect I will continue to grow quickly. It is one of our survival traits.*"

"*Can you breathe fire?*"

She projected a thought of extreme humor. "*Why would you ask such a question?*"

"*Humans think of your kind as mythical creatures we usually call a dragons, and in human stories dragons can breathe fire and are very dangerous and frightening.*"

"*I admit this might be a useful capability, but we do not breathe fire. Do you think this belief that we breathe fire will motivate humans to kill us?*"

Perseus hadn't thought about that possibility, but it would probably be one of many problems they would have to overcome. It suddenly occurred to him that he didn't have the luxury to feel sorry for himself. Everyone around him, Penelope, the hands, Ittikana, and even the future of the HB, all required his attention. And the thing he found most surprising was that he really believed that he was the only one they could count on. His confidence was growing and his depression over the call to his parents was already fading. He would deal with them later.

CHAPTER 17

BY THE MIDDLE of September, things had settled down considerably. There hadn't been any more direct attempts to sabotage the HB operations, but everyone was still on edge and prepared to fight fire with fire if necessary. Penelope, however, was finding it suspiciously impossible to schedule stock trucks to haul the HB cattle to market.

After breakfast one morning, Penelope asked Perseus to hang back so she could discuss something with him.

"Perseus, I can't find any of our usual trucking resources willing to haul the HB cattle. They say they're completely booked up. I don't recall Dad ever telling me anything like that happening in the past. And yesterday, out of the blue, I got an unsolicited call from a guy who claimed to be with a logistics firm. He told me he would be able to arrange livestock transportation for our operation."

"Did that seem suspicious?" Perseus asked.

"Yeah, it did. I think it might be another attempt by Bart to create some sort of last-minute disaster for us. It could be anything from stress to our livestock during shipping to outright rustling.

Maybe I'm just over reacting, but it's all starting to wear me down. Do you have any ideas?"

"I don't think you're over reacting at all. We should be expecting the worst from Bart. He's evil. Let me talk to Tommy. You know, the Choctaw have several cattle operations, so they must have connections, hopefully ones that Bart can't get his dirty fingers on."

"Yes, that's a good possibility. Let's try it."

Tommy said he would talk to his grandfather, and by the next day, he had located one of Bus's friends in Alabama who owned a small trucking company and was willing to schedule his trucks. They just needed the transport dates. After consulting with Slim, Penelope chose three separate dates spread over four weeks: September 26, October 10, and October 24. Depending on the size of the trailers and the number of cattle they loaded on each, they would require up to three trucks for each run.

Penelope called an agent from a major meat processor that her father had often worked with over the years. He was shocked to learn of Bud's untimely death and assured her that he would do a contract with the HB. When the contract was prepared, he called and offered her an excellent price.

"I know Bud was meticulous about his animals, so I'm sure they'll be high quality beeves. I'll send you all the paperwork tomorrow, including the address of the feed lot in Kansas that you can pass on to your transport company. She couldn't wait to tell Perseus.

At supper that evening, Penelope shared the news with everyone. She realized they all had a vested interest in this year's success and would be particularly relieved to hear about the excellent price offered.

"I think we oughta put a guard in each a them trucks, or at least one a the three," Slim said. "You just know Bart is gonna try an' pull somethin'."

"Perhaps you're right," Perseus agreed. "I think we should ask Tommy if he can round up a couple of his people. Bart's got his hooks in too many guys around these parts to trust anybody off the reservation."

"I spect yer right about that," Slim offered.

"This is the time we should be extra vigilant," Penelope warned. "If anything happens between now and the delivery, we're in trouble."

They all agreed. Everybody was wearing a gun now, except Angelica, and even she kept one close by in the house. "You be sure I can use a gun," she said confidently, and nobody disagreed.

Penelope came down to the barn that evening to help Perseus with Ittikana. They had been allowing Ittikana to fly at night to give her the opportunity to increase her strength and agility. She was somewhat reticent to venture out, concerned about Perseus' explanation of the potential dangers that lurked out there, but she loved to fly. She used these opportunities to explore her new world. She told Perseus and Penelope that she was both amazed and alarmed by how humans had overrun the land. Perseus told her that this part of the world was considerably less populated than the cities. He described cities to her as tall buildings and apartments packed with humans, which she found hard to believe.

On a couple of her nocturnal surveillance flights, a few people had spotted her in the night sky and were, predictably, alarmed. When they called the sheriff, they were hard pressed to define what they had seen, but he dutifully sent deputies to investigate. It was difficult to track her, though. After all, nobody really knew what they were looking for, and by the time the authorities arrived, she was long gone.

That evening, Ittikana surprised Perseus when she announced that she wanted to go back to where he found her.

"I want to search for others of my kind who may have been shaken loose from the rocks also. I know you will not want me to go, but it is important to me."

He passed the announcement on to Penelope. *"You're only two months old, Ittikana,"* Penelope said. *"Do you really think you are ready for this kind of trip?"*

"I am ready. I know there will be dangers, but I must find any others who may have been exposed by being released from the rock. They cannot survive unless they are provided water as I was."

Perseus knew he couldn't stop her. *"How do you know where to go?"*

"I can't explain it, but I know. The stars will guide me."

"We will be worried while you're gone. Please be very careful."

She made her purring sound and nuzzled them both, and then she moved several yards away from them and took to the air.

"I hope we see her again," Perseus said. Privately, he thought her chances of getting to the cave area and back again were slim. If she became exposed, humans would likely shoot first and ask questions later. Her appearance would no doubt terrify people. The number of harmful scenarios she could potentially encounter was more than he could bear to think about.

"There's something I want to tell you," Penelope said.

Perseus pulled himself out of his dark thoughts about Ittikana's fate and looked at her expectantly.

"I plan to go up to the feedlot in Wichita to inspect the facilities. I want to make sure it's the kind of place we want to send our cattle in the future. I realize I don't have much choice this year, but I have to plan ahead. I'll go up with the second or third truck convoy. I want you to stay here to watch over the HB while I'm gone. Would you do that for me?"

He could tell from her voice she was trying to sound self-assured and in control, but the announcement didn't sound like a ranch owner giving orders and instructions to a hired hand. He realized that she wanted his support and some encouragement.

"That sounds kind of risky, Penelope. Are you sure you need to do this?" he asked his voice full of concern. He knew she was trying to put on a brave face, but he could tell she understood the risk. She was no doubt trying to fill her father's shoes, and he admired her for that.

"Yes, I think I need to do this, Perseus. Will you help me?"

"Of course. You know I will. We'll have to take extra precautions though. If something were to happen to you, all would be lost." He held her gaze. Now he had two special lives to worry about, Penelope's and Ittikana's.

She leaned into him and raised herself up on her toes to kiss him. Their kisses had become more ardent recently, making it ever more difficult to restrain their unspoken desires.

CHAPTER 18

ITTIKANA FLEW HIGHER and higher into the night sky, until she could see for many miles in every direction. She could see lights everywhere, pinpricks of evidence that humans were present. There were so many, and yet Perseus had told her that this area contained relatively few humans compared to the numbers dwelling in their cities. The images of a human city he had projected to her were overwhelming. So many beings concentrated into the confines of these wonders of human creation. She had to admit they were impressive, but also frightening.

She looked up toward the stars and quickly determined her bearing. Their positions and relation to various points of direction were ingrained in her brain. She did not understand the details of how her navigation abilities worked, but she was certain she could trust in them. She made a slight adjustment to her direction and pressed on into the night.

The farther northeast she traveled, the darker the land below her became. She knew this meant fewer humans, but she needed more details. So, she began to descend and started sending ultrasound clicks toward the ground, listening for the sound waves to bounce back. She was able to form a mental image of the terrain, which was comprised of a series of undulating hills and valleys. As she flew on, she could sense the landscape was gradually rising and the hills and valleys were more pronounced. She was approaching the mountains, and she wanted to fly lower to get a better view of the area. When she was about 60 miles northeast of the HB she thought she was close to the location where Perseus had found her and she flew even lower, deftly skimming the contours of the ridges and ravines. She was focused on locating the place she sought, but she was also alert for any hint of other wyverns that might be in this area. As she searched, it occurred to her that the terrain was probably quite different now than when the location memory-map was transferred to her embryonic brain.

She was beginning to tire, so she decided to descend to rest and take a closer inspection of the surroundings. She instinctively settled on a ridgeline, which would allow her to take flight quickly in any direction. She scoured the land from her lofty vantage point, but nothing looked familiar. She felt reasonably sure she was close to where her memory told her she should be, but it all looked different somehow.

The Ouachita Mountains are a series of folds, forming scores of heavily forested ridges and ravines throughout the range that often look quite similar. This, coupled with the erosion of eons of storm water, contributed to her confusion.

She sampled the air with her super-sensitive nose and caught something that smelled vaguely familiar coming from down in the ravine. She weighed the potential risks of descending to the bottom. Down there it would be much more difficult to make a quick getaway in an emergency. There were no sounds or scents of danger, so she thought she could at least make a flying pass along the bottom to get a closer look.

She spread her wings and descended from the ridge, catching the still warm rising air. She approached the bottom slowly, moving closer with each successive pass. Finally, when she thought it was safe, she landed on a wide sandy bank of the stream at the bottom. She did not know this was the same place that Perseus, Penelope, and Tommy had camped when they found her. The storm had washed away all traces of their being there.

Following an impulse she could not explain, she moved along the stream in her awkward crawl, until she arrived at a small cave opening. She stopped and stared at it. This, she thought, was the source of the vague scent she had detected up above. She moved closer, then peered inside. The scent was stronger in there.

She scanned the small space, her eyes well-suited to night vision, and she saw fragments of a material she was familiar with: the chrysalis-like sacs that encased wyvern embryos. She took it all in, trying to decipher the meaning of the scene. Were these fragments the result of hatchings, or were they evidence of some predatory decimation of her sisters?

She noticed the narrow opening at the back of the small cave and moved in to take a closer look. The passage was too small for her to pass through, but she could see partway into the chamber beyond. There were three chrysalises lying in her view. They were all shriveled in an advanced stage of decomposition. She knew these sisters had been freed from their rock bonds but without any exposure to water, they had not survived.

She returned her attention to the remains in the outer chamber and studied them carefully. One looked relatively intact, save for the rents in the sac that might indicate a hatching. The others looked torn into several pieces as though scavengers may have gotten to them. Of course, the ravaging could have taken place after the hatching. No way to tell, she decided.

She wasn't sure whether to feel hopeful or disheartened. She thought she had established at least one thing: more of her sisters had been released and may have survived. She might not be alone in the new world dominated by the humans. This thought lifted her spirits.

She exited the cave and discovered that it was nearly dawn. She didn't want to chance flying in the daylight, so she reentered the cave. She would rest here until darkness once again claimed the land.

Ittikana awoke to the sound of humans talking. Alarmed, she moved as far back into the cave as she could manage and curled herself into a tight crouch, covering herself almost entirely with her wings. She could hear the words but could not understand what they were saying because she could not see them, and the rock impeded her ability to focus her thoughts.

The human sounds grew louder until they seemed to be just outside the cave entrance. She saw a human head poke through the opening and look around. She held perfectly still, with only one eye exposed from behind her cover. She focused her thought pictures on this human. *"Do not enter this cave. There is danger in here."*

The human let out a yelp, and the head quickly disappeared from the cave entrance. There was more talking just outside, then they seemed to be moving away. After several minutes of quiet, Ittikana moved quickly to the entrance and cautiously scanned the area outside. She had to leave. She would be trapped in here if they came back. They might be harmless, or not, but even in the best case they would be very frightened if they saw her. She was aware the humans considered her appearance as monstrous. This did not offend her. After all, Ittikana thought humans were quite ugly.

She cautiously crawled out of the cave and listened carefully. She could hear the humans a short distance upstream, so she turned in the opposite direction. There was very little room for her to get airborne in the ravine. She thought it would be possible, but difficult and noisy. Her wings would no doubt be clipping the overhanging trees, and she would have to flap her wings furiously to get her bulk off the ground which would make considerable noise as well. The commotion would draw attention to her presence and the humans would likely see her. Perseus warned her not to allow herself to be seen until they had figured out a plan for telling the world of her existence.

The situation was making Ittikana very anxious. She didn't want to disappoint Perseus. She trusted him and depended on his advice and tutelage. She moved down stream as quickly and quietly as she could manage, unsure of her next move. She took stock of her surroundings and tried to determine how much time would pass before the end of the day. It was cloudy and she was in a ravine, which made it difficult to locate the sun. There was no cover other than the overhanging trees and the steep walls of the ravine, so she had to keep moving. She wanted to put distance between herself and the humans.

Ittikana could see a large outcropping of rocks some distance ahead, so she stood up on her hind feet to get a better view of them. She thought she could climb the rocks to get a better look at the terrain, and they would also provide her with a much-improved platform for taking flight, if that is what she ultimately had to do.

She reached the rocks and steadily clawed her way to the top where she found an opening to another cave. This entrance was situated such that it was completely hidden from sight except from this very spot. Perfect. She could conceal herself here until the darkness of night provided her with the cover to explore further. As she made herself comfortable, she realized she was hungry. She would hunt this night.

CHAPTER 19

BART HAD BEEN keeping close tabs on the activity at the HB. He had surreptitiously installed remote security cameras at various strategic locations around the property which allowed him to monitor the comings and goings. He also had informants at the feed store, the cooperative, the grocery, and other places where Penelope or the HB staff might be seen. He wasn't taking any chances that his plan to take over the HB would fall apart. The place would be his.

So far, things had gone mostly as he had planned, except for Bud's death. That was supposed to have been a simple accident where Bud plowed into two or three of the McAllister steers and banged up his truck. Bart would then hold the lost steers over Bud's head as just one more bit of harassment. But the damn fool went and got himself killed. He realized this was going to have a much bigger impact on the desired outcome than anything he could have imagined. Bud's daughter was now the sole owner of the HB, and perhaps this simplified things.

The main problem now was Penelope's reaction. She blamed him, and that little piss-ant working over there was no doubt encouraging her to hold him responsible. Originally, Bart wanted to get the HB and that sweet little bitch to boot, but he was beginning to realize that getting the girl wasn't going to work out, and that required a change of plans.

He contacted his two most trustworthy henchmen, Billy Joe and Spence. These guys had been with him since he was a teenager. Bart grew up in Choctaw County and was known as one of the wild, out-of-control kids who were always getting into some kind of trouble. His parents were into crystal meth and had blown themselves up one day while cooking up a batch of the stuff. He managed to elude the child protection services officials, living like a wild Indian, some said.

He and his buddies started working on local cattle ranches as teenagers and became proficient at the job. But Bart had always augmented his legitimate income with various forms of larceny, from stealing tools to rustling cattle. As he grew older, the crimes got bigger and now included embezzlement and fraud. He had always been a smart guy and a natural leader, reinforced with liberal applications of menace and brutality.

Billy Joe and Spence arrived at Bart's private cabin on the McAllister place soon after Bart summoned them.

"I'm going to change things up a bit," he began. "Looks like the HB was able to get trucks after all, probably through them damn Indians. So, I want to take one of them truckloads and dump the load out in the western counties somewhere, somewhere we can find 'em later. We'll know when they're leavin' 'cause we got them cameras set up. I found out they're takin' 'em up to Wichita, so get a couple of the boys to intercept 'em up north. They'll probably be runnin' more than one truck, you know, a convoy, so be sure to take the last truck."

"How we gonna get 'em to stop?" Billy Joe asked.

"I paid off the inspector that's gonna be out there when they load. He's gonna put one a them little devices we've used in the past under the dash in the cab of the truck. That will shut down the rig when the boys following it send the signal with their little black box."

The two men laughed. "That's great," Spence said. "You're as smart as they come, boss."

"I got one more change to the plan," Bart said. "We're gonna' take that little bitch from the HB down."

"What do ya mean boss?" asked Billy Joe. "Are we talking about doin' her in?"

"Yeah, that's exactly what I'm talkin' about," Bart replied with a sneer. "I've had enough of her defiance and arrogance, treatin' me like I was trash. I'm pretty sure she ain't gonna get enough trucks to take all them steers at once. I think they're gonna need at least two runs. We let everything go just fine the first haul, so they get to thinkin' everything's okay. That'll also give us a chance to see what she's doin' when them trucks are rollin'. Sooner or later, she's gonna go on up to Wichita to check things out. Now that her daddy's dead, she's gonna have to do that sort of thing herself. One way or another, we'll get her on the second or third run. I already got a place in mind on the res for stashin' her. We'll make it look like the Indians done it."

"I don't know, boss," Spence said, scratching his head under his hat. "You sure that's a good idea? I mean, especially considerin' all them other things that we caused recently. Don't you think ever'body's gonna figure we done it?"

"They can think all they want. I'll have an alibi, as usual, plus witnesses to my whereabouts when this all goes down. I'll claim you was with me. With her out of the way, the HB property will eventually go into probate and my claim will be settled in court. The HB will be mine."

"You boys keep yer eyes and ears open," Bart continued. "I don't want any surprises. They'll be a shippin' them calves in the next week or so, so we got work to do."

CHAPTER 20

EARLY ON THE morning of September 26, three trucks pulling stock trailers arrived at the HB. Penelope and her team were already waiting at the pens and loading chute. They started work extra early that morning to make sure the cattle were sorted out into separate groups according to their age. The oldest steers would ship in the first convoy. As soon as the first trailer was backed up to the loading chute the HB team began the loading process.

As always, they tried to move their cattle slow and easy to keep the animals as calm as possible. Penelope and Günter were in the pen with the cattle, guiding them into the Bud pen area a few at a time. Perseus and Chilo were stationed inside the Bud pen, along the chute, to keep the cattle moving toward the ramp, while Slim and the truck driver where at the ramp to make sure the animals entered the semi-trailer.

Penelope was encouraged to see that two of the trailers where the drop-belly type. These trailers provided up to five separate compartments for keeping the number of animals in each compartment at a specific number which reduced bruising and stress. Limiting the number of cattle in each compartment also allowed them to lie down during transport. She decided not to use the upper rear compartment, called the dog or dog house. She wanted to make sure her cattle were treated humanely, but putting cattle up in the dog required using a steep loading ramp, which made it difficult for the animals to load and unload.

Bud had invested in the specific type of equipment that facilitated the low stress loading and unloading of cattle. The HB used a system called a Bud Box which encouraged the cattle to use their natural instincts to move voluntarily to where the rancher wanted them, rather than forcing them along using cattle prods. The number of cattle put into the Bud box was determined by the number of cattle that could fit through the ramp system at once. When those animals were in the trailer, the next group was moved into the Bud Box pen. The name of the loading system, Bud, had nothing to do with Bud's name. That was just a coincidence.

The loading process went smoothly, and by 11:00 all three trailers were ready to roll. Slim explained to the drivers that they intended to put an armed guard on each truck. Bus Abbott had already alerted his friend in Alabama that this would be a requirement, so the drivers didn't put up any resistance to the extra passenger. Penelope hired a local security firm to fulfill the shotgun role. The firm was owned and staffed by members of a local Choctaw tribe. It added extra cost, but everyone agreed that it was better than losing cattle if Bart decided to try something.

At 11:35 the security guards arrived and the trucks began the rumbling run down the gravel drive heading for the stockyard up in Wichita. All of the HB staff stood outside the main barn and watched the trucks until they were out of sight.

"Why do I feel so nervous about this?" Penelope asked nobody in particular.

"You gotta right ta feel nervous, Miss P," Slim said, still looking down the empty drive. "That Bart is the devil hisself. No tellin' what he might try."

"I think you've done everything you could to ensure those cattle arrive safely," Perseus said. "And don't forget, you took out insurance on them as well."

"Yes, well the insurance and the guards, and even these trucks, cost extra. Money off the top of our earnings," Penelope said. "But you're right. I guess now we should focus on the next load. Still, I'll feel a lot better when I get the call telling me they arrived in Wichita without incident."

They all headed toward the main house for lunch. They had been up since well before dawn and were famished. Angelica prepared a special lunch for them, including carnitas, vegetables, beans, rice, and tortillas, plus fried chicken and fresh baked bolillo bread. They all ate with hearty appetites and lingered long after the normal lunch time to discuss the morning's processing.

The conversation eventually drifted toward Ittikana's whereabouts. They were all anxious about her status. She had been gone two weeks, and Perseus was very concerned for her safety. He wanted to go looking for her, but knew he had to stay with Penelope to help her through the stressful process of getting the cattle delivered and sold. He could see that Penelope was also worried. She thought Ittikana would only be gone a day or two.

"I knew that one day she would have to be on her own, but she's just so young, at least in terms of human age," Perseus said. "It's hard to imagine we might never see her again."

"If'n she's been seen, dead or alive, you can be sure we'd a heard about it," Slim said. "She ain't the kinda thing that goes unnoticed."

When everybody finally got up from the table to begin the afternoon's work, Penelope tugged on Perseus' shirtsleeve and gave him a look that he understood meant to stay behind. She asked him to follow her into her father's office.

"I guess this is my office now," she said sadly. She walked around the room, gently touching things here and there.

"What is it, Penelope?" Perseus asked softly. He thought he already knew the answer.

"I'm feeling so sad, Perseus. It's all I can do to keep going when I get up in the morning. All the stress of getting the cattle to market, the trouble with Bart, and even Ittikana being gone, it's all so exhausting, emotionally I mean." She stood staring out the window her thoughts all askew.

"What can I do for you, Penelope? I hope you know I'd do anything for you."

"You're already doing it. You've been a rock. Could you just hold me for a while?" She turned to him.

The look on her face nearly broke his heart. She was trying to be so brave, but he knew she must feel like her whole world was falling apart. He moved close to her and pulled her into his arms. She held him tight with her head resting on his shoulder. He felt so protective and strong when he was around her. She gave him purpose and stirred other feelings he couldn't really define just yet.

CHAPTER 21

ITTIKANA HAD LOST track of time. She had been searching the ravines in the mountains for several nights, looking for places that might provide shelter for others of her kind. There was ample evidence that others had been shaken loose from the rock and emerged from their protective casings, although she was aware that many, perhaps most, had not emerged so much as having been forcibly removed. This growing realization saddened her greatly.

The egg remnants would likely have contained her sisters. Her mother would have deposited scores of incased individuals throughout the area, using several different locations to ensure the survival of at least some of them. Ittikana's search had revealed that this place contained a large number of small caves, typically near the bottom of the ravines, which separated the numerous geological folds characterizing these mountains. It was becoming increasingly evident that time had eroded the ravines below the cave openings, leaving them high and dry. The newly released progeny needed water to revive them.

A few of the casing remains that Ittikana found had somehow made their way out of the cave and close to the water near the bottom of the ravine. Fewer still had managed to get wet, either from rainfall or by entering the water in the stream. She realized the only way this could have happened is for something to have pulled them outside. In her case, this turned out to be her human friends. Most of the others had no doubt been dragged out by wild animals.

The thing that kept her searching was the tantalizing evidence that at least a few of the casings looked as though they had been breached from the inside. She had also recently picked up a scent that she was sure indicated one of her own was alive and not far away. In addition to her visual search, she was now sending frequent mind messages in the hope of making contact.

The nights were getting cooler, and there had been signs of wet weather approaching from the southeast. She had not had any other close encounters with humans since that first day, although she had sometimes heard them from her secluded hiding places in the rocks and caves. She would only come out with the safety of the night.

This day, as she emerged from a protective overhang scoured out by the nearby stream, darkness was well on its way toward dominating the sky. She climbed the rock face above the overhang and began to send out her thought signals. *There! What was that?* She thought she detected a similar signal. She immediately took off into the early evening sky, flying in concentric circles to search an increasingly wider area. She heard it again and immediately headed in the direction of its source.

"Hello, I am your sister. Keep sending me your thoughts. I want to find you. Hello, are you there?"

"Yes, I can sense your thoughts. Where are you?"

"Just keep sending me your thoughts. I will find you."

It did not take Ittikana long to zero in on the other's location in a clearing at the top of a nearby ridge. She circled around to make sure there was no danger nearby, then landed just a few yards away. She folded her wings up near her body and took her

first long look at what she believed to be her sister. The other
wyvern returned the appraising gaze before standing up on her
legs, spreading her wings, and stretching her neck in a screeching
greeting of joy. Ittikana immediately repeated the gesture, then
crawled over close so she could touch and smell her kin.

They were both overwhelmed with happiness and relief to have
found each other, bombarding one another with thought messages.

"Wait. Stop. Our thoughts are all tangled together," Ittikana said.
It was immediately obvious that this other wyvern was younger
and still trying to sort out her memories, and the stress of trying to
make sense of her current environment and situation compounded
the problem.

*"I have many questions and much to tell you, but first tell me how
you fare. Are you fit? Can you fly yet?"*

*"Yes, I am fit, although very hungry. I can fly but have only been
trying to do so for three sun cycles. You appear older. You are larger
and you appear to be a strong flier."*

Ittikana replied, *"I have been out for almost three moon phases.
I came from this same place and was found by humans who took me
into their care. I have been living with them ever since."*

This information obviously startled the younger wyvern.
*"Humans? My memory of humans recalls them as dangerous and
violent. Are you certain they are human?"*

*"Yes, quite certain. These humans are good, but they have warned
me that many of their kind are not. They told me that humans now
dominate the land and are more numerous than seems possible. I have
seen evidence of this myself, and I have been careful to fly only at night
so that I am not discovered. I am sad to inform you that I have not
found others like us. You and I seem to be the only ones, at least in this
area. According to my humans, we have been hidden from the world
for a very long time."*

The little wyvern took all of this in, generating no thoughts
in return.

"First, I suggest we get some food. You will need strength to return with me. I no longer believe there is much possibility of others in this area. We need to return to my humans. They will be worried about me."

"Are you certain you can trust them?"

"Yes, but other humans might well be dangerous, so we will continue to avoid encounters with them. Come, I will show you a good place for hunting deer. We are not supposed to hunt the humans' cattle. These animals are not in our memory, but they look something like the great bison. If you try to take these cattle for food, it will anger the humans."

"It seems the world is a much different place."

"The humans prefer to call us individually by a name. Mine is Ittikana. They told me this name means friend in the language of the aboriginal people of this land. You should think of a name for yourself."

The little wyvern's thoughts were confused by the concept of a name, but she was willing to think about it. Ittikana knew they would need to spend more time here before attempting to return to the human home. She knew the little wyvern was not yet up to the journey.

CHAPTER 22

THE SECOND LOADING and shipment of cattle at the HB was accomplished without any serious problems. The animals were all in good health, there were no injuries during loading, and there had been no sign of Bart in the last two weeks. Penelope was beginning to relax just a little, but they still had another load of cattle to get up to Wichita on October 24, and she decided this is the convoy she would join.

Perseus still had not seen or heard any news about Ittikana. He was tempted to assume the worst, but he was heartened by the fact that there had been no big news story about a dragon or monster on any of the news outlets. She must still be out there looking for others of her kind. Everyone who knew about her, the HB crew, Tommy, and his grandfather, had kept her existence a secret.

Tommy stopped by the HB the day after the second shipment of cattle left the ranch to tell Perseus that his grandfather wanted to speak with him.

"He's had another vision," Tommy told Perseus.

"Yes, I would love to talk to him, but I shouldn't leave the HB, at least not until all the cattle are safely shipped and arrive at the feedlot. You know Bart is still after me."

"Yeah, I know. Grandfather told me he was willing to come here, but he wanted to get your okay first."

"Of course, he can come here. Do you have any idea what his vision was about?"

"No, he didn't tell me, but sometimes I can see some of the things he does."

Perseus stared at Tommy expectantly. "Well?'

"I think he is going to tell you about a trial you must go through, something that could change your life."

Perseus couldn't help but chuckle. "Oh really? You mean something more trying than what I've already been through? I don't know if I can survive anything much more difficult."

Tommy wasn't smiling. "I think maybe you won't," he said seriously.

Now Perseus wasn't smiling either. "Are you kidding?"

"Grandfather will tell you what he's seen, then we can try to figure it out. You know, sometimes his visions are a little obtuse." At that they both laughed.

Penelope spotted them at the barn and came down to join them.

"Hi, Tommy. What's up? Why are you guys laughing?"

"I may not have long to live," Perseus said casually.

She gave him a queer look. "Oh, I thought it was something funny."

"Grandfather had another vision that involves Perseus," Tommy told her.

Penelope's eyebrows shot up. "Oh, well now, that's usually something life-changing, isn't it?"

Two days later, Bus Abbot arrived at the HB being chauffeured by Tommy in his old, beat-up pickup. Penelope saw them park down at the barn and rushed to join them. She wanted to hear about this vision. If it involved Perseus' future, it would probably have some impact on hers as well. Perseus was still in the barnyard area finishing up his chores, when he heard Bus's old truck stop just outside the barn, coughing and sputtering when Tommy turned off the ignition.

He jumped off the wagon he had been filling with feed from the grain bin and walked toward the main barn. He rounded the corner wiping sweat from his brow with a kerchief.

"Man, you sure can't sneak up on anybody in that old truck," he said smiling.

"Timing belt just needs a little tweaking," Tommy said quite seriously.

"Good morning, Mister Abbott," Perseus said to Bus.

"Achukma unnahinli," Bus replied in the Choctaw language. "That means good morning."

"I figured so," replied Perseus. "I was hoping it didn't mean, I have bad news." He smiled broadly, but noticed Bus was not smiling.

Penelope caught up with them and greetings were exchanged all around. She moved close to Perseus and took his arm. "Would you mind if I sat in on this?" she said in a way that both Perseus and Tommy knew meant, "I will be joining you for this revelation."

"No, of course not," Perseus replied, hoping Bus wouldn't have a problem with it.

Although it was mid-October, the day was quite warm, so Perseus suggested they all go into the bunk house where there was air conditioning. They all took seats around the rustic table, which conveniently included four chairs. Bus looked all around, never having been in this place before. He thought it looked singularly white-male-cowboy and nodded his head slightly in approval.

"This is a masculine space," he pronounced. "It is good."

"I come down here to play cards, Bus," Penelope announced defiantly. All three men gave her a bemused look.

"You are a strong woman," Bus quickly replied. "Though you are no doubt a rose among the thorns down here."

She blushed. "You're such a gentleman, Bus."

"Well, let's get down to business," Perseus said. "What is it you see in the future that involves me, Mister Abbott?"

All eyes were now on Bus. "First, I must tell you that visions are often like a puzzle. They require much reflection and effort to uncoil their true meaning. Some people think of them as a prediction, but that is not the true nature of a vision. A vision is an attempt by a spirit to guide the receiver toward something. There are many spirits, some are good and helpful, while others are tricksters, and there are also a few who are evil."

Bus fixed his gaze on Perseus. "The spirits have a strong attraction to your future and a role they think you must fulfill. I am perplexed that they would select a white man for bestowing this guidance, and I have thought about this for a long time. I am sure you were meant to play a part in the future of our nation, but it is still not clear what that role is."

Bus paused, his eyes became unfocused, his eyelids half closing, as if he was going into some kind of trance. His breathing slowed, and in a different tone of voice, almost a chant, he said, "You will be faced with three tests."

Now all eyes were on Perseus, who realized he was holding his breath.

"The first test will determine the strength of your courage and will lead you into harm's way." There was a simultaneous gasp from Tommy and Penelope. "In the second test you will be reborn, and you must decide who you will be. The third test will determine the strength of your character, and you must choose between two paths that may decide the fate and future of many."

Bus expelled a loud breath and slumped toward the table. Tommy caught him by the shoulders. "Grandfather." He lightly shook Bus's shoulders. "Grandfather, are you alright?"

Bus recovered quickly and sat up straight. He looked around the table, a bit disoriented. Then, "Yes, yes, I'm fine, Grandson." Bus looked into Tommy's eyes. "You know that you are also meant to play an important role in these tests. I have seen this." He looked at Penelope. "And so are you, Miss Wesley. I am tired now. Tommy, could you please take me home?"

"Yes, Grandfather."

The others helped get Bus to the old truck and thanked him for coming out to see them. Bus was clearly exhausted from the experience. Tommy promised he'd return later.

Perseus and Penelope stood outside the barn and watched the old truck until it was out of sight. She turned and took one of Perseus' hands and saw that he had a dazed, faraway look in his eyes.

"Hey, mister, you still with us?"

It took him a moment to answer. "Yeah, I'm still here, but I feel pretty weird if you want the truth."

"Me too. That was kind of freaky. Do you think there's anything to what he said?"

Perseus looked deep into her eyes. "Well, the whole thing with the wyvern happened, and the three of us were all part of that. I don't know what to think. This vision seems a lot more personal. I mean, three tests. It sounds like something out of a fairy tale. And why me? Can you think of anybody less likely to be the object of some spirit's attention . . . and having responsibility for the fate of many others, or whatever Bus said?"

"Who are you, really?" she asked, still watching him intently. "You roll into this little, one-horse town one day, the least likely guy I can think of to end up staying and working here at the HB. Then you turn out to be a really capable horseman, a very nice man, and you start to capture my heart."

"I did? I mean, I am?"

"Yes, you have. And then there is the whole Choctaw connection, the first vision, and the mystical quest to find the Sint-Holo." She continued to look at him as if she was expecting some kind of answer.

"I'm just a regular guy," he insisted. "My parents threw me out of their house because I wasn't living up to their expectations, so I was homeless, a drifter, clueless. Meeting you was the best thing that ever happened to me. I would really like to spend the rest of my life with you."

Oh, God. He hadn't meant to say that. It just came out. This probably wasn't the best time to say something like that, although he meant it with all his heart.

"You really mean that?" she asked, moving a little closer to him.

He could feel her breath on his face. The brims of their cowboy hats collided, so keeping her eyes fixed on him, she deftly took hers off, allowing her to move even closer.

"Yes, I mean it." He suddenly wondered if this was one of the tests, but she reached up and kissed him and the only thing left in his mind was her.

"If you two ain't got nothin' else ta do other than suck face, we shore could use some help out in the pens." Slim's voice quickly put a damper on the moment. They abruptly shifted their focus to him sitting atop his horse with a Cheshire-cat grin on his face. "Does this mean you'll a be movin' out a the bunkhouse?"

Perseus, acutely embarrassed, stammered unintelligibly at something on the ground near his feet.

"No, Slim. Perseus will still be staying in the bunkhouse, at least for now," Penelope said wryly. "What do you need out there?"

"We're a movin' the last batch of cattle into the loadin' pens. Would be a heap easier if we had another horse or two."

"We'll be right there. Come on Perseus, let's saddle up."

Tommy came back just before supper. Penelope invited him to dine with them, and he happily accepted. Angelica had made enchiladas that evening, which seemed to be everybody's favorite. The conversation focused on the day's ranching activities and progressed to making a mental list of tomorrow's work. After supper, Slim and Günter went down to the bunk house, while Perseus and Tommy stayed up at the main house.

The three companions retired to Bud's office. They all still thought of this room as Bud's, even though it was now where Penelope managed the business of the HB operation. Angelica brought in a large cup of coffee for each of them and closed the door as she left. They sat quietly for a while, sipping their coffee.

"How's Bus?" Penelope asked.

"Oh, he's fine," Tommy replied. "He was just worn out from the trance he went into. He doesn't usually get that far into a vision when he's talking about it. By the time he tells someone about a vision, he's already had it and had plenty of time to think about how to interpret it. Today was pretty unusual."

"What do you think about all this, Tommy?" Perseus asked. "I mean, I feel kind of weird being the target of these visions. Like your grandfather said, I'm a white guy and nobody special."

"Well, I kind of think you're special, for a white man that is." Tommy gave an impish grin. "You know, life has a way of just throwing things at us and we have to decide what to do with those things. Life is like a game. You gotta keep making your move or you're out of the game."

Perseus smiled. "I had a friend back in Virginia who told me pretty much the same thing. He was old and wise. How did you get so worldly-wise?"

"It just comes natural to us Indians. Did you ever watch the Lone Ranger? Ever notice how wise Tonto was? The Lone Ranger couldn't have made it without him." Tommy offered all this with a wry grin.

"Yeah, yeah. But you're right, a person has to take life as it's dished out; you know, fate and destiny. Your grandfather's vision, though, makes it all seem so profoundly monumental. I think I'd rather just plod through my life without knowing that what I do and the choices I make have so much gravitas attached to it all. What if I do have to face these tests and I make bad decisions?"

"You'll have to cross those bridges when you get there," Tommy said helpfully.

"You're going to do just fine, Perseus," Penelope said. "I've been thinking about what Bus said, and we all face these kinds of tests throughout our lives. We all have to make choices. You're a good person, so I know you'll do whatever you feel you have to do in each circumstance. I have faith in you."

"Me too," Tommy added.

"Oh great. No pressure!"

"By the way, I noticed you don't seem to be wearing a gun anymore," Tommy said. "What's that all about? I thought you all decided you would always wear a gun in case Bart or his hoodlums show up."

"He says there's no point wearing one because he doesn't know how to use it," Penelope said, sounding frustrated.

"I have a gun with me if I'm away from the house or barnyard," Perseus said defensively. "It gets in the way when I'm doing my chores."

CHAPTER 23

BART HAD BEEN biding his time, waiting for the right moment to strike. He knew the HB would have to bring in a third group of trucks. There were still cattle to be transported. He hadn't anticipated the security guards riding in the trucks, so the hijacking part of his plan had to be cancelled.

One of Bart's henchmen rode up to him out in the pens. "Them stock trucks from Alabama just rolled into town. They'll be going out to the HB first thing in the mornin'."

"Okay, good job, Spence. Let's start gettin' things ready. Find Billy Joe and tell 'im to get on out to the reservation and check out that sheep shed we staked out. We'll need to get those supplies we gathered up out there too. We'll meet tonight after supper to go over everything. Got it?"

"Yessir." Spence rode off to begin getting things ready. He still thought this plan was too dangerous, even reckless, but he wasn't about to refuse whatever Bart ordered.

October 26th dawned with light clouds skittering across the sky. Penelope and the HB crew met the transport trucks and began the process of loading the last of the cattle. They were all grateful that the autumn morning was cool, making the work a little easier and the cattle less stressed from the incessant heat. The loading was uneventful, and the trucks were ready to roll well before noon.

Penelope sent the trucks ahead, telling them she would join them at the truck stop in Hugo. She was going to pick up the security guards and bring them with her. It tuned out picking them up and taking them to the trucks saved her a few dollars. She gave her final instructions to Slim and Günter, who were going to be staying behind.

Now, she was ready to leave. Perseus followed her to the pickup truck to say goodbye and to assure her that everything would be fine back at the HB. They shared a brief kiss and said their goodbyes.

"Maybe I should come with you," he said.

"No, I need you to stay here, make sure the place stays in one piece." She smiled. "I'll be fine. I'll have security guards with me. What could go wrong?"

He watched as her truck rolled down the long driveway, creating a cloud of dust that eventually swallowed the vehicle. He was uneasy about this trip to check out the feedlot in Wichita. He supposed it was good business, but he wondered if maybe they were getting a little too relaxed about the whole Bart menace.

Two miles down the road, Penelope saw a truck with a horse trailer blocking the narrow pavement. There was a man at the back of the trailer, apparently trying to get his horse out. It looked like the trailer had possibly jackknifed, and she spotted a tire lying on the road next to the rear of the truck. It was lucky the trailer hadn't come off the hitch and rolled into one of the deep ditches on either side of the road. She was going to have to stop. There was no way to get around because of the ditches. Perhaps she could help.

She pulled her truck to the side of the road as far as she could and turned off the ignition. She was so focused on the apparent accident in front of her, she hadn't noticed that another truck had pulled up behind her. As she stepped down out of the cab, she saw a man emerge from the other truck, his hat pulled down low over his face. She was surprised she hadn't seen this vehicle but didn't think much of it until the man got close enough for her to see that he was wearing a ski mask. It took a few more seconds for her to register what was happening, but by then it was too late. Her gun was sitting on the seat of her truck, out of reach. She scrambled to get back into her truck, but the man grabbed her and threw her to the ground.

Penelope lay on the hard pavement, stunned from the hard fall. Before she could gather all her senses, a bag was thrown over her head and her hands were being tied behind her back. She couldn't believe this was happening. She should not have tried to make this trip alone. She should have known better.

Two hours after the stock trucks left HB, Perseus received a call from Tommy.

"Perseus, Penelope never showed up at the security company. Do you know where she is?"

"What! No. If she didn't pick up the security guards, the only other place she could be is at the truck stop. She was going to meet the trucks down there."

"She not there. One of the truck drivers called me asking where she was. They're ready to roll."

"Damn. I don't know. Let me think a minute."

"Why don't I call the security company and tell them to go ahead and send the guards to the truck stop so we can get the cattle rolling. The drivers already have all the necessary paper-work. This is probably another plot to keep them from getting to Wichita."

"Yes. Okay, that's a good idea, please do that for me, Tommy. I'm going to go over to the McAllister place and find Bart. I'm sure he's behind this, whatever it is."

"Hold on, Perseus. You can't go over there by yourself. What are you going to do, smack him around some until he tells you what he's done with Penelope? He'll kill you . . . or beat you senseless at the very least."

"I don't care, Tommy. I've had it with that creep. Somebody has to stand up to him. We've got to find out what's happened to Penelope."

"I know, I know, but let me help you. Please, just wait until I get there. I'll call the security company and get that straightened out, then I'll come right over. Will you please wait until then before you do anything stupid?"

There was a long silence. Perseus was so angry he knew he wasn't thinking straight. "Alright, I'll wait until you get here, but hurry."

"I will. Why don't you tell everyone else there at the HB what's happened in case Bart tries something else? All of you need to be on high alert."

"I will. Thanks, Tommy."

It was nearly 3:00 when Tommy arrived at the HB. He could see that Perseus was on the verge of panic with worry about Penelope. Slim, Günter, Chilo, and Angelica were all up at the house trying to keep him from doing something stupid. Tommy noticed that Perseus was wearing a revolver on his belt again.

"Have you called the sheriff's office yet?" Tommy asked.

'Yes, just about fifteen minutes ago. They said they would send some deputies out on the country roads to see if maybe she was broken down or in a ditch or something. I'm sure she would have called if she was stranded."

Just then they all heard someone driving up to the house and went outside to see who it was. It was the elected sheriff, himself, who got out of the SUV cruiser. He immediately noticed that everybody was packing a gun, which is what he had expected. He had decided to personally get involved in this situation before a shooting war started.

"Good afternoon, everyone," he said calmly.

"Any news about Penelope?" Perseus asked anxiously.

"No, I'm afraid not, son. I'm sure there's something not right going on, but we need to go about finding her in a level-headed manner. I imagine you're itchin' to go over there to the McAllister place and pick a fight with Bart Oglethorpe, but that's not going to happen."

"Sheriff, you know he's behind this. You have to know that," Perseus pleaded.

"Maybe so, son, or then again, maybe not, but I agree I need to go talk to him."

"I'm going with you," Perseus insisted.

The sheriff scratched the side of his head, as if he was giving the matter some thought. "I don't suppose there's any way to keep you from going, short of locking you up. You can go, but I'm not going to allow you to start anything. Do you understand?"

"Yes, sir." He turned to the others. "You guys all stay here in case Penelope comes back. I'll see you a little later."

When the sheriff and Perseus arrived at the McAllister Ranch, there were told that Bart was out near the stables working with horses. Bart spotted the cruiser heading toward the stables and rode out to meet it. He dismounted Diablo as the sheriff and Perseus got out of the cruiser.

"Hello, Sheriff," Bart said. "How are things at the county jail?"

Perseus thought Bart sounded like he and the sheriff were old friends, and he wondered if maybe they were, and that this was all part of the scheme. He was ready to explode.

"Hello, Bart. We're here to see if you know anything about Penelope Wesley's whereabouts."

Bart feigned confusion. "I haven't seen Penelope for several weeks, Sheriff. What's up?"

"She's missing. Was supposed to go on up to Wichita with her cattle today, but she never showed up at the truck stop. No sign of her or her truck anywhere, just seems to have disappeared."

"Disappeared? Why, that doesn't sound like somethin' she'd do, Sheriff. Maybe she just went on up to Wichita by herself. I haven't heard a peep outta that girl for some time now."

Perseus couldn't take it any longer. "You're a liar. We all know you had something to do with her disappearance, just like you caused her father's death and all the other disasters that have been happening at the HB. And somebody shot at me and Penelope. Who else around here would try to get rid of me?" He was now shaking with rage.

Bart was smirking. "You know, this little twerp rolled into Hugo a few months ago out of nowhere. He's like a fish outta water in these parts. He's just a little sissy boy who's pertendin' to be a cowboy. What's he got to do with the HB and Penelope anyway? You oughta be askin' him where she is."

Perseus launched himself at Bart with a fury that surprised both Bart and the sheriff, but Bart easily pushed him away, knocking him to the ground. The sheriff quickly stepped in and pulled Perseus away, ordering him to wait in the car.

Perseus felt so helpless and frustrated that tears began to well up in his eyes. Maybe he was just a sissy. He was worried sick about Penelope, but there didn't seem to be anything he was capable of doing to help her. He had to get control of himself and think.

When the sheriff returned to the cruiser, Perseus tried desperately to convince him that Bart had to be behind Penelope's disappearance. The sheriff didn't disagree with him but told him that there was nothing he could do without evidence. He needed something more than just a hunch. Meanwhile, he and his deputies would conduct a thorough search all around the back country around Hugo.

Perseus decided to just shut up. He wasn't going to depend on the sheriff to find Penelope. He didn't know what he was going to do, but he would come up with something . . . something that included keeping track of Bart.

After the sheriff dropped him off at the HB, Perseus told the others about the confrontation with Bart. They all agreed Bart was behind Penelope's disappearance, but nobody had any useful ideas about what to do. Perseus went to the office and came out with another pistol, this one's a semi-automatic. He was struggling with the magazine, trying to figure out how to load it, when Tommy took the pistol from him and finished loading the gun.

"Do you know how to use this thing?" he asked.

"Not really. You just aim it and pull the trigger, don't you?"

"Before you go out a shootin' ever thing in sight, I'd better teach you a thing or two," Slim said, his eyes squinted. "You're more likely to shoot yerself with that there type of gun if'n you don't know what yer doin'."

Perseus nodded and handed him the pistol. He was also carrying the revolver, but he thought he could figure out how to use that one. It was less complicated. He started pacing, everyone watching him nervously.

"Do you have a plan?" Tommy asked.

Perseus stopped pacing and looked at Tommy angrily. "No, not exactly. But I'm going to go find Bart, and when I do, I'm going to start shooting off pieces of his body until he tells me what he's done with Penelope.

They all stared at him, then Günter started laughing. "Well, that's quite a plan. I'd like to be there to see that."

Tommy moved up close to Perseus and put a hand on his shoulder. "Okay, let's start putting some kind of plan together. First, let's wait until it's dark, whatever we decide to do. If Bart or his thugs see you coming, they'll be the ones shooting you to pieces."

Perseus nodded in agreement. In truth, he didn't really know what he would do, but he was desperate. He couldn't let himself think too much about what kind of trouble Penelope might be in.

"Let's wait until it gets dark," Perseus said, "then we'll go over to the McAllister place and watch for Bart. If he leaves, we'll follow him."

"What if he leaves before dark?" Günter asked. "Now that the sheriff's been there, he's got his alibi established. He might think he can get around unnoticed."

"I'm going to call some friends at the res and ask them to help us out," Tommy said. "We can try to get a couple of guys over to the McAllister to keep an eye on who's coming and going. I'll see if some others can just start searching around in the back country. If they haven't taken her out of the county, we might have a pretty good chance of finding her."

"That's a great idea, Tommy," Perseus said.

"Why don't me and Günter take our horses out past the HB and over close to the McAllister? We can keep an eye on their back door case they try a goin' cross country."

"Yes, that's a good idea too." Perseus was beginning to feel like there were some things they actually could do. He looked at his watch. It was 6:00. "We've got about an hour before it starts to get dark. Meanwhile, I'll try to think of something I can do to find Penelope."

They all felt sorry for Perseus. They knew not knowing what was happening to Penelope was driving him crazy, and not being able to do anything about it was only making it worse.

CHAPTER 24

TOMMY HAD MANAGED to organize a sizable posse in the short time he'd been recruiting. Slim and Günter were watching the McAlister from the backside and had reported seeing Bart leave just a short while earlier. They told Perseus he had been heading into the res, but they had lost him. They couldn't imagine where he could be going. Tommy alerted his posse of Bart's last known location.

It was now 8:00 and darkness had taken possession of the sky. With the news about Bart, Perseus and Tommy were hanging back at the HB rather than running off chasing shadows. They had decided there was a better chance of figuring out where Bart was if they were just patient. Sitting on the tailgate of Tommy's pickup, a heavy silence hung in the air as they pondered the situation.

From above them, a strange sound, interrupted their contemplation. There was no moon, and the night sky was further obscured by loose, scudding clouds drifting overhead. When the sound grew louder and clearer, they became alarmed and jumped from the tailgate, ducking close to the bed of the truck. Suddenly, two other-worldly silhouettes burst into view, stirring up a cloud of dust below them as their wings beat the air for a landing just yards away.

Perseus and Tommy jumped to their feet. "Ittikana!" they both shouted. They waited for the two wyverns to land completely and fold their wings in close to their bodies, then they ran up to greet them. Perseus knew right away which one was Ittikana. She was larger and was a distinctive golden color. When she saw the humans, she rose back up and stretched into her usual screeched greeting.

"Hello, Ittikana," Perseus said aloud. "I'm so glad to see you. I see you brought a friend."

She lowered herself and nuzzled both of the humans. "*I am glad to see you as well,*" she said through her thoughts, first to Perseus, then to Tommy.

"*This is the only other one of my kind I was able to find,*" she said. "*She wants her name to be Star. I told her that humans wish to know us by a name. She is quite anxious about being here with humans, though.*"

Perseus was passing along the thoughts to Tommy to speed up the conversation.

Tommy projected his thoughts to Star. "*Your name in the Choctaw language is Fichik, which means Star in English.*"

Star looked at Tommy curiously. "*You communicate well,*" she projected. "*However, it doesn't matter what human speech words you use, it is still Star in your thoughts to me. You will understand what we communicate in your own way.*"

"*I understand,*" he replied. Tommy explained his conversation with Star to Perseus.

Perseus told Ittikana that Penelope was missing and that he was sure the man, Bart, had kidnapped her. Ittikana could discern from the emotions in his thoughts that he was very angry and worried about her safety. She became angry as well. She felt very protective toward her humans.

"I am very frustrated, Ittikana. I don't know how to find Penelope. I can't help her if I don't know where she is," Perseus said.

"I can find her. I can fly over this land and project my thoughts to her. If she can receive my thoughts, she will be able to respond. Even if we cannot understand each other due to the distance or obstructions, I will know she is there."

New hope surged through Perseus' mind. *"You can do that? Yes, of course. Oh, please, Ittikana. Go try to find her, please."*

Ittikana told Star what they needed to do, and she agreed to help. They both stretched out in preparation for flight, and with a great rush of air, the two wyvern ascended into the inky night.

Perseus noticed how much larger Ittikana had grown in the nearly four weeks she had been away. She was probably 12 feet high when she stood up on her legs and stretched her neck. Her wingspan could easily be 16 feet. It was that gaping, tooth-filled maw of hers, which she prominently displayed when she let out one of those screeches, which made her look quite fearsome. He was glad she was his friend.

Perseus and Tommy paced around the truck until they finally realized that they should start calling the others to update them. They called Slim and told him that Ittikana had returned with another wyvern, and was searching for Penelope, and reminded him not to reveal the existence of these creatures to the others in the posse. There was no time to explain. They needed to focus on finding and rescuing Penelope.

It didn't take long for Ittikana to detect a trace of Penelope's response. She had been broadcasting her thoughts from the time they left the HB. She was using the same technique she had used in the mountains, flying in expanding concentric circles and communicating, *"Penelope, tell me you are receiving my message."* Penelope's emotional state came through to Ittikana as intensely blue, indicating fear.

She narrowed Penelope's location down to be a small structure almost directly below her. Her night vision was acute, so she was able to locate a crude shack at the edge of a large open space among the trees. She fixed the image of the structure in her mind, then flew back to Perseus.

Perseus and Tommy were ready and waiting when she returned. She had a difficult time trying to explain how to get to the location, able only to project an image of the structure and the direction of its location from the HB. At first, neither Perseus nor Tommy knew what to do, but then Tommy suddenly thought he remembered the little shack.

"I think it could be an old sheep shed on my grandfather's farm, although there are many of these shacks on the reservation," he said.

Perseus thought for a few seconds. He was becoming more anxious by the minute. So much so that it was difficult to concentrate. "Well, that's better than nothing. Maybe we could start heading there and ask Ittikana to follow us. If we need to make a course correction, she can give us directions."

Although both wyverns were tired, they agreed to assist the humans to the exact location. Tommy gave Perseus directions to his grandfather's land. It had been a few months since the bar-b-que, and Perseus couldn't remember much about getting to the place. Ittikana and Star flew overhead, but as they drew closer to an old gate marking the dirt path entrance to the sheep shed, she knew they were going to the right place. She communicated this to Tommy, who relayed the information to Perseus. The wyverns landed some distance from the shed and waited for the humans to catch up.

"We should stop the truck before we get there and walk the rest of the way," Perseus suggested. "We'll want to sneak up on them."

"Right," Tommy agreed. "I'll turn off the lights now." There was a three-quarter moon rising slightly above the horizon, making the landscape reasonably navigable without the truck's headlights.

"I'm going to stop just up ahead. It's a bit of a hike from here, but it's so quiet they'll be able to hear us if we drive much closer."

"Okay. Let's hurry."

They parked the truck and started closing in on the shed at a fast trot. Within ten minutes, they could see the dull glow of a lantern's light ahead and slowed down to a walk. They were both breathing hard, not only from the exertion of the hike, but from a growing fear of what dangers might lie ahead. The ramshackle structure faced an open field. The light came from two windows and a wide doorframe in the front of the shed, all three of which were open to the elements.

They crept closer to the shed, coming in at an angle to minimize their exposure. They stopped suddenly when Perseus held up a hand. The dim lantern light inside the shack now revealed Penelope sitting on the dirt floor, her back against the wall. It looked like her hands were tied behind her back. Perseus was overcome with emotion as he looked on in horror at the woman he loved. He was ready to rush in, guns blazing, but knew better than to do so.

Seeing the look on Perseus's face, Tommy gently rested his hand on Perseus' shoulder. "Easy, Kemosabe," he whispered. "Let's take it one step at a time."

Perseus nodded and let out a sigh so deep it felt like it came from the bottom of his soul. He knew he needed to calm down. They remained still for a of couple minutes as they assessed the situation and began to formulate a plan. They determined there were at least two men in the shed because they could hear them arguing. As they crept nearer, they saw Bart and the other man, but there didn't appear to be anyone else inside. They inched closer until they could clearly see Bart and the other man.

The argument was getting more heated, and the other man suddenly pushed Bart hard and reached for a pistol hanging from his belt. Tommy and Perseus watched in horror as Bart quickly produced a large hunting knife and stabbed the man in the chest. Even from where they observed the scene, they could see the other man as he looked up at Bart in disbelief, his pistol falling quietly to the dirt floor. Bart withdrew the knife and then drove it back in with brutal force. The other man dropped to the floor, moaning, and holding his wounds.

Bart grabbed the man by his shirt collar and dragged him outside. He shoved the man to the ground and kicked him in the head several times until the body was still.

Perseus, in shock at what he has just witnessed, forced himself to act. He pulled out his gun, the semi-automatic he'd retrieved after Slim set it down at the house. "Alright, Bart. That's enough. Put your hands up."

Bart looked up, obviously taken by surprise. But rather than put his hands up, he rushed at Perseus with the knife. "You little bastard," he roared.

Perseus stood his ground and pulled the trigger. Nothing happened. He tried again, but the safety was on and he didn't know how to release it. He saw Bart charging at him, quickly closing the distance, and realized he was going to die.

Tommy fired his gun and missed, but the blast was enough to stop Bart in his tracks. He surprised both boys when he turned and ran back into the shed. They both ran after him, stopping short when they saw that Bart had grabbed Penelope and was holding her roughly in front of him, his knife at her throat.

As if frozen in time, they all stood facing each other.

"Bart, let her go. It's over. Let her go and you can walk out of here and just keep on going," Perseus demanded. "You don't want to hurt her, not really."

"Shut up, you damned little piss-ant. I've had all I can stand of you. I'm going to kill this bitch if you don't drop those guns." Nobody moved. He had his forearm tightly around Penelope's neck. It was obvious that she was being strangled, as she gasped for breath. "Drop 'em!" he roared, causing both Perseus and Tommy flinch.

They did. Perseus couldn't stand to see Penelope being choked to death. He was breathing hard, so hard they could hear him from where they stood.

"Move over here, slowly. Up against this wall," Bart commanded as he moved in the opposite direction, changing places with them. He still held Penelope pinned between his chest and forearm. When they were against the wall, Bart slowly bent down and picked up Tommy's gun, then pointed it at Perseus.

Bart started laughing, a hideous, fiendish laugh. "Did you creeps really think you could survive messing with me?" He shot Perseus, who immediately fell to the ground. Penelope screamed. Bart turned the gun on Tommy, but before he could pull the trigger there was a tremendous crash behind him. He spun around to see something that looked like it had come up from the bowels of Hell itself.

Ittikana stood upright, spreading her wings only slightly, but obliterating the entire front of the shed. She opened her fang-filled maw and released a deafening shriek of rage. Bart pushed Penelope toward the beast and started to raise the pistol, but in the blink of an eye, her barbed tail swung around from behind and caught him under his ribcage. She lifted him up off the dirt floor then clasped him by his back, just under the shoulder blades, with both of her thumb claws. He screamed in pain and terror. She bent her neck down and stuffed his head into her jaws, clamping them shut.

There was a nauseating sound of tearing flesh and crushing bone, then the headless body of Bart Oglethorpe was pulled away and eviscerated as Ittikana pulled her ten-inch tail barb down the length of his torso. When she released his body from her thumb claws, what was left of him fell to the ground. As Penelope and Tommy watched in fascinated horror, she commenced to devour Bart's entrails with vicious abandon.

Penelope crawled her way over to where Tommy crouched next to Perseus. Tommy began untying the rope that bound Penelope' hands. They didn't want to watch the carnivorous scene before them but couldn't take their eyes off it.

"Oh my God. What is she doing?" Perseus cried.

Tommy and Penelope spun around to see Perseus struggling on the ground next to them. His left side was covered in blood.

"You're alive!" Penelope cried. "Oh, Perseus." She reached over to hug him, but he yelped in pain.

"Oh, I'm so sorry," she said recoiling.

"I can't believe she's eating him. Are you guys alright?" Perseus asked.

"Penelope is a little beat up, but I'm alright," Tommy said.

"I'll be okay, Perseus. My wrists are raw."

"Where are you hit?" Tommy asked

"In the side. Hurts like heck, but I don't think it's too bad. Pretty sure I have a broken rib." He looked down at the wound. "I suppose I could bleed to death," he continued with a smirk on his face.

Their conversation was interrupted by the loud, disgusting sound of regurgitation. Ittikana was apparently puking out her meal. When she was finished, she looked up at them. They all just gaped at each other for several seconds.

Ittikana broke the spell. "*Humans are not very good to eat. My memory knew that, but my anger got the best of me. Apologies.*"

"*It's alright, Ittikana,*" Perseus said. "*Thank you for saving our lives.*"

"I could not do less. You must tell me more about these new human weapons. They appear to be much more lethal than any we know about from the past."

CHAPTER 25

THE RESERVATION POSSE was standing about 20 yards away, dividing their terrified attention between the horror in the shed and the nightmare standing between them and their means of escape. They watched in mystified awe as Tommy suddenly exited what was left of the mostly destroyed shed, helping a bloody Perseus move away from the disaster. As if all of this wasn't mind boggling enough, the white rancher-woman they were all searching for emerged from the rubble stroking the thing they had just watched eat Bart Oglethorpe as if it were a pet dog.

"Hi, everybody. Thanks for helping us and coming out here," Perseus said with sincere gratitude. "We're going to need some help getting things cleaned up. I could use a lift to the hospital too."

Nobody spoke a word.

"I'll explain everything, but could somebody please take Perseus and Penelope to the hospital?" Tommy asked. Nobody moved.

Penelope looked at Tommy and said, "I'm fine. I don't need to go to the hospital. I'll do just fine at home."

"Okay, Penelope, if you think that's best. Now, let me explain. These two beautiful creatures are what our people call Sint-Holo.

Turns out they're real, the old legends were true. They helped us find Penelope. It's a long story, but I'll fill you in with all the details later. Right now, we need to get these two humans to a hospital. It's important that none of you tell anybody else about what happened here tonight or about Ittikana and Star." He pointed to the wyverns. "That's who these two are. That's Ittikana." He pointed to the monster who ate Bart. "And that's Star." She hissed in response, causing everyone in the posse to flinch.

Finally, somebody spoke up. "What the hell, Tommy? Are you telling us these two are actually Sint-Holo?"

"Yes. I can tell you a lot more, but, please, I'm going to need your help. Think about it. We can't have this mess get back to the white authorities. I'm sure you know these were bad guys, Bart and whoever the other dead guy is over there. By the way, Bart murdered him. We saw it happen. I want you to help me get rid of them and their truck. We'll burn what's left of the shack. Perseus will say that his gunshot wound was an accident. We're going to make up something to tell the sheriff about Penelope's temporary disappearance: she went on to Wichita by herself, had her phone turned off, something like that.

"After we get all that sorted out, I'll explain why Perseus and I think we need to keep the lid on the re-appearance of Sint-Holo from our legends. It's up to you guys. Can you help me out on this?"

"Does your grandfather know about these two creatures?" somebody asked.

"Yes, he does. He went out to the HB where Ittikana has been in hiding. He also wants their existence to be kept secret, at least for now. You might remember last spring, at the bar-b-que, he invited Perseus so that he could tell him about a vision he had that involved Perseus looking for the Sint-Holo."

"I'm bleeding to death over here," Perseus said, reminding everyone that he was still waiting.

There was a general murmur of recollection and assent, and one of the guys from the posse stepped forward to help Perseus and Penelope to his truck. As they were preparing to leave, the lights of another vehicle were seen coming toward the old sheep shed. Tommy and Perseus panicked.

Perseus got back out of the truck, bending over in pain as he did so. He hobbled over to stand next to Tommy, but before they could gather their wits, the vehicle was right there with the others. Tommy sighed with relief.

"It's Grandfather's truck." He hurried over to help his grandfather. "What are you doing out here?"

"I might ask you the same thing, Grandson," Bus said evenly.

"It's a long story. The short version is that Bart Oglethorpe kidnapped Penelope and we found her here, thanks to the help of Sint-Holo." He waited to see the expression on his grandfather's face.

"She is here then?"

"Yes, they're right there," Tommy said, pointing. It was quite dark, so the older man couldn't make out the shadowy forms. "I'll take you over to meet them. I think you'll be quite surprised."

"Them? Are there more than one?"

"Yes, there are two now. Ittikana went looking for more of her kind up in the mountains where we found her. She just returned tonight with the only other one she could find. She got back just in time to help us find Penelope."

As they approached Ittikana, Tommy projected his thoughts to her, explaining that his grandfather wanted to meet her, that she had not yet hatched the last time he saw her, and that it was his vision that inspired Perseus to go looking for her.

Bus stopped just a few feet away from Ittikana and looked intently at her. Star moved closer to get a better look at this older human. Tommy realized that his grandfather was weeping.

"*I am honored to meet you, Grandfather,*" Ittikana told him. "*I can see in your mind that you are one of the special ones from our memories. You are a story teller, and you have kept our story alive. Thank you. Your grandson has been very kind to me, and we have become friends. Both he and Perseus tell me that the world has changed much since our kind last lived in this land.*"

"*Yes, I do not know if your kind can survive in this world,*" Bus told her sorrowfully. "*But I am blessed to have had the chance to see you with my own eyes. I would be willing to help you in any way I can.*"

"*You are already helping. By telling our story, you keep us alive, if only in the minds of humans. I came back tonight to tell Perseus, Penelope, and Tommy that we are going back to the mountains. We will live there, no matter what happens. We may find more of our kind; or we may not. If we cannot find a male, we will eventually disappear forever. The future is always uncertain for us all, is that not true?*"

Perseus and Penelope joined Bus and Tommy. "What is she saying, Mister Abbot?" Perseus asked.

"She says she came back tonight to say goodbye. They're going back to live in the mountains."

"I thought that might be what she wanted to do." He told Penelope and Tommy.

The three companions went to Ittikana and put their hands on her chest. They each said their tearful goodbyes. She thanked them for all they had done for her and expressed her hope that they might all be together again someday.

The others were now all gathering around, wondering what was happening. Somebody asked Bus.

"They are saying goodbye. Sint-Holo is talking to them with her mind. She is as smart as any of us, probably smarter."

"You mean she can talk? I don't hear anything," someone said.

"She communicates with thoughts."

Just then, the wyvern moved away a short distance and prepared to take flight. They both raised up on their legs, stretched their necks, and spread their wings. A screech of farewell split the quiet of the night as they hurled themselves into the air. Everyone watched as the two Sint-Holo dissolved into the inky blackness.

"I'm still bleeding to death over here," Perseus again reminded his companions.

CHAPTER 26

PERSEUS WAS TREATED for his wounds at the local hospital and released the next morning. The bullet had struck him in the left side, glancing off of one of his ribs, breaking it in the process, and then passed through his upper arm. The damage to his flesh was relatively minor, amounting to two impressive lacerations, one on his side and one on his arm. He required a total of 37 stitches. He was in pain, but he assured his friends that it was tolerable with the help of the analgesic prescription he was given.

Penelope decided not to have her wrists treated at the hospital due to the obvious questions such a wound would raise. They were scraped raw from the rope but were easily treated at home with an over-the-counter antiseptic and analgesic spray. She was sore for a few days from the rough treatment, but that was bearable with the help of some over the counter pain relievers.

Tommy and the reservation posse disposed of Bart and Billy Joe's remains, using a borrowed backhoe to dig a deep hole in a remote location of Bus's farm. Bart's truck was dismantled and the parts were distributed among the boys in the posse. The sheep shed was burned to the ground.

Penelope contacted the sheriff to tell him that she had not been missing and apologize for all the trouble. She didn't know what she was thinking by leaving her cell phone at home. The sheriff said he wasn't surprised, considering all that she had been through with her father's death and trying to get the cattle to market. Then he asked her if she'd seen or heard from Bart. She told him she hadn't, but if he was gone, good riddance. Her sentiment didn't surprise the sheriff.

All the cattle made it to Wichita and the HB received a fat check. It covered all the year's expenses plus a healthy profit. Penelope put aside a large part of it in reserve, just in case anything came up with Bart's loan. She wondered if he had any kin who might inherit the loan document. Better safe than sorry, she thought. There was still plenty of profit left over to finance next year's operation, and even pay her staff a little bonus.

Things had settled down to the usual grind on the HB. There was always plenty of work to be done. Perseus was still healing from his wounds, so he was only doing some of his lighter chores. He had been quiet since the ordeal, and Penelope wondered where their relationship was going to go from here.

About a week after the kidnapping incident, Perseus decided to call his parents again. He thought he should tell them about his injury and update them on how things were going in his life. He assumed life for them had probably not changed. If nothing, they were creatures of habit. He had changed though . . . a great deal.

"Hello."

"Hello, Mother. It's Perseus."

"Yes, oh. Just a minute. Let me get George. Just hold on."

He heard her put the old landline phone down. That was odd. Why had she called him "George" rather than "your father?"

At least a minute passed before he heard the handset being picked up again. "Hello, is this Perseus?" It was his father.

"Hi, Dad. Yes, it's me."

"Listen, Alice and I have been talking since you've been gone. We have decided to tell you something you need to know going forward. We are not your biological parents. We adopted you when you were an infant. We have also decided that from here on out, you need to make your own way through life. You're of legal age now, and we feel we did our job the best we could in raising you. As you know, we are quite disappointed in how you've turned out."

He was stunned speechless.

"We've retained a lawyer. Alice thought it best to have a third party handle the legal action in order to keep everything objective and all. You will be receiving a package of documents that explain everything and includes the original adoption forms and so forth. You originally came from an orphanage out there in Oklahoma, where you've coincidentally chosen to live. So, maybe you can find out something about your biological parents, although from what we can remember they both died. That's how you became an orphan. You'll only have to sign a statement of receipt."

There was a pause. "What's the legal action?" Perseus' voice was thin. He could barely breathe.

"We are disinheriting you from our wills, Perseus. You are no longer welcome back here. We no longer consider you our son. Our lawyer will answer any questions you may have. I'll just say good luck."

His father hung up the phone. Perseus sat at the table in the bunk house staring at nothing, too shocked to do or think anything. *Did that really just happen? His parents just declared him no longer their son! Was that even possible? He was adopted. His real parents were dead.* These thoughts just kept circling around in his head, over and over again.

He slowly got up from the table and went out to stand in the middle of the breezeway. His stomach recoiled as the news sunk in. How could this be? Without really thinking about what he was doing, he saddled Balius. The pain of mounting momentarily brought him out of his trance, but once the horse started moving, he slipped into an altered state of mind.

Penelope came down to the barn to see how Perseus was doing and was shocked to find that Balius was gone. He shouldn't be riding in his condition. There was nobody else around the barn area. Slim and Günter must be out working in the pastures. She immediately saddled her horse and set out to find Perseus.

She found him an hour later, out in the old, abandoned building where they had kept Ittikana. His horse had not been tied up and was wandering around grazing some distance away. She tied her own horse and entered the cabin, where she found him sitting on the floor in the far corner. It seemed he hadn't noticed her coming inside.

"Perseus?" He didn't answer. "Perseus, are you alright?"

He slowly looked up at her with a blank expression on his face but said nothing. She walked over and sat down beside him.

"What's happened? I can tell something's happened. Please, Perseus, tell me."

"I called my parents. I wanted to tell them about my injury and that I was happy here and to see how they were doing." He stopped talking, just staring at nothing.

"What happened, baby?" She touched his cheek gently, and he began to cry. Tears streamed down his face.

"They told me I wasn't their son, that I was adopted. They said I was on my own now, not welcome back in their home. They're sending me some kind of legal papers that say they're no longer my parents. My dad told me my real parents are dead. They wouldn't even say hello to me on the phone. It was like I was just nobody." He broke down into sobs, which caused a stabbing pain in his side from his broken rib. He grabbed his side and between sobs moaned.

Penelope stroked his hair and tried to soothe him. "Oh, baby, darling. I'm so sorry. I don't know how they could do such a thing to you. I'm here for you. I'm here. You're not alone, baby. I'm right here." She was crying now too. It was breaking her heart to see him this way. What kind of people were they? How could they do this to him?

When he had finally cried himself out, he continued to sit there with his face in his hands. Penelope was still stroking his hair and neck. She heard someone riding up outside. There was a small knock on the door and Slim asked if everything was alright.

"Come in, Slim," Penelope said.

He could immediately see that things were not alright. He took his hat off and looked to Penelope for some enlightenment.

"Slim, could you please go back and get a truck out here? Perseus shouldn't be riding with his broken rib. Maybe you could take our horses back with you?"

"Yes, ma'am. I'll do that right away. You gonna be alright here 'till I get back?"

"I think so. There's a bottle of brandy in my father's, my study. Could you bring that back with you, please?"

"Yes, ma'am." He nodded and quietly slipped out the door.

Forty-five minutes later, Slim drove up in the big 350 with Günter and the bottle of brandy in his hand. They both took off their hats when they entered the old shack and Slim handed the bottle of brandy to Penelope, who placed it down next to her.

"I brung some glasses too," he said sheepishly.

"Perseus received some very upsetting news today. His parents disowned him, told him he was an orphan, and that they were done with him." Her voice broke as she finished this short announcement.

Perseus said nothing.

Günter cleared his throat. "Percy, you know we're your family, if you'll have us, I mean."

"That's right. You're like a little brother ta me." Slim added.

Perseus looked up at the two rough men, then he looked over to Penelope, her eyes glistening with concern and love. Something snapped inside him at just that moment, something positive and liberating. He started nodding his head. The others all exchanged glances, not sure what was going to happen.

"Thank you," Perseus said. "I feel like you're my family, I really do. You're the best people I've ever known, and that's finally just sunk in. I'm actually very lucky. This personal disaster has been happening for several years now. I somehow knew it was coming, but was in denial. My parents have always seemed so detached and remote. Now I know why but that doesn't make it hurt any less. One thing I realize though, is that I've been happier here than I've ever been in my whole life."

"I'm not going to let this news crush me. I'm going to rise above it and move forward."

He situated himself, wincing as he did so. "Slim, why don't you pour us each a glass of that brandy?"

"I'd be plum tickled," Slim said with a broad smile.

When they all had a glass, Perseus raised his and the others followed suit. "To my dear friends and my family."

They all took a drink. Perseus reached for Penelope's hand, held it up to his lips and kissed it. "Thank you. I was spiraling into a dark place, and you came and rescued me."

"Oh, Perseus. You rescued me, remember? I would never let you feel alone." She leaned over and kissed him.

"Will you marry me?" he asked suddenly.

Her eyes popped wide open. Slim and Günter exchanged surprised looks and started laughing.

"Are you serious?" she replied.

"I love you. I'm pretty sure you love me. Will you marry me, Penelope Wesley?"

"Yes, I will, and we'll build a family of our own."

Slim and Günter started cheering and everybody drank a toast to the happy couple.

Penelope looked closely at Perseus. "Are you sure you're alright?"

He took both of her hands in his and looked at her intensely. "Yes, I am sure. It was a shock, a big shock, but I realize now that this has been coming for some time."

He pulled her close. "I think I've just passed the second test." He smiled conspiratorially.

CHAPTER 27

SEVERAL WEEKS PASSED, and the weather grew colder as preparations for Thanksgiving went into high gear. Perseus was mostly back to full mend, both physically and emotionally. The wedding was planned for the following April, although Perseus had moved into the main house the night of the disastrous news from his adoptive parents. By mutual agreement, he was sleeping in a guest room. They wanted to wait until they were married to begin the family making process, and Perseus also needed time to figure out who he really was.

Perseus now knew he was not really a Fawcett. He was a little disappointed that he wasn't the great-great-grandson of Percy Fawcett, the famous explorer. As a child, that belief had always given him a kind of vicarious pride and a reason to believe that he might someday also be a famous adventurer. But now his focus was on finding out who his real parents were. He wanted to know his real last name when he and Penelope got married. This was important to him, and Penelope understood.

A few days after the life-changing phone call, Perseus received a thick package of documents from the law office of Morris & Beckenstein, as promised. He signed and returned the document that acknowledged his receipt of the package. The documents included a copy of the adoption certificate, medical records, school reports, his high school graduation certificate, and a copy of the papers that described his disinheritance. He was disappointed there was no note or further explanation from his parents—his adoptive parents.

The one thing he hoped he would find in the package was his birth certificate, but it was not included. The name of the adoption organization was listed on the adoption application. That would at least give him a place to begin his investigation. He soon discovered that finding information about birth parents was like looking for hen's teeth.

Perseus started the process by locating the adopting organization in Tulsa, Oklahoma. Fortunately, Oklahoma is one of the few states where access to records by adult adopted children is less onerous than in many other states. After gathering information online about how to go about gaining access to birth information, he discovered that he would have to go to Tulsa to file a petition. That was the easy part.

Ten days after filing, he received a notice that the petition had been received by the county court and he had been assigned a date to meet with the judge to whom he would have to explain why he believed it was necessary to unseal the adoption records. He was scheduled to go before the county judge on December 4th.

On Thanksgiving morning, Perseus asked Penelope if she wanted to go for a ride around the ranch. The big feast was scheduled for 3:00 and Angelica was attending to most of the preparations, preferring Penelope stay out of the kitchen until it was time for the last-minute preparations and the serving. So, Penelope didn't feel guilty for accepting the invitation to ride.

Perseus had both horses ready ahead of time, so when Penelope arrived at the barn, all she had to do was mount up. It was a partly cloudy, breezy morning, making the cool morning air feel several degrees colder. They were both using stampede strings to keep their hats from flying off with the wind and were wearing lined denim jackets.

"This is a perfect day for a pleasure ride," Penelope said.

"It feels odd to be riding just for the fun of it," Perseus observed.

"Yes, we certainly don't do that very often around here. I'm glad you suggested this, Perseus. Where do you want to go?"

"I was thinking we could head out to the river and just ride along the bank. I've never done that before."

"That sounds great. I know a good place for riding and looking. Some of the shoreline in the southern section is pretty marshy, but just up north a way it gets a lot more solid."

"Okay, lead the way."

They rode and talked about their future together. They discussed the cattle operation and some of the things they might change on the ranch. Perseus shared some of his ideas about making improvements to streamline the processing end. He wondered if maybe they could lease breeding bulls rather than keeping them year around. He admitted he was still uneasy around them. They shared their thoughts about the wedding too.

"Well, I won't have a very long guest list," he said with a wry chuckle. "I'd like to invite Syble, if that's okay."

"That would be perfect. She's the one who is kind of responsible for us meeting."

"Yeah. I think we should invite Tommy, of course. Maybe Bus too."

"Of course. I don't have many on my list either. I can only think of two high school friends I'd invite. My aunts and uncles are pretty far removed from my life. I barely know them, but I suppose it would be a big deal if I don't invite them."

They came upon an old ramshackle cabin nearly hidden among the trees. It was situated on a small rise about 100 yards from the river bank.

"What's this?" Perseus asked. "Is this part of the HB?"

"Yes. There are a couple of old dwellings like this on our land. This was one of the old home sites my distant relatives built when they settled this area. I don't know much about this one, or who lived here."

"Can we look inside?"

"Sure, why not?"

They dismounted and tied their horses. The place seemed as old as the land itself, looking as if it could turn to dust at any minute. The hewn timbers were covered in green moss, with thick vines growing up one of the walls and into a tree that had become part of the cabin itself. Much of the chinking had disintegrated long ago, leaving dark gaps between the timbers. There was no door, only an opening overgrown with weeds.

"Looks rather spooky," Perseus said. He put his hand on one of the timbers that formed the wall by the door. He was surprised at how sturdy it still felt. He peered inside, but it was too dark to make out much of the interior.

"When did your ancestors settle in this territory?"

"It was sometime in the late 1800s."

"So, this place is probably well over 100 years old. They don't make 'em like this anymore." He turned to see her reaction.

"Yeah, for obvious reasons."

"I don't know. We could clean it up a bit, some paint, some curtains. . ."

She smacked him on the arm, and he winced. "Oh, I'm sorry, Perseus. Does your wound still hurt?"

He laughed. "No, I'm just being silly." He pulled her close and kissed her.

"You know. You're right though," she said. "I don't know anything about this place, or any of the others like it on the ranch. There is a lot of history here, family history. All I know is that this property was probably bought by someone in my family from an Indian who had been given the land during the allocation period. There's got to be a story behind this place."

"Maybe we could do a little research and dig up something interesting. I'm sure there are records stashed somewhere in your house, or maybe at the county clerk's office. I have a whole new perspective about families and their history now. I'll help you try to piece it together."

He looked at his watch. "I suppose we'd better start heading back. We don't want to hold up Thanksgiving dinner."

CHAPTER 28

ON DECEMBER 4TH Perseus sat quietly on a bench inside the
Tulsa County District Court waiting for a judge from the Probate
Division to hear his petition. He was nervous. Penelope had
offered to come up to Tulsa with him for moral support, but he
told her he wanted to deal with this on his own. He didn't tell her
that he thought it was just too personal at this point to share with
her or anybody.

Finally, his name was called and he followed the bailiff into
the courtroom. Both giddy and apprehensive, he was feeling a bit
light-headed. After the perfunctory preliminaries were attended to,
the judge took several minutes to silently review his petition, then
he took a good, long look at Perseus.

"Your adoptive parents have essentially disowned you," he
announced. "Were you a troublemaker of some kind? Why do you
think they have done this?"

"No, sir, I mean, your honor. I was their only child, and
I would say they did a good job of raising me. They are both professors at Howard University in Washington DC, and I think they
were just absorbed in their own lives. I mean, they always took
care of me and everything, and I lived a privileged life while I was

with them, but at around age 19 things changed. They wanted me to be more like them; at least that's what it felt like. I guess the problem was, I didn't know what I wanted to do. Two days after my twenty-first birthday they told me to leave, that I couldn't live there with them any longer. They let me keep the car they had given me on my eighteenth birthday, and I had some money saved up, so I headed out west. But I ran out of money in Hugo."

"I got a job as a cowboy at a local ranch, and that seemed like something I could do; and I liked the work. About six weeks later, when I called to tell them where I was and that I was alright, they told me to grow up. The next time I talked to them, they told me I was adopted and that they were disowning me. I don't remember exactly what they said because I was so shocked. They had a lawyer send me some documents that disinherited me. They also told me my parents died when I was an infant."

Perseus was silent for several moments. He needed to collect himself; he didn't want to start falling apart there in front of this judge.

"After that, I felt cast adrift. I need to know who I am. I mean, if I'm no longer Perseus Fawcett, who am I? I want to know my real name. I want to know something about who my parents were. If they died when I was an infant, I'm guessing they didn't give me away. I probably became an orphan because they died in an accident or something. So, I think they would want me to know who they were. Don't you?"

He angrily wiped a tear from the corner of his eye. He refused to start crying.

"So, your honor," his voice quavering slightly, "I want to see my original birth certificate. If it please the court." He'd heard that last phrase in the movies, so he threw it in for good measure.

When Perseus looked up at the judge, he could see a sympathetic expression on his face. He wondered what he was supposed to do next. The judge was now looking down at the papers in front of him and writing something.

"I am going to issue a court order that will require the State Registrar to provide you with an uncertified copy of your original certificate of birth," the judge declared. "Since your adoption was finalized after November 1, 1997, and since you are over 18 years of age, and since you are not aware of having a biological sibling under the age of 18 currently in an adoptive family, and since your parents are deceased, I am able to grant your petition." The judged looked up at Perseus, who now stood in stunned surprise, tears streaming down his cheeks.

"Good luck to you, son. I hope this helps you find yourself."

That was it. All he had to do was go to the State Registrar and get the birth certificate. Where was the State Registrar? He asked someone at the information desk in the courthouse lobby and was told it was in Oklahoma City. He decided that he would drive back home through Oklahoma City and pick it up.

Soon, he discovered it wasn't that easy. He would either have to make an appointment or submit the application on-line or apply by mail. Any of those options would result in up to 10 weeks before he could actually hold the certificate in his hands. Frustrated, but relieved that he could actually get a copy of his birth certificate, he told himself he could wait another few weeks.

He called Penelope to share the good news. She told him she was very happy for him, and to hurry home. On the two-and-a-half-hour drive back to Hugo, down the Indian Nation Turnpike, he daydreamed about who his parents were, what they might have been like, and what they looked like. If he was lucky, maybe he could dig up some photographs. Maybe he had grandparents, uncles and aunts—maybe even a whole family of relatives!

The days passed slowly for Perseus. Christmas came and went, and January dragged on. In the first week of February, the new calves started coming. The weather was cold, especially at night, and the ranch work picked up considerably, helping to move the clock and calendar more quickly. His life was definitely good and his future bright, but he was still anxious to get his hands on that birth certificate.

Finally, on the 5th of February, the document he'd been waiting for arrived in the mail. Penelope stood next to him while he opened the envelope as though there was some sort of sacred artifact inside. He took a quick look at the cover letter, but didn't read it, then he unfolded the birth certificate. Penelope noticed that his hands were trembling and put her arm around his waist.

He studied it for a long time. "I was born in Pottawatomie County, in Shawnee, Oklahoma, on April 1, 1997. It says my name was Percy Alan Hadjioannou. My father's name was Robert Hadjioannou. Good grief, I can't escape being Greek. Race: white. There's no age listed. Occupation was performer, and in the industry block it shows: circus." He exchanged a look with Penelope. "My mother's name was Irene Abbott, race: Native-American. She was 24 years old, born in Oklahoma." He lowered the certificate. "Native-American. My mother was a Native-American." He looked at the certificate again. "There's nothing in the length block, but I weighed 7 pounds, 3/4 ounces. According to this, my mother had no other children."

He looked at Penelope, a thousand things swirling around inside his head. "I'm part Indian. My mother was an Indian. And my father was a circus performer." His sounded excited and baffled at the same time. He studied the certificate again, looking for some hidden meaning in this information. "Look, this was their address."

"Can I use your computer? I want to look up this address."

"Yes, of course."

They hurried into the office where Perseus sat down at the desk and typed out the address on Broadway Avenue. When it came up on Google Maps, he switched to the street view and stared at the house where his parents had lived. It was a small, neat white-clapboard house with a covered front porch supported by red brick columns. It was located in an older neighborhood with large, mature trees growing in the yards of homes that looked similar to the one his parents had lived in.

He zoomed out on the map to get some idea of where Shawnee was located in the state and was surprised to discover that it was a suburb of Oklahoma City. He wondered why he was born in Tulsa if they lived near Oklahoma City. Yet another mystery.

His emotions were like a kaleidoscope churning inside his head, making it difficult to sort out his feelings. It was so fulfilling to have this precious information right here in his hands, but now there were so many other questions. One question that now dominated his thoughts was how his parents died. He realized he would have to do more research to get the answers. He would need to locate a death certificate for both of them.

Penelope was watching him, trying to gauge his reaction. She wasn't sure what, if anything, she should say or do. Perseus suddenly shot her a look as if he'd just had a startling epiphany.

"My mother was a Native-American and her maiden name was Abbott. Do you suppose she might be some relation to Bus and Tommy?"

Penelope's brows arched. "I don't know, but it would certainly seem possible. Why don't we ask?"

"Of course," he said, as if this were the most ingenious idea he had ever heard. He pulled his cell phone from his pocket and initiated a call to Tommy.

"And my father was in the circus," he said in a whisper as he waited for Tommy to pick up. Penelope had to stifle a laugh at the expression on his face. He looked like a kid on Christmas morning.

Tommy answered the call. "Tommy," Perseus shouted. "I'm an Indian. I'm an honest-to-God Indian."

"What?" Tommy said, utterly confused. "What are you talking about?"

"I just got my original birth certificate. It came in the mail. Penelope and I are looking at it right now. My mother's maiden name was Abbott, and the certificate says her race was Native-American. Irene Abbott, 24 years old, Native-American. I'm looking at it right now. And guess what. My father was a circus performer. His name was Robert Hadjioannou. Do you suppose we're related? I mean, you and me."

Tommy was quiet on the other end.

"Hello. Are you still there?" Perseus asked.

"Yeah, I'm still here. I'm thinking, trying to absorb what you just said. Her name was Irene Abbott, you say?"

"Yes."

"Holy shit," he said, after another pause.

"Really?" Perseus switched to speaker mode so Penelope could hear too.

"I think she was my aunt. Grandfather had a daughter named Irene. It was his youngest daughter, my father's little sister. Grandfather never talks about her, but he told me once that she ran off with some white man from the circus when they were wintering over here in Hugo. He said she had broken his heart and he never heard from her again."

"Wow, I . . ." Perseus' voice trailed off. "Do you suppose your grandfather would talk to me about her?"

"I don't know. Probably. I think he will be pretty happy if it turns out you're one of his grandsons, and not actually a white man, well, only part white."

CHAPTER 29

THE MEETING WITH Bus was an emotional experience for everyone in the room. Bus verified that the Irene on the birth certificate was almost certainly his daughter. He verified that the man from the circus who had taken her away was named Hadjioannou, although he had no idea what the man actually did. He told Perseus that his daughter was always talking about getting off the reservation and making something of her life.

He laughed bitterly. "So, she ran off with a man from the circus, a white man, and got as far as Shawnee."

"I looked up their address, Grandfather," Perseus said. "It looks like they were living in a nice house, in a nice neighborhood. They must have been doing alright."

Bus just harrumphed. Perseus felt good about calling Bus, Grandfather. It felt comfortable and Bus seemed to like the idea of finding a new grandson.

"Well, now I understand why you were part of my vision. I just wasn't able to understand why a young white man would play such a prominent role. The meaning of most visions is difficult to determine. This one was about your homecoming."

Bus brought out an old, beat-up box from a closet in his bedroom. It contained old photographs and mementoes of the family. He rummaged through the box until he found a small stack of items wrapped with a string. As he took each object from the stack, he examined it carefully and provided a description to the others. There were pictures of Irene from childhood through her teens. There were drawings she had made for her mother and father, some done in crayon, some in pencil. Her high school diploma was among the artifacts.

Perseus was particularly taken with his mother's high school photo, and he couldn't bring himself to put it down. This was probably close to what she looked like when she gave birth to him. To Perseus, she looked like an Indian maiden out of a storybook, with her large brown eyes, long dark hair, and a smile that seemed to indicate that she was genuinely happy that day. Her head was tilted in a very pretty way. Everybody noticed him staring at the photo.

"I think you should keep that picture of your mother, Grandson."

Perseus didn't look up. It was a very emotional moment. Penelope leaned in close to him and put her head on his shoulder so she could also admire the picture. It made her think of her own mother and father, and how difficult it was to lose your parents, much less to never have known them.

Perseus took time over the next few weeks to uncover information about the death of his parents. He discovered they were both killed in a motorcycle accident just six months after his birth. The authorities were not able to identity next of kin, another mystery, so he was placed in the child protective services system and subsequently adopted by the Fawcetts.

He began to consider changing his name. His anger over what his adoptive parents had done to him had subsided considerably since discovering the identity of his birth parents, but it still seemed reasonable to change his name to his birth name.

It was about this time that the disappearance of Bart and Billy Joe began to bubble back up. The sheriff came out to the HB one morning wanting to go over the details of the day that Penelope had gone missing. Seems there were a number of loose ends in the investigation. He wanted Penelope and Perseus to answer some questions.

They invited him into the living room. "Has there been any word at all about what happened to Bart and Billy Joe?" Penelope asked.

"There's been no trace of them since that day," the sheriff said. "No credit card or ATM usage, no withdrawals from their bank accounts, no sign of Bart's truck, nothing."

Perseus and Penelope sat quietly.

"There has been some talk, though. One of the hands at the McAllister seems to think that Bart and Billy Joe were with you the day they disappeared, Penelope. Says he's sure of it."

"Well, I assure you, Sheriff, I would have nothing to do with those two, much less be with them on the day that I was moving the last of my cattle up to Wichita. I think you know how I feel about Bart Oglethorpe. As far as I'm concerned, he caused my father's death, and he's been behind several other attempts to disrupt our operation here at the HB."

"Yes, I'm well aware of the problems between you two. Fact is, though, you never were in Wichita, at least not at the stockyards. There's no record of you being there, and we all know you didn't meet your drivers as planned. You may recall that my office was notified that you were missing the same day that Bart and Billy Joe were last seen."

"Yes, well I explained that I went to Wichita on my own, which caused everyone to worry, but I was still distraught over my father's death and not thinking straight. I can't imagine any logical scenario where anything I did that day would result in my being with Bart and Billy Joe."

The sheriff decided to take another tack. "Perseus, where were you the day and night that Penelope was considered missing?"

"I was here at the HB, Sheriff. After you dropped me off, I stayed right here. The whole HB crew was here waiting to hear something of Penelope's whereabouts. We didn't want to leave the ranch for fear that Bart or one of his thugs might do something destructive. We were so concerned about the ranch and our personal safety we all carried side arms everywhere we went, and we did everything in pairs. You know, somebody took a shot at us just before Bus was killed. I can show you the bullet hole in the barn."

This revelation seemed to surprise the sheriff. "You didn't report that incident?"

"No, we didn't, Sheriff," Penelope answered. "We were pretty sure reporting it wouldn't result in any action. We knew who was behind it, but we had no way to prove it."

"There's some who think you were determined to get revenge for your father's death." The sheriff was looking at Penelope. "These incidents you're describing could be construed as a motive for retaliation."

Perseus and Penelope exchanged looks, then fixed their gaze on the sheriff. "Do you really think that either one or both of us are capable of taking on Bart Oglethorpe and his thugs, Sheriff?" Penelope asked. "He and his gang beat the crap out of Perseus and Tommy Abbott at the Red Barn. We're afraid of them. If they've gone, then we're not going to miss them, but if you're suggesting that we, we, what? Got rid of them somehow. Well, I just can't believe you'd think we would even know how to do such a thing."

The sheriff sighed deeply, nodding his head. "I don't think you got rid of them but I'm just doing my job, Penelope. There's talk. You know? It's a small county and a small town. Something's happened to those two, probably something bad, so I have to look into it."

"I understand, Sheriff," Penelope said, sounding more sympathetic now.

"Alright. Thank you for your time," he said, getting up. "How's your wounds, Perseus?"

"Much better, Sheriff. Thank you. Almost good as new."

The sheriff stopped, seemed to just remember something. "There's a rumor going around that you have some kind of giant flying creature at your beck and call. Do you know what that's all about?"

Perseus hoped his face didn't give away his sudden panic. "A giant flying creature?" He gave a nervous laugh. "Seriously? No, no. Something like that would be pretty hard to keep a secret. Maybe those rumors have something to do with the Sint-Holo legend that we heard about at Bus's bar-b-que last spring. Penelope, Tommy Abbot, and I went camping last Fourth of July up in the Ouachita Mountains. Some guys at the reservation were kidding us about going up there to look for it. It's supposed to be kind of like a dragon."

The sheriff chuckled. "Well, that's pretty farfetched for sure."

When the sheriff left the house, heading for his cruiser, Penelope and Perseus breathed a heavy sigh of relief. They hugged each other.

"Do you think anything will come of this?" Penelope asked.

"I don't know, sweetheart, but I'm willing to bet I know who's talking about this. It's that guy, Spence. I don't know what he hopes to gain from it, but I doubt there's too many others in this county who would care much about Bart and Billy Joe disappearing."

The days got more and more hectic as increasing numbers of cows gave birth to their calves. With Bud gone, the workload had to be distributed among Penelope and the crew, including Chilo.

In addition to the ranch work, Penelope was getting more anxious about planning the wedding. Perseus suggested perhaps they should put the wedding off until things slowed down.

"Perseus," she replied with a mischievous grin, "are you getting cold feet."

"No. Are you kidding? I'm ready right now, this minute. Let's go into town and get the County Clerk to do the job. We can pick up a bottle of cheap champagne on the way home."

She smacked his arm, and he feigned pain from his healed wound. They both laughed and then they hugged.

"We'll just have to squeeze the planning into our busy schedule," Penelope said. "I've already sent the invitations out, and we're going to do the reception here. Angelica assures me she has everything under control. Have you arranged for the preacher, the ring, and the best man?"

"Yes, ma'am, I have. Doesn't sound like there's that much more to do."

"Are you kidding? There's the flowers, the pictures, the bridesmaid's gifts."

"Well, you just let me know if there's something I can do, and I'll see to it. By the way, did you send an invitation to Syble?"

"Oh, no," Penelope cried. "I completely forgot. Maybe we could go into town tomorrow and invite her in person. Let's go to her café for dinner."

"Oh, a fancy night out on the town, eh?"

The next evening, they walked into Syble's Café. It was busy, but Syble stopped what she was doing and came over to greet them. "Well, I haven't seen you two in a long time. The word is out you're gettin' hitched."

"Yes, we are, Syble," Perseus said, "And we want to invite you. You're the one responsible for us meeting and for me getting a job out there at the HB. It's on a Sunday afternoon. So, do you think you could make it?"

"Are you kidding? I wouldn't miss it." She looked like she was on the verge of tears.

"Great. Here's the official invitation." Penelope handed her the envelope. "We want to have dinner here tonight. Got any food left?"

"Of course. There's a booth right over there. I'll be by in a minute to clean it up."

Penelope and Perseus enjoyed the house special of pot roast and potatoes for supper, something that Angelica rarely made at the HB. Syble gave them a large piece of apple pie to share for dessert. They all tried to catch up on the local gossip in small, quick snippets as Syble rushed around trying to keep all her customers happy. The top gossip headlines included Penelope having some connection to Bart's disappearance, Perseus conjuring up creatures from Hell, and that Perseus was actually an Indian.

"Wow!" Perseus said to Penelope. "There sure aren't any secrets in Choctaw County, are there? Who do you suppose is leaking all this information all over the place?"

"I'd still place my bet on Spence for spreading the Bart disappearance thing," said Penelope. "He's probably one of the two men who bushwhacked me on the road that day I was supposed to meet the truck drivers."

"I'm surprised he just doesn't forget about it and lay low," Perseus said. "The only way he could know anything is if he was involved in your kidnapping. Making an issue of it identifies him as one of the conspirators."

"I don't think he's smart enough to put all that together, sweetheart."

When they were finished, they thanked Syble and said good-bye. It was dark outside, with only one streetlight providing just enough illumination to find their truck. The café had already been busy when they arrived, so they had to park on the side of the building in a rutted patch of gravel that served as the overflow parking lot.

As they neared their truck, two men stepped out from the shadows of another truck. They walked quickly toward Penelope and Perseus and stopped between them and their truck.

"Oh," she gasped.

"I was wondering if you two were ever gonna come out of your hole at the HB." They recognized the voice as belonging to Spence. They couldn't see the men's faces due to the darkness and their hats being pulled low on their foreheads.

Perseus stepped in front of Penelope protectively. "What do you want, Spence?"

"I know you two had somethin' to do with Bart and Billy Joe just disappearin' in ta thin air. You didn't think you were gonna get away with it did you?" His voice was thick and ominous.

"Why would you think that we were involved in their disappearance, Spence?" Perseus asked.

"Let's just say I know for certain this Wesley bitch was with Bart and Billy Joe the night they disappeared."

"Oh. Could that be because you were the one who kidnapped Penelope, tied her up and took her out to the old sheep shed on the Abbot farm on the reservation? Is that how you know?"

The two men just stood there for a few seconds, saying nothing.

"If I were you, and I definitely would not want to be you, I would keep my mouth shut and leave town."

"You little bastard," Spence growled as he lunged toward Perseus.

Perseus quickly reached into the inside pocket of his denim jacket and pulled out a .357 revolver. He wasn't the same naïve, timid, and soft kid who this man had beat up in the Red Barn several months ago. He rushed up to meet his aggressor, grabbed the front of his jacket, and rammed the barrel of the pistol into the man's throat, the hammer making a menacing click as Perseus pulled it back. Spence stopped dead, spreading his arms out wide.

"I hate bullies," Perseus said in a low, steady voice. "I really hate dumbass thugs who like to go around threatening others, picking on people they think they can push around. I really hate you, mister. Do you know how easy it would be for me to pull this trigger? Do you understand how much I want to blow the back of your head off?"

Spence said nothing. "Answer me!" Perseus roared.

"Yes, yes. I do. Please don't pull the trigger. Please. Jackson?" Spence called out to his partner, hoping he would do something.

"She's got a gun pointed at me, Spence. I can't do nothin'."

"You see, Spence, we're not going to take it anymore. We're not going to be victims any longer. This is going to end. Do you want to know what happened to Billy Joe? Bart stabbed him to death. I watched him do it with my own eyes. Stabbed him several times, then let him fall to the ground and kicked him in the head until he was dead. I was going to shoot Bart, but my gun didn't fire. He ran inside that sheep shed and grabbed Penelope, holding that same bloody knife to her throat until we dropped our guns. Then he took one of those guns and shot me.

"He shot me, Spence. But he didn't kill me, did he? Because if he did, I wouldn't be here wanting to blow your brains out, would I?" Perseus pushed the gun harder into the man's neck. "How does it feel to be on the other end of the stick, Spence?"

"Somebody, please do something. Don't let him kill me."

Perseus was so completely absorbed with Spence that he hadn't noticed that a crowd had gathered behind them. Nobody was saying anything, and nobody was making any move to stop what they were witnessing.

"There's a bit of a crowd behind us, sweetheart," Penelope told him gently.

Perseus didn't care. He was dealing with a whole lifetime of being afraid, of being picked on, of being rejected. He wanted to terrify this bully, and then he wanted to kill him.

Spence was crying now, but his tears didn't move Perseus one iota.

Finally, Penelope moved over and lightly placed her hand on his shoulder and spoke very softly. "I think you've made your point, my darling. Don't ruin your life by taking this man's. I want to marry you, and I can't do that if you're in jail."

Perseus pushed Spence away, still pointing the pistol at him. His hand was rock steady. He was a rock of righteous indignation. "Get out of here before I change my mind," he said in an even tone.

Spence and Jackson turned and scrambled back to their truck. The small crowd backed away to let them exit the parking lot. When the two men were gone, the people standing there began to murmur.

"About time somebody put those guys in their place."

"You okay, son?"

"Isn't he the guy those two beat up at the Red Barn a while back?"

They all slowly turned away and got in their own vehicles or returned to the café. Penelope and Perseus were alone in the dimly lit parking lot.

"You calmed down enough to drive?" Penelope asked him. "Why don't you let me drive?"

"Yeah, that would be a good idea." He didn't move. "I'm sorry you had to see that. I went kind of crazy."

"Are you kidding? I wouldn't have missed that for all the tea in China. You were a badass. Whew! I'm going to marry a badass. You know, I had my gun out too, cowboy. I'm tired of being harassed and bullied too."

He looked at her, surprised by her reaction. "You're a badass too, aren't you? Wanna go to the Red Barn and have a few shots?"

"I think we'd better quit while we're ahead, mister. Let's go home and make out. I feel kind of aroused after all that excitement."

They both laughed nervously as they got into their truck. By the time they made it back to the HB, the adrenaline rush had come to a crashing halt. They agreed that the café incident would be broadcast all over Choctaw County within the next 24 hours through the gossip network. They weren't sure how much of Perseus' description of the sheep shed violence had been heard by people standing behind them, but they expected another visit by the sheriff was highly possible.

CHAPTER 30

THE DAYS TURNED into weeks, and, before they knew it, the wedding day had arrived. Life had settled into a busy routine at the HB with work being the primary focus of their lives. Despite their concerns, the sheriff never came back to talk to them, and there were no reprisals from Spence and Jackson.

The wedding was a small affair, with only a few dozen guests. The ceremony took place at a small, non-denominational church in Hugo. Penelope had Perseus dress in a black, western-cut suit and a new black felt hat, which she bought for him as a wedding present. She was attired in a sleeveless, form-fitting white lace maxi dress, with a crown of daisies in her hair. Her mother's single strand of pearls adorned her neck. Since it was still cold outside, she wore a trim, white denim jacket. Everyone agreed they made a storybook couple, a' la Louis L'Amour fashion.

Perseus managed to scrape together enough money to purchase two plain golden bands, which Penelope assured him were the best, most beautiful rings in the whole world. Tommy Abbot, now his cousin, was his best man and threatened to come to the wedding dressed in full traditional Choctaw regalia. Penelope asked her best friend from high school to be her maid of honor.

After a short ceremony at the church, everyone gathered at the HB for the reception. Angelica had outdone herself in preparing a wonderful feast for the guests. Syble insisted on providing the wedding cake, which was devil's food with white icing. Of course, Slim and Günter were there, as were Chilo and Angelica. Bus and a handful of new relatives also attended. Beer and champagne were available and consumed in copious quantities.

There was no time for a honeymoon. The demands of the ranch at this time of year made going away for a few days impossible. Perseus teased Penelope that he thought they should spend their wedding night in the bunk house, but he did have a surprise for her. When the reception party was in full swing, he told her to go get her honeymoon things, it was time to go. They said goodbye to their guests, who cheered them on their way.

Perseus opened the pickup truck door for her. "Where are you taking me, sir? You know we can't be away tomorrow."

"Yes, I know. I have a surprise for you. Don't worry, we'll be back here in time to do our chores."

Her interest was piqued, but she couldn't imagine where they could possibly go that was close and appropriate for a wedding night. All things considered, she wasn't really very concerned. They had both waited a long time for this night and were excited to finally be united in love and marriage.

He pointed the truck out toward the back of the ranch, over the rutted trails and fields. He finally pulled up to the old cabin where they had kept Ittikana.

"Oh, my goodness," she squealed. "You expect me to spend my wedding night in this old shack?"

"Just wait and see. If you don't like it, we'll head back to the house."

When they got to the door, he picked her up in his arms, wincing slightly form the still-tender rib, and carried her over the threshold and into the cabin. She couldn't imagine when he had the time to do it, but the interior had been transformed into a bright, clean, and cozy cottage. There was even a fire burning in an old potbellied stove in one corner. He'd conspired with Slim to sneak out of the reception and get the fire going.

Fresh, clean straw covered the floor, and on top of the straw were three colorful rugs. There was a comfortable-looking poster bed with turned-down white sheets and a thick comforter. Fluffy pillows were arranged at the head of the bed. Next to the bed stood a bedside table overflowing with fresh flowers. There was even an old-fashioned wash stand, complete with a ceramic wash basin and pitcher, and large, fluffy towels hanging on pegs.

In the middle of the room, atop a small, farmhouse table, was a vase of long-stemmed, white roses. Next to the roses were a bottle of champagne in an ice bucket and two stemmed glasses. Lanterns hanging from hooks cast a soft glow around the room, giving the place a homey feel. The scent of rose incense pleasantly masked the old musty smell.

He set her down next to the table. She put her hands up to her cheeks and took in the whole space, making a 360-degree inspection.

"Oh, Perseus. It's beautiful, perfect! This is better than anything I could have ever imagined. When did you find the time to do all this?"

He shrugged his shoulders. "It was a labor of love."

She flung herself into his arms and kissed him passionately. "It's wonderful. Thank you, sweetheart. Let's go to bed."

"I guess the roses worked," he said, smiling broadly.

Their union that night, was passionate, but slow and deliberate, as they took the time to explore each other's body and learn the intricacies of each other's pleasure. At last, they fell asleep, intertwined in each other's arms, and blissfully exhausted.

CHAPTER 31

SHORTLY AFTER THE wedding, Perseus turned 22. He awoke next to his new bride, marveling that this beautiful woman was actually his wife. He lay in bed reflecting back on his life just one year earlier. He recalled the disappointment he felt about his parents, his adoptive parents, forgetting his birthday, and his April Fools' Day joke. Funny, it seemed like such a long time ago, like maybe another whole lifetime ago.

He wondered if they ever thought about him anymore. He wondered if he would ever forgive them. Although he was excited to have discovered his true roots and something about his biological parents, the Fawcetts were the only parents he'd ever known. He tried to remember something about his real mother, but he'd been too young.

He shook his head. What the heck was he doing? That was the past. Today was his birthday, and there was a very beautiful, naked women lying next to him. He reached over and touched her. She moaned sleepily in response and opened her eyes to find him watching her. She smiled.

"Happy birthday, my love."

Now, that's more like it. "Thank you. I am happy."

"What do you want to do for your birthday?"

"Well, you could get up and come down to the barn to shovel horse shit with me. That would be nice."

She smacked his arm and giggled. "Let's ask Chilo to do that for you today. I don't think he would mind. We could just stay in bed for a little while this morning."

"Hmm, now that sounds like a good way to begin the next year of my life. Sure beats how my birthday started out last year."

As April turned into May, Perseus became increasingly concerned about his grandfather, Bus. The old man's health was failing. He was having fits of coughing that wracked his entire body, but he refused to see a doctor.

"There's no sense in spending money on a doctor just to be told that I'm gonna die," he would say. "I've lived a long life and I'm ready to go to the Great Spirit."

Tommy and Perseus both thought Bus probably had lung cancer, but there was little they could do about it except try to spend as much time with the old man as they could manage. Perseus spent most days working 10 hours or more with the HB cattle. Tommy was doing all the work on his grandfather's farm; a farm he was certain he would inherit all too soon. Privately, they hoped Bus could make it until his big annual bar-b-que, scheduled for May 25th.

Bus had been pressing Perseus to apply for a Certificate of Degree of Indian Blood, a CDIB. Bus told him he was chahta, one of the people, and qualified to become an official member of the Choctaw Nation as a member of the panther iska, or clan.

"In our society, the mother determines which clan you belong to," Bus told him. "That was my wife's iska, and so it was your mother's." Bus took Perseus' hand. "I am proud to have you as my grandson, and it would please me if you would officially recognize your heritage. So many of our people have perished or integrated into the white man's world, and now they have faded out of memory."

"Do you dislike the white people so much, Grandfather?" Perseus asked.

"No, not at all. I judge people for who they are, not what they are, but the chahta have a history, a very long history in this land. We have traditions, a language, and a culture that is ours and ours alone, just as the white, black, brown, and yellow people have theirs. I believe it is important to retain our identity, and to be proud of it."

These words weighed heavily on Perseus. It had never occurred to him that this would be something he would ever need to think about, until now. It was crazy. It still hadn't completely sunk in; he was half Indian. What should he do?

Perseus wondered how Penelope would feel about him becoming an official member of the Choctaw chahta. Were there implications for their children? He freely shared his thoughts on the subject with her. She was very supportive but told him that it was something he had to decide for his own reasons.

He began to have recurring dreams about walking down a narrow path in a dense forest. In the dream, he would always arrive at a fork in the trail with no clear indication of which path he should follow. In some of the dreams, the direction he chose led him to a dark space where the path simply ended. In other versions he would ultimately find himself at the edge of a precipitous cliff, while still other versions found him surrounded by an angry mob throwing rocks at him.

When the dreams came, he would wake up feeling disoriented and anxious. He understood that the dreams were a reflection of the struggle he was having about taking steps to become a recognized member of the Choctaw Nation.

One day in early May, while he was preparing to move the breeding bulls out to the cow herds, he made the decision to apply for the certification. He knew this would please Bus, and he finally concluded that having the CDIB card didn't mean that he had to do anything else if he didn't want to. He thought it would be a nice gesture of acknowledgement of his heritage for his grandfather and his mother's memory.

Tommy told him that if he decided to apply, he could do it all online. He needed his birth certificate, his mother's death certificate, his adoption papers, and proof of identification. He would also need his grandfathers' CDIB card number. It would be the Bureau of Indian Affairs that would process the application and make the final determination. Becoming a member of the Choctaw Nation would be a tribal decision and a separate application process. He would first have to be considered for a trial membership.

With Tommy's help, Perseus submitted his application. Tommy suggested he call the regional office of the Bureau of Indian Affairs, located in Muskogee, and explain that his grandfather was very ill and why he would appreciate any help he could get to expedite the processing of the application.

The call did not go well. The person at the BIA end of the call was curt and unsympathetic. Tommy told Perseus he would contact the tribal council member who represented their district and see if he could do anything to help.

"He's a very nice man and knows Grandfather personally," Tommy assured Perseus. "He's even been to several of Grandfather's bar-b-ques. Even if we can't get this done in time for the bar-b-que, it will make Grandfather happy to know that you're doing it."

"I'm sure it will, but it would be great if I could show him the actual card. This has all happened so fast. It's only been a couple of months since I received my original birth certificate. It's still hard to come to grips with the revelation that I'm part of your family. It's almost like a dream."

"Speaking of dreams, I wonder whatever became of Ittikana and Star," Tommy mused. "You suppose they're still alive?"

"I think so. If they ran into trouble with humans, we would have heard about it on the news. I'm pretty sure they can take care of themselves. I've been thinking about them too. I'd love to see Ittikana again. Maybe they've gone into Sint-Holo mode, you know, keeping low. What was it Grandfather said, ". . .in the deepest caves, in the deepest waters?""

"Yeah, and if we ever go back up there, let's hope it's not her time to feast." They both laughed grimly. They both had a flash-back of Ittikana tearing Bart's head off and ripping him open. "We don't want to be out when she's hungry," Tommy added.

It was May 25th, the day of Bus's annual bar-b-que. Bus was weak with the effects of his ailment, but he was in good spirits. The crowd was looking like it would be larger than usual. Word had gotten around about his condition, and Tommy believed that many people were coming to say goodbye. Even the Choctaw tribal chief and the local tribal council representative were there.

Bus was sitting in the old wooden chair on the porch of his house, just as he had done the previous year. He was wearing his traditional hunting jacket, his beaded shoulder sashes, and beaded belt as well. Tommy was standing beside him. This year, however, there was a long line of people waiting their turn to get close enough to speak to him for a few moments.

Perseus could see, as he and Penelope approached, that Bus looked tired, even haggard, but he was smiling, seeming to enjoy all the attention. When Bus spotted them, he motioned for them to come forward. Tommy helped them get through the crowd.

As they made their way, Bus spoke in the Choctaw language. "This is my long-lost grandson, my daughter's son." He switched to English. "Come, come. This is Perseus and his wife, Penelope."

By now, just about everybody in the county knew the story of Perseus: how he coincidentally ended up in Hugo, became a cowboy at the HB, discovered he was actually part Choctaw, and, most amazing of all, he was related to Bus Abbot. News like this traveled fast in these parts. The crowd parted like the Red Sea as Penelope and Perseus made their way up to Bus.

Penelope was carrying an apple pie, which delighted Bus tremendously. Once again, he asked Tommy to put the pie away in the kitchen for later. When he reemerged from the house, he found Bus telling everyone about the vision he had and how he couldn't understand why a white man had been so prominent in this vision. But it turned out to be Perseus, and he knew the moment he first saw him, right here in this very spot last year, that he was someone special and somehow connected, not only to himself, but to the Choctaw people. Of course, it turned out to be true. This was his grandson.

In telling this story, Bus seemed to come alive. All his tiredness evaporated. He bragged about his other grandson, Tommy, and how it was Tommy who found Perseus in Hugo, and recommended he take the job at the HB that Penelope offered him. He took her hand as he related this part of the story.

"And now, she is my granddaughter by marriage. It is remarkable."

Many in the crowd applauded and shouted encouragements and greetings.

Then Bus became serious as he looked out over the crowd, obviously preparing to say something profound. The crowd hushed and the people in the back pushed forward to better hear what he might say.

"Then the most amazing thing happened," he continued in a more subdued voice. "I could see this young man's dreams. He was being summoned, but he did not know that. I told him the story of Sint-Holo." There was a collective gasp among the crowd. Tommy and Perseus couldn't help but smile. The old man was on a roll.

Later, these three young people standing right here," he gestured to Penelope, Perseus, and Tommy. "They went searching for the creature of our legends." There was a pregnant pause. The old man knew how to play the crowd. "Some say they found the creature. Some say they saw it with their own eyes a few months ago. Who is to say, but it is clear that these are special people. They are very special to me."

There was enthusiastic applause, then people began maneuvering to get close. The rest of the afternoon followed the same itinerary as last year, with the afternoon bar-b-que, the dancing, and the socializing. This year, however, Tommy, Perseus, and Penelope seemed to be the main attraction.

By the time Bus was ready to tell his annual story to the children, the day had grown late. It took him longer than usual to go back up the hill to his house. This year, there were many more attendees at the story time. The children, as always, got the front row seats, but behind them were scores of adults eager to hear the story.

Once again, Bus told the story of Sint-Holo. This time, though, he was able to add considerably more detail about the creature's appearance and its relationship to the people, the chahta. The children were enthralled, and the adults were curious. Had the rumors about Perseus controlling the Sint-Holo been true?

After the story, Tommy held up his hands to quiet the crowd. "We have an important announcement to make. Could I get everyone's attention please? Bus looked up at him quizzically. "My cousin, Perseus, has an announcement he would like to make."

Perseus cleared his throat. He suddenly realized he was quite nervous. "As you must now know, I have recently discovered that my birth mother was Irene Abbott, Bus's estranged daughter. She and my father, who she met at the circus when it was here many winters ago, ran off to get married." Perseus decided not to mention the fact that his father was a white man. "Of course, this means that Bus is my grandfather."

"I have thought long and hard about what this astonishing news of my origin means to me and to my family." He paused a moment to collect himself. He realized that he was becoming very emotional. Penelope took his arm to encourage him. "I have applied for my CDIB card and want to request, here today before the chahta, that I also be accepted for consideration as a trial member of the Choctaw Nation. If accepted, I would be a member of the panther clan."

There was applause and murmurs throughout the crowd. Bus stood up and embraced his grandson. They were both now openly crying, and everyone was glued to the emotional scene on the porch.

There was a sudden rush of wind, stirring up the dust, then, without any warning, Ittikana landed on the rooftop of Bus's house. People began scattering, some screaming, as she gathered herself and brought her wings in close to her chest. Perseus couldn't believe this was happening. He immediately began communicating with her.

"Hello, Ittikana. What are you doing here? You're scaring the people."

"Tell them I come in peace. I mean no harm to anyone."

Perseus shouted to try to calm everybody down. He noticed that, ironically, the children had not moved. They sat, openmouthed, in wonder and awe. Several of the young people who had made up the reservation posse the night everyone was searching for Penelope, were going through the crowd, trying to reassure them the creature was not going to harm them. Tommy was also doing his best calm the people down.

At last, the crowd settled into an uneasy state of relative calm. More people from down the hill were now hurrying up to see the spectacle.

Perseus held up his hands. "Listen to me. Please. This is Ittikana, which you know means friend. She has recently come back into our world after many centuries. She is probably what the people used to think of as the Sint-Holo, but she is not a danger to the people, at least not the good people. She is also intelligent. She speaks through her thoughts."

"I am going to ask her to say hello to you. Do not be afraid. Her way of saying hello is a little startling."

He spoke to Ittikana, and, after a long pause while she seemed to be studying the children at the front of the crowd, she rose up on her hind legs, stretched her wings and neck, and screeched her unique greeting. Then an amazing thing happened. The children all got to their feet, raised their hands in the air, and imitated the wyvern's greeting, screeching at the top of their lungs. Then as one, they all laughed joyously and waved at Ittikana. They loved her. Perseus wondered what she had said to the children, for he was sure that's what she must have done.

The larger crowd had now become mesmerized by the spectacle of this amazing creature they were sure must be Sint-Holo resurrected. They watched as Perseus communicated with the creature. She was only slightly larger than the last time he'd seen her, but on top of Bus's roof, she appeared quite monstrous.

"*I am surprised to see you, Ittikana. Why have you come out of hiding to visit in front of such a large number of humans?*"

"*I wanted to see you, Perseus. I have heard you in your dreams of late, and I know you have been struggling with a decision you found difficult.*"

"*You can detect my dreams from so far away?*"

*"Yes. You and I have a bond, a special bond. I was not aware of
this until I left. It is difficult for me to explain because I do not fully
understand it myself, but when you have a certain kind of dream,
I also have a similar dream. You see, I was also struggling with a very
profound decision. At first, I thought I would attempt to communicate with you in the dreams, but in my attempt to do so, I realized
that I had actually made my decision. And I also knew you had
made yours."*

*"Do you mean my decision to formally accept my heritage as a
Native-American?"*

*"Yes, that is what I mean, and I wanted to personally extend my
approval of your decision. As I said, I also made a decision. I realized
that hiding in caves for the rest of my life is not an honorable way to
live. I am not certain how yet, but in some way, your decision and
mine are connected. So, I have come here today to reaffirm my bond
with you and to ask you to help me and others of my kind to live in
harmony in this world, a world which seems very complex and confusing to us."*

Perseus nodded his head, then looked at his grandfather, who
was still staring up at Ittikana. "Grandfather." Bus shifted his gaze
to Perseus. "Ittikana comes to us asking for help, to live among the
chahta in peace and harmony. Why don't you talk to her?"

At first, Bus looked confused. But then he looked back to
Ittikana and began to speak to her in his mind. She leaned her
head closer to him and began responding. Meanwhile, Perseus
asked for the crowd's attention. He tried to explain who Ittikana
was, how he, Tommy, and Penelope had found her, and that she
was very intelligent. He also told them the reason for her visit, and
he explained why she had every reason to be concerned for her
safety and the safety of the others of her kind. This last bit of the
announcement caused quite a stir. *There were more?*

Tommy helped out by explaining how these creatures were born with handed-down memories of how the world was in eons past, and that the world was considerably more complicated today.

Perseus wanted to emphasize her request. "Ittikana told me that she has chosen you, the Choctaw people, and she is asking for you to live in harmony with her and her kind. Can we do less?"

There was much murmuring in the crowd. Bus turned and put a hand on his grandson's shoulder. Perseus thought his grandfather looked serene.

"She is an amazing creature, Grandson. She believes in you and is counting on you and our people. This is a great day, I think. You have made me very happy and proud. Thank you."

They embraced each other, and then Bus held out an arm, gesturing for Tommy to join them. After a moment, Perseus caught Penelope's eye and motioned for her to come to him as well. The children were next to join the group embrace, then, one by one, all the others in the crowd did the same.

Ittikana watched this and was moved by the group expression of unity. She broke into Perseus' thoughts. *"I am pleased to see these humans expressing empathy and support. It affords me with hope for the future."*

"I have missed you, Perseus. I hope we have the opportunity to see each other again soon. I must leave now. The others are anxiously awaiting the news of how I was received by the humans."

"How many others have you found?"

"Only two more. There is a total of four of us now, but we intend to travel farther east and continue to look for others. We will stay out of sight and avoid humans, if possible, unless we are here in this land."

"Please tell Star hello for us. Would you tell Penelope goodbye?"

"I have already done so, and she told me that she and you have mated. This is good, you belong together. You should warn the people that I am leaving."

"I will. Goodbye and good luck, my sister. Be safe."

She made a purring sound. "*Goodbye, my brother.*"

Perseus announced that Ittikana was about to leave and that the departure would be fairly dramatic. As she began to spread her wings and stand on her hind legs, everyone took a step back. The people were all startled, but pleased, when she managed to broadcast a farewell into all their minds simultaneously. She crouched, then sprang into the air with a loud screech, bringing her wings down hard to gain altitude. She rose up into the growing darkness and flew out of sight.

EPILOGUE

The world kept on turning after that momentous day at the bar-b-que, and life continued as it always had. Trouble would come and go in Choctaw County, as trouble tends to do everywhere. But, for a time, the bad guys, who always make life less joyous for everyone around them, were gone, and the good people of the county, of every race, color, and creed, went about their lives in relative harmony.

The HB Cattle Company grew a little more successful each year. The issue of the loan never coming up again, although Penelope always kept enough cash reserve in the bank to cover the loan, just in case. Slim was made foreman of the operation and two more hands were hired for him and Günter to boss around. Chilo and Angelica arranged for a niece and nephew from New Mexico to come to the HB to begin training. They would need somebody to replace them when they grew too old to continue with their duties. Chilo, with help from the others, built another small house next to their quarters to accommodate the growth.

Penelope and Perseus turned out to be very good at making babies. They eventually produced five children, including twins.

They continued to work the ranch along with the hired-hands, and they taught their children to ride and rope and manage cattle.

Penelope kept her maiden name of Wesley since she was the last of the family to carry the name, and Perseus made the unusual decision to change his name to Wesley as well. After thinking on it for a while, he realized he had no real attachment to either Fawcett or Hadjioannou. He considered taking his mother's name of Abbott, but ultimately decided that becoming a Wesley was the correct decision. He thought it would make things less confusing for their children and help ensure the family name of the ranch endured.

He cherished his new Choctaw family as well. Having real blood relatives close by made him feel whole and part of something which had been missing in the early part of his life. Tommy was more like a brother to him than a cousin, and when he finally married and started having children, Perseus delighted in getting the two families together for holidays and special occasions. The chaos of the gatherings made him realize what he had missed in his own childhood.

Penelope and Perseus began restoring the old buildings scattered around the HB. They spent time digging through family and county records, trying to piece together the Wesley family history. Perseus was often confronted with the painful reality of the dichotomous relationship between his Indian-self and his white-man-self, inherent in the facts they uncovered about how the HB land had been acquired.

He also learned from stories told by his grandfather just how difficult things had been in the early years for that side of his family, and for the Choctaw people in general. He gained a better understanding about why there was an ingrained mistrust and resentment of the white man among many of the chahta. It often made him feel conflicted, but he took some comfort in the fact that the Choctaw Nation was currently doing fairly well. They had their own government and were making strides in maintaining their culture and traditions. He was proud of his Native-American heritage.

Bus passed away in October after Ittikana's visit to the bar-b-que. He had been elated over the appearance of the Sint-Holo that day. He told Perseus and Tommy that it was the single most significant event of his life. He told them that Ittikana had thanked him for his vision, which ultimately resulted in her rescue and her opportunity for life. She told him he was a treasure among his people and that she was honored to have met him. He told this story to others over and over, and he told his grandsons that he could now die happy.

Tommy continued to live in Bus's house, even after he was married, although he had to make some improvements and add on to the house once the children began to arrive. He also continued the annual tradition of hosting the bar-b-que, which over time became a Choctaw national event, requiring substantial expansion of the accommodations. The story of Sint-Holo, now also known as Ittikana, was told to the children each year. Of course, now a new story was told of the day the Sint-Holo returned.

Ittikana would visit Perseus and Penelope at the HB a few more precious times. These were private affairs, often motivated by questions and issues the wyvern needed human help to resolve. They trusted Perseus and looked to him for his guidance. Over time, Perseus realized there was little he could do to protect these amazing creatures, and this broke his heart.

Ittikana continued to search for others of her kind, but none were ever found. The wyvern tried to maintain a low profile in the mountains, staying out of sight and avoiding humans when possible. Nevertheless, there were a few unfortunate encounters. As their existence became widespread knowledge, many people became obsessed with finding them, often to no good end. There were inevitably some humans who wanted to exploit them or destroy them, and life for the wyvern became increasingly challenging. They were creatures which no longer had a comfortable place in the natural order of a modern, so-called civilized, world. In the end, they retreated deeper into the wilderness, disappearing back into the realm of legend.

Author's Notes

A friend of mine suggested I write a Western novel. At the time I thought that would never happen. I couldn't imagine a story about the Old West that hadn't already been told, probably several times over. And, frankly, I'm partial to sci-fi and fantasy stories. Although I manage to insert something of that ilk into everything I write, a Western just didn't seem to be the kind of genre that lent itself to a cross pollination with others.

A western needs to have good guys and bad guys, cowboys and Indians, outlaws and sheriffs, robberies and gunfights, you know, the usual stuff we're all familiar with in stories like The Lone Ranger and Tonto. Actually, I'd been thinking my next book would be about a dragon. I like dragons and love reading books about them. Despite my misgivings, I still found myself struggling to come up with a way to work a dragon into a Western. I'd have to sleep on it. . . .

You see, most of the concepts and images for my books come to me in dreams. It's been that way from the beginning. One night, during the time I was still trying to determine what my next book would be about, I had a dream about a creature that existed thousands of years ago, a creature that was part of the Native-American mythology. In the dream, there was an old man, an Indian, telling children a story about this legendary creature.

When I awoke the next morning, the dream was still quite vivid in my mind, and it triggered a recollection of some research I had done about Native-American lore for my book, *Journey To Eden*.

During that research, I discovered all sorts of interesting Native-American stories about spirits, tricksters, giants, and fantastic creatures. Maybe I could work a dragon into a Western after all. Now, I had two legitimate ingredients of a western; Indians and some fantastic creatures from their own stories.

If you are familiar with Greek mythology, you may have detected some similarities with this story's main character, Perseus, and the mythic hero, Perseus. After reading *Cloud Cuckoo Land*, by Anthony Doerr, I did some cursory research on Greek tales. That's when I stumbled onto the mythical story of the hero's journey of Perseus. This story has all kinds of great hero concepts, including a call to adventure, an amazing journey, a one-eyed hag, all kinds of hero-worthy trials, self-doubts, help from allies, a dark cave, threats from bad guys, and ultimately the hero overcoming all.

I decided I wanted to use the name Perseus for my primary protagonist. I realize it's not a typical cowboy name, but I was looking for one that would be a principal aspect of my hero's character, a name that would result in an inherent adversity he would have to overcome again and again. In this story, Perseus didn't like his name, but by dealing with it as he went through life, he became stronger. In the end, everyone associated him and his name with strength and perseverance, a true hero. As a side note, if you have read other books I've written you know that I frequently give unusual names to many of my characters.

I finally decided that I would try to put all the pieces I had dreamed up into a modern-day Western setting. I began to believe it just might work, and the modern setting would be more approachable than a story of the Old West. I chose Oklahoma because I knew this was one of the major areas the United States Federal government set aside to relocate Native-Americans driven off their ancestral lands as a result of the Indian removal policies of the nineteenth century. A quick check confirmed that half the state of Oklahoma is considered "rediscovered reservations" covering 19 million acres and consisting of 39 tribal nations, including the Choctaw. So, there would be plenty of Indians.

I chose 2018 as the time when the story takes place, because this is one of the periods when fracking, *an oil extraction process*, was at its peak and thought to be the cause of a surge in local earthquakes. Oklahoma also ranks second in beef cattle production in the United States, so there would be plenty of cows and cowboys out there. I chose Hugo as the town around which the story takes place because it's conveniently located in the Choctaw Nation. It's the county seat of Choctaw County, it has cattle ranches nearby, and it's reasonably close to the Ouachita Mountains, which is where I decided to locate the dragon in this story.

Sint-Holo is an actual creature out of the dark legends of the Chahta Yakni, the Choctaw Nation. Nope, I didn't make that up. I felt it was important for this story to have a creature that was an actual part of the local Native-American culture. A contemporary Native-American named Hunter Harris wrote down the story of Sint-Holo as it was told to him by his elders. Mr. Hunter emphasizes the importance of telling the story exactly as it has always been told, unchanged from generation to generation.

Of course, to make the story a little more interesting, I had to figure out how the creature might become reborn. I was pleased to discover that the Choctaw stories make a provision for such an occurrence. According to Hunter's story, "The Elder Speaks", the chief elder at a special gathering warned the people that, among other evil spirits, the Sint-Holo has returned. This announcement, I presume, was intended to be metaphorical, but it was all I needed to proceed.

Since my version of Sint-Holo's resurrection had to be literal, I felt obliged to do some serious research on the scientific possibility of such an event and came up with cryptobiosis, an extreme reduction of metabolic activity, which can be reversed. I realize that some readers get hung up on these technical explanations that stretch reality, so, yes, it's still implausible, but it's a what-if story, right?

Now, I had all the elements of a modern Western, except for some bad guys, but they're pretty easy to dream up. *The real world if full of very bad people from which to choose a story's villain.* I chose the fictitious Black Bart as the main villain of my story partly because of a friend I served with in Vietnam, the same person who suggested I write a Western, by the way. When we were in the Air Force together, he was a young, rugged, well-built guy, with dark hair and movie-star looks. He's not actually a bad guy in real life, but he was the one who came to mind when I was dreaming up Black Bart.

Of course, a Western usually has a romantic back story, and so I introduced the attractive, yet sturdy cowgirl, Penelope, who, by the way, was also a mythological character. She was the wife of Odysseus. Remember when Perseus was just beginning his journey, the phone conversation with his friend, Jim, and Jim's confusion over the journey of Perseus versus the odyssey of Odysseus? Okay, that's probably asking too much of my readers.

Penelope Wesley may be a stretch for many of my city-slicker readers, but there are plenty of wholesome, country gals out there in this country. Back in the small cowboy town where my wife and I built our ranch, we had a neighbor who raised three good-looking daughters who could ride and rope and raise livestock.
I thought of them when I was defining Penelope's character.

I wanted the Native-American characters to represent people who still struggle with the past but have both feet in the present. I loved developing Bus. He's a character who was quite capable of living for the moment but still able to maintain his strong connection with the cultural identity of his past. To me, he represents the archetype of the Native-American elder who reflects all that was good and worthwhile in the old ways of the chahta, the people.

I don't actually know a person like him, but I wish I did. I wanted his grandson, Tommy, to be intelligent, level-headed, and dependable. I tried to make them both come across as Americans who live and work and play and dream much the same as Americans of every background.

I hope you enjoyed reading this story. I certainly had fun writing it. I think, just maybe, I pulled off the challenging quest of telling a story about how a dragon might find its way into a modern-day Western. Perhaps these notes will provide you with some insight into how a tale like this one is crafted. On the other hand, it may just be further evidence of my addled brain at work.

About the Author

JOHN R YORK grew up in a rural town in central Ohio and has fond memories of working on the extended-family farms during the summer months of his youth. He served in the Air Force with the 3rd Air Rescue and Recovery Group in Viet Nam and in Thailand with the 40th Rescue and Recovery Squadron toward the end of that unpopular war.

John eventually attended college at Florida Atlantic University and received his bachelor's degree in computer science and worked in that industry for the next 24 years. The beginning of this period was when the Internet was being born, and he was lucky enough to have been involved in many of the historic efforts to create and evolve those technologies.

Along the way he and his wife, Paula, built their beloved Hellanback Ranch (HB) in the back country of San Diego County. This was their little piece of paradise where they raised livestock, planted wine grapes, and started a winery. Ramona, the little town a few miles from the ranch, was a great place to live, and over the years they became very involved in the community. The time came however, when ranching and winemaking were a bit overwhelming, and the Yorks made the painful decision to sell the ranch. They relocated to New Port Richey on the west coast of Florida so that John could focus on writing.

John got the idea to start writing novels around 2014. He had done a lot of professional writing dealing with management and technology during his career, but always loved telling stories. It was in his blood, as he would say. In 2016 he retired and has been writing ever since. John has published books in several different genres. He also loves to cook, play the piano and sing, and has composed several songs. John is still involved with winemakers back in California, and enjoys mentoring those who are just getting started in that industry.

If you enjoyed this book please leave an honest review on your favorite bookstore's website.

Visit me at JYorkHB.us2. authorhomepage.com and sign up for my newsletter so you can be among the first to know about my upcoming books, book sign—ings, readings, and more.

I invite you to hang out with me on Facebook at john.york.9277

Other Works

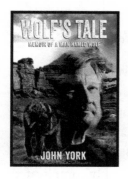

Wolf's Tale: Memoir of a Man Named Wolf (Nov 17, 2017)

From his earliest childhood, Wolf O'Brien enthusiastically wanders into unexpected twists and turns that life places before him. His propensity to impulsively plunge into situations that he considers "something worth doing" results in many unlikely adventures. As an old man writing his memoir, he struggles with recalling all of the stories that he has told over the years and the details of those stories. As he labors through the process of capturing all his memories into his book, however, an amazing new adventure unfolds before him.

Paperback: 9780999387009 | 431 pages | $14.99
Kindle: B076JW61TZ | $7.99

Mild Meld   (Mar 13, 2019)

One day near a small town in Southern California, in a canyon where the O'Brian's ranch is located, a faint, nearly subsonic sound began to make itself apparent. At first, the sound was relatively easy to ignore, but over time it seemed to bore its way into Wolf O'Brian's consciousness. Eventually, the sound became so insistent it compelled Wolf to try to find the source. What he discovers is beyond belief—a portal leading to a parallel world. Wolf and his friend, Chase O'Brian, ultimately find themselves in the complicated and challenging position of trying to save the world.

Paperback: 9780999387023 | 466 pages | $18.99
Kindle: B07PKFXBMM | $7.99

The Eighth Day: A New Order   (Aug 8, 2020)

Ryker O'Brian is a talented young man returning home after three years of education and training in Washington, DC. Ryker returns to a joyous homecoming at the remarkable and mysterious compound known as Mind Meld where his life is immediately complicated by the extraordinary events that are about to unfold in an already troubled, near apocalyptic world.

In the midst of the crisis, an extraordinary cosmic phenomenon occurs, resulting in an opening to other worlds through a rip in the space-time continuum. The event will change the world, all worlds, forever. The amazing heroes of this story are thrown together in an unlikely alliance, determined to help the nation rise from the ashes of a world near collapse.

Paperback: 9780999387047 | 443 pages | $18.99
Kindle: B08FHDK75L | $7.99

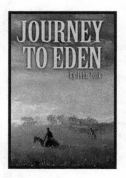

Journey to Eden   (May 3, 2021)

The year is 1847, four very different people, Shadow, (a Dakota Indian), Archibald Weed (an albino), Anna (a "Fancy Girl"), and George Blackhorse (a dark skinned Native American) serendipitously meet and begin a journey on the wild upper Mississippi River to a place they call Eden. They seek freedom, equality, and the opportunity to pursue their dreams. They all have one thing in common. They are all half-breeds.

Paperback: 9780999387061 | 450 pages | $18.99
Kindle: B094GH6K8Y | $7.99

Billy Bean's Ghost   (Nov 17, 2021)

Billy Bean lives alone in the small attic apartment of an old, unoccupied mansion. His cheap rent is subsidized by an agreement to watch over the place while the owner is away. During his weekly inspections of the old mansion, Billy discovers a treasure, a Steinway concert grand piano. He is so inspired by the magnificent instrument that he tentatively begins playing again, but there is a slight catch. Each time he plays this marvelous piano, he hears an imploring voice inside his head.

The mysterious voice compels Billy to visit psychiatrist, Abigale Applebee, who agrees to help him sort out what kind of mental health problem he's experiencing. They soon discover the voice is not the result of a psychosis, but rather something far more sinister. Led by the voice, Abby and Billy unexpectedly uncover the horrific secrets of a long-forgotten cellar below the house. But who is going to believe them?

Paperback: 9780999387078 | 167 pages | $14.99
Kindle: B09M922LFR | $7.99
Audible: 5 hrs 31 min | $13.96 member; $19.95 non-member